CW00660900

GARDEN
OF SECRET &
SHADOW

To all the dreamers. Let your dreams guide your path. You never know where they might take you. Who knows, they may help you to write a book about vampires...

Quick Word Definition:
***Haint Blue**- the tradition of painting porch ceilings blue was started in the Southern United States by the Gullah who believed that ghosts (known as haints and pronounced haunts) could not cross water. Painting the porch ceiling "haint blue" is believed to keep ghosts from entering the home.*

prologue

MY STOMACH GROWLS loud enough to wake me from a dream. I don't remember the last time I ate. The cabinets have been empty for a few weeks, which means today will be the same as yesterday, a no food day. Most days are. Weekends, summer, and holidays are the worst.

A soft giggle echoes through the door to the back corner of the small closet. My safe space. My hiding place.

Another giggle, followed by a deep sigh, creeps under the door. "That's it, baby. Keep going." My mother is doing what she always does when we need money, entertaining a gentleman. At least that's what she calls it. She makes me hide, so they don't know I'm here.

The sound of bouncing springs and deep grunts, followed by a loud cry, makes me cover my ears. I hate this part, but I know from experience it means it's over. I don't know how much time passes before a door slams, telling me he's gone. My stomach growls again, this time feeling like someone is punching me from the inside.

"Amelia?" The door creaks open, letting dull light seep inside. "Are you awake, baby girl?"

"Yes, ma'am."

"Good. How about we go get you something to eat?"

I smile a toothless grin. "Can I have a Happy Meal?" One of the kids in my class was talking about Happy Meals a few weeks back, and it's all I've thought about since.

Mama smiles back. "I think we can do that."

The lantern we use in place of electricity casts shadows throughout the dark bedroom. I slip into the same clothes I've worn for the past week. They're covered in dirt and stains, evidence of not being washed in months.

"Come on, Amelia. Let's go get you that Happy Meal." She grabs my hand, pulling me out the front door.

"Hey, sexy," an older man, blocking the majority of the hallway, says. "How you been?"

"Real good. Just taking my baby out for some food."

"Cool, cool. How about I come see you later?" He props his hand on the wall, towering over the two of us.

Mama runs her hand down his chest, stopping not

far from his heart. "Sure thing. I could use some *company* from a big strong man like yourself."

The man steps aside. "Alright, sugar. I'll come see you when I can." He winks and smacks her on the butt as we pass by.

Mama pushes my face downward, hiding me from his view. We exit the dilapidated building and enter the familiar streets of the French Quarter. It's a short walk to Happy Meal heaven, and I can't control my excitement at seeing the Golden Arches.

"Two Happy Meals, please," she tells the teenager behind the counter.

"Two?" I whisper.

"Nothing but the best for my baby." She ruffles my hair as the girl sets two boxes and two drinks on the counter.

We find a seat in the back, and I open the box of heaven. Inside is a hamburger, fries, and a toy. "Eat your food, then you can have your toy."

"Yes, ma'am." I take a bite of the hamburger and realize there's nothing but bread and cheese.

"What's the matter?"

"Nothing," I answer, pretending to enjoy the meager sandwich.

Mama grabs the burger from my hands. "Where's the meat?" Taking my box, she spills it on the table, scattering the fries everywhere. "Are you fucking kidding me?"

I watch in horror as she takes the unopened Happy

Meal, along with the one I was eating, back to the counter. I cover my ears, knowing what's about to happen.

She throws both boxes of food at the cashier and leaps over the counter in a fit of rage. I pull my knees close to my body, making myself as small as possible. This is all my fault. Why did I ask for a Happy Meal? *Mama, stop. Stop. Stop. Please...stop.* The cries fill my mind as I watch the spectacle take place in front of me. The noises that leave her mouth sound more like an animal than my mother. In a matter of minutes, police are inside the building and pulling her off of the workers.

I don't wait to see the aftermath. I take off, running out of the restaurant and back to the only place I know, home.

Luckily, the courtyard and hallways are clear of obstruction, making for an easy escape. I don't slow down until I'm inside the apartment and back in the safety of my closet.

This was my life until the age of twelve. Mama entertained men, spending time in and out of jail, until the day everything changed.

Tammy Lockhart never came home.

ONE

the new guy

THE DOOR CREAKS OPEN, revealing an older white-haired woman. She's no taller than me, which isn't saying much. She flashes a warm smile. "Can I help you, dear?"

"Um, hi! I'm interested in the apartment you have for rent." I point to the "For Rent" sign attached to the front porch post. Printed underneath, in small letters, is the word *Haunted*. "Is it still available?"

"Of course." She opens the door to a dimly lit set of stairs with doors leading off the main hallway. "Would you like to see it?"

"Right now? Wow. Yes, please." I've tried to snag more apartments than I can count in the French Quarter, only to find they've been rented before I get there or are so far out of my price range that I'd need a job making over six figures to afford it. Properties don't stay on the market long, especially on Royal Street, the heart of the antique district.

"It's the first one on the right, up there. Number four." She points to the second floor, and I try to contain my excitement. The first door on the right means there's a balcony overlooking the street below. She pulls a key from her apron pocket. "Bring it back when you're finished."

"Yes, ma'am. Thank you." This woman doesn't know me from Adam, yet she's letting me tour a vacant apartment on my own. "Are you sure you don't want to come with me?"

She laughs. "No, dear. I don't do stairs. It'll be fine. I trust you." She enters the apartment directly underneath the one I'm going to see, leaving me alone in the dim entryway. I run my fingers along the carved woodwork that lines the staircase. Thank God no one slapped a coat of white paint over it through the years. The wallpaper looks original to what I'm guessing is a house that was built at least a century ago. Faded yellow stripes, covered in orange and turquoise flowers, are the victim to years of nicotine stains and hands rubbing across the linen as people ascend and descend the stairs.

Don't get your hopes up, Amelia, the voice of reason sings through my mind. No doubt, this place is well out of a grad student's budget. Even with my weekend job as a barista, I don't make enough to afford an apartment like this. I reach the second-floor landing and head straight to apartment number four. The skeleton key fits perfectly, clicking as the door opens with a loud creak.

My breath catches as I look around the oversized, fully furnished room. Soft pink wallpaper greets me in the main room that leads into a small dining area. The furniture looks original to the house, and I'm instantly in love. A pink tufted velvet couch sits against the wall opposite the balcony. Wide-plank oak floors show years of use and are the host to a plush lime-green rug in the center of the room.

The furniture and decor throughout the rest of the apartment match the aesthetic of the first room. I can barely control my excitement. This is everything I've been looking for. The dorm is not meant for doctoral students, and being one of the oldest students there, I've turned into the dreaded dorm mom. It's a job I don't want.

I make one last pass through the apartment before heading down to find out how much it's going to set me back each month. The bedroom closet is large for a home of this age. Surprisingly, it's a walk-in. What's in the back corner is almost a deal breaker, almost.

"What did you think?" the older woman asks, opening her apartment door for me.

"I love it!" I clear my throat. "I mean, it's nice. How much is the rent?"

"I'm asking five hundred, plus a one-hundred-dollar security deposit."

I stare at the woman, not sure I heard her correctly. "Five hundred dollars a month?"

"The man who lived there before told me I should ask more. When he left, I raised the rent by fifty dollars. Do you think it's too much?"

This, ladies and gentlemen, is the perfect definition of a conundrum. Apartments in the Quarter cost anywhere from fifteen hundred to two thousand per month. Dammit, good Amelia wins. "No, ma'am. In fact, I think you could get three or four times that amount for this apartment."

She laughs. "What would the point of that be? The building is paid for, and my expenses are low. Are you interested in renti..."

"Yes!" I interrupt. "One hundred percent, yes. I'll take it."

"Perfect!" She claps her hands. "The first of the month is Friday. Do you think you could move in that soon?"

"I could move in tonight if needed."

"That won't be necessary. Friday will be fine." I hand her back the skeleton key. "No, you keep it. It's yours anyway."

"Do you need me to fill out paperwork for a credit check and background check?"

"Hun, I don't even know what half of those words mean. I'm a good judge of character. You're going to be fine." She reaches her hand toward me. "Esther James." She shakes my hand.

"It's a pleasure to meet you, Ms. Esther. I'm Amelia Lockhart."

"What a beautiful name. I think you'll be the perfect addition to our home." The door closes, and I stare at her door in shock. Did I just rent an apartment in the Quarter, on Royal Street for a literal steal? Yes. Yes, I did! Stuff like this doesn't happen to me.

The rest of the week passes painstakingly slow as I count the minutes until I get out of the dorm and into the apartment. The skeleton key practically burns a hole in my pocket, begging to be used.

First thing Friday morning, my clothes and the few items I've collected over the past few years are packed into two suitcases, and I head toward my new home. My twenty-year-old Nissan is small enough that I'm able to squeeze into a spot directly in front of the apartment building.

"Good morning, Amelia," Ms. Esther says, as I open the front door to the building. "I forgot to tell you that the key fits the front door. However, it looks like you figured that out."

"Yes, ma'am. I did." I drag my heavy bags through the door, careful not to scratch the wood any more than it already is. I hand her six hundred dollars in cash. "Here is the security deposit and this month's rent."

"That's perfect! I'll write you a receipt later if that's okay."

"Yes, ma'am. I'll stop by on my way to class."

"I thought you were a student. It's good to have

some fresh blood in here." She smiles before heading back into her apartment.

Unlocking the door, the smell of home hits me. Despite the musty smell all old buildings in the Quarter share, the light shining in the French doors welcomes me. It doesn't take long to unpack my few clothes, hanging them in the front of the closet. My eyes are drawn to the back corner, where the ancient, almost deal-breaker, box sits. It's long enough to fit a person inside. If I didn't know better, I'd swear it was a coffin. I laugh at the thought and continue arranging the bathroom to my liking.

"Have you had a chance to write a receipt?" I ask Ms. Esther on my way to class.

"I have." She hands me a piece of notebook paper with the word receipt scribbled across the top, along with a date and her signature. "I hope this will work for now. My receipt book is empty."

"It's perfect. Thank you."

"Was everything okay in the apartment?"

"It was. I do wonder why there's a huge box in the bedroom closet. It looks like a coffin."

She laughs. "A coffin? Why would there be a coffin in there?"

I join the laughter. "I hoped you might know."

"The last tenant must have left it behind. I'll ask Garrett to get it first thing tomorrow. He's the handyman."

"Thank you." I close the door and walk the ten-minute commute to class. This is too good to be true. I can't believe I found the greatest apartment in New Orleans for the cheapest rent possible, and it's only ten minutes from the university.

Being a doctoral student in European history makes my peer group very small. When the door opens unexpectedly, everyone turns and stares as a new member enters the room. A man I've never seen before walks in, places his backpack a few desks behind mine, and sits down.

"Welcome, Mr. Chamberlin. Students, this is Harrison Chamberlin. He's going to be joining us mid semester as a transfer student from the University of South Carolina. Please make him feel welcome." Most people turn back toward the front without acknowledging him. Before I have that chance, he waves. Shit.

Two hours and one boring class later, Harrison walks out of the classroom a few steps ahead of me and holds the door open as I approach. "After you, ma'am." His accent is so thick, I feel like I've gone back in time.

"Why, thank you, sir." One of my toxic traits is imitating accents when I'm speaking to someone with a particularly strong one. My words sound like a true Southern Belle. "I'm sorry, that was rude. I didn't mean to make fun of your accent."

"It wasn't rude at all. I appreciate a good accent every now and again. Can I walk you home?"

"Um, no. I'm not trying to get murdered, but thank you for the invitation." He laughs a low, deep laugh.

"I assure you I am a gentleman, and no murdering would be taking place." He smiles, lifting one side of his mouth higher than the other. "Doing you harm is not something I would ever think of doing."

"Okay. Thank you, anyway. I'm going to walk." I keep moving and turn to wave. "I'll see you around." He waves back as I take another look at the handsome gentleman who may or may not have just volunteered to murder me. He's at least a foot taller than me, which isn't unusual. Being five feet tall, on a good day, means everyone is a foot taller than me. His hair is tied in a man bun, with messy sprigs sticking out on the sides. Green eyes continue to watch me as I walk toward Royal Street and my new, cheap escape.

I grab a quick bite at a small café not far from my apartment and head home to continue working on my thesis. Why I chose to do my thesis on the study of mythological creatures from the medieval period in Europe is beyond me. Other than a few ancient texts I've found in the library, not much is printed or can be found on the subject. Most of what I've found is the same information, just altered for each text.

No matter what night it is, the French Quarter is always loud and mostly one big party. Tonight is no exception. Royal Street isn't as bad as Bourbon, but people are milling around below, clearly having had too many hurricane drinks. I open my balcony doors, allowing the street sounds to fill the room. I don't mind the noise. It's far enough below that it doesn't bother me, yet close enough that I don't feel isolated. Standing on the balcony, something next to the streetlamp catches my eye. I squint, trying to determine the details of what I'm seeing. Whatever or whomever it is seems to be staring back at me and into my apartment.

I take a step back, still trying to determine what it is, when it moves away from the lamppost and closer to the house, staying hidden in the shadows.

What the hell? I'm being paranoid. I close and lock the doors and head into my new bedroom. The coffin is still in the corner of the closet and, according to Ms. Esther, will be gone tomorrow. I find an old blanket and cover it for no reason other than it's weird.

The partying is winding down below as I close my laptop and finish writing for the night. For the first time in a few weeks, I managed to write more than a few sentences. I feel accomplished.

I crawl into the furnished bed and sigh at the comfort that surrounds me. This mattress feels like sleeping on a cloud. The dorm mattresses are barely thick enough to keep the ancient springs from stabbing me in the back, and before that, my bed was the floor. I could get used to this.

Lying in bed, the reality of where I am hits me. When Tammy stopped coming home, I lived every day, every moment in fear. I was a twelve-year-old child, forced to figure out how to survive. Only a handful of people knew my secret until I turned eighteen and left for college. No water, no power, barely any food—I was nothing more than a ghost, abandoned by the one person who was supposed to take care of me.

Thinking of how much my life has changed since then, brings the emotions I buried years ago to the surface. *Don't let them see your weakness. Don't let them see your pain.* The mantra that plays in my head on constant repeat echoes through my mind, and for the first time since I can remember, I ignore it, giving the tears permission to fall.

I wake the next morning to the sun shining through the blinds. Small flecks of dust float through the beams of light, telling me it's time to get up and go to class. My mind flashes to the new student, and I can't help but wonder if he'll try to walk me home again.

Moving faster than yesterday, I cut my commute down to eight minutes and arrive before class starts. I'm surprised to find Harrison sitting at the desk next to the one I've claimed as my own for the past two years. A fluffy, overpriced drink of some sort is waiting on my arrival.

"What's this?" I ask, sliding into my seat.

"A peace offering," he answers with a smirk.

"Does that mean I was right? You were planning on murdering me yesterday?" I take a sip, filling my palate with deliciousness. "Oh, my God. What is this? It's amazing."

"It's a caramel apple frappe espresso."

I take another sip. "I make these for a living, but this is the first time I've drank one. No wonder people are willing to pay six dollars and wait in line for hours for a coffee." I take another drink, nearly finishing it in one sip. "Thank you."

"You're welcome." Class passes quickly, and I have a hard time paying attention. Most of my time is spent watching Harrison take meticulous notes of the lecture. His handwriting reminds me of examples I've seen in ancient books. The script is flowy, beautiful, and perfect.

As soon as we're dismissed, I grab my laptop, shove it into my backpack, and move toward the door. In a move from yesterday, Harrison slides quickly in front of me and holds the door open, ushering me outside.

"May I walk you home?" he repeats the familiar question. "Before you say anything, your safety is my highest priority. I usually save murdering for at least the third date."

"Since this is only the second time we've met, I'm going to assume I'm safe. I'd be honored if you walked me home, kind sir." I mimic his thick accent.

"Lead the way, ma'am." I give Harrison the history of each building we pass and how it relates to our current course of study. Not surprisingly, most of the buildings in the French Quarter can be traced to French or Spanish influence and host a history to match. Harrison hangs on every word, studying each detail of the buildings I point out.

"This is me," I motion to the two-story home that

houses my new apartment. "Thank you for not murdering me."

"My pleasure. I'd be honored to walk you home again tomorrow."

"I don't know. I feel like I'd be pushing my luck with the timeline of your murder schedule."

Harrison laughs before bowing slightly. "I'll see you in class tomorrow, ma'am." He waits until I'm safely inside before leaving the front walk. I don't know whether to be flattered or terrified.

coffee and ghosts

FIVE O'CLOCK on Saturday morning comes way too early. I roll over, slapping my phone several times before the alarm finally shuts up. Being a grad student doesn't pay the bills, at least not yet. Who am I kidding? My completed doctorate degree probably won't pay the bills either.

Cars are already lining the coffee shop drive-through as I head inside. *Think what you could buy if you saved your money instead of buying overpriced coffee!* I mentally shout at the line as I pass through the waiting cars.

"Amelia! You're late," my boss barks at me. "We're busy already."

"Sorry, Jen. I overslept," I lie. We've had this same conversation every Saturday for two years. I'm not late, in fact, I'm right on time, but I don't argue. I never argue. Nope. Amelia Lockhart is a chronic people pleaser, thanks to Tammy Lockhart and the childhood trauma she instilled deep inside.

"It's fine. Get back here. We need you." I take a second to clock in before heading to my usual spot and to begin filling orders. Being a barista isn't a fulfilling occupation, but it's provided me with spending money and will pay the rent for my new home.

Four hours later, my back aches, my feet hurt, and I need to pee. Today has been busier than usual thanks to a unicorn drink that went viral, and everyone is convinced they need to try it. To me, it looks like purple baby poo.

The next order that comes through catches my attention. It's a caramel apple frappe espresso, the same drink Harrison brought me yesterday. I glance around the room, halfway hoping to see him.

Jen took the order, and the single "H" she wrote on the cup gives me hope. I take my time, making sure every ingredient is perfectly measured and blended to perfection.

"H," I call, setting the drink on the counter. A tall man with dark brown hair steps out of the back corner, and my hopes are instantly shattered. It's not Harrison.

"Amelia, we need milk and unicorn straws. I can't leave the register. Can you grab some from the back?" Jen barks more orders at me, and of course, I don't argue. Moving to the back of the store, a familiar face catches my eye, making me explode with nervous energy.

Harrison is in line to order. *He's just here for coffee, Amelia. Nothing else.*

I've delivered the milk and straws and been back in place at least thirty minutes before his order makes it to me. I'm disappointed to see it's nothing more than black coffee. I don't know what I expected, but black coffee isn't it. "Harrison?" I call to the waiting area.

He steps up, wearing a dimpled smile. "I didn't know you worked here."

"Yep. Two years now." I hand him the coffee. "That was a long wait for black coffee."

"I'm not a fan of all the fancy mix-ins. I save those for the girls on my murder list."

"Go ahead, make jokes. I'm keeping a tally of the number of times we've spoken for self-preservation purposes." I can't hide my smile.

"Good." He returns the smile, looking me in the eyes and causing butterflies to instantly take flight in my stomach. "It was good to see you again, Amelia." I watch him leave, still unsure what to think about Harrison Chamberlin. Did I tell him my name? I don't have time to think about it as four more orders for unicorn frappes make their way to me.

After one of the busiest coffee-making days we've ever had, the line finally slows ten hours after my day began. By the time I park in front of the apartment house, the sun has completely set, and the weekend party crowds are already out, wandering the street.

My feet move in slow motion, as I unlock the

antique door. The moment I enter, something feels "off." Ms. Esther's door is standing wide-open, and her television is blaring the evening news at top volume. "Ms. Esther?" I stick my head inside to see her lying on the couch.

If it weren't for the awkward position her body is in, I'd swear she was asleep. Her feet are hanging off the front of the couch, and her chin is pressed to her chest with one arm twisted behind her in a strange position. "Oh, my God. Ms. Esther?" I nudge her arm.

She doesn't respond, and I try again, this time shaking her arm. Her eyes pop open, and she sucks in a deep breath. "What's wrong?" she whispers.

"Your door was open. I was afraid something was wrong."

She struggles to sit up. "Oh, I'm fine. My blood pressure drops sometimes, causing me to take an unplanned...nap." She looks around the room. "Was anyone here when you came in?"

"No, ma'am." I follow her line of sight. "Was someone here earlier?"

She sits up completely, steadying herself on the arm of the couch. "No. I must have been dreaming again. Thank you for checking on me."

"Can I get you something to eat or drink? Orange juice, maybe? You look really pale."

She pats my leg. "That's sweet, but I'm fine. I feel much better now. I've been tired today. Getting old can do that to you."

I stand, moving toward the door. "If you change your mind, just yell for me. I should hear you."

"These old walls are soundproof. You wouldn't hear anything." Her words strike me as strange, but I don't question her. "Close the door behind you, please." I do as she asks, making sure the door is closed tightly before heading upstairs.

My new bathroom is the host of a claw foot bathtub, and I decide to do something I've never done—take a bath. The moment my body sinks into the water, an embarrassing sigh leaves my mouth. I rarely got a chance to clean up when I was young, and when I moved to college, the dorms only had showers.

Sinking into a tub of hot water feels heavenly. I lay my head back, and exhaustion sets in immediately. Dreams fill my mind the moment my eyes close. Visions of Ms. Esther's apartment flash through my mind. She's lying on the couch like I found her, except she's not alone. I look around, searching for the source of the feeling, finding the room empty. A large planter in the corner of her room crashes to the ground, pulling me out of the dream and back to the now lukewarm water of the bathtub.

Every noise and creak of the old house draws my attention as I hurry to dress. I've never been one to get scared easily, thanks again, Tammy, but something doesn't feel right. I slip through my front door and hear the sounds of a television turned to full volume once again.

"Ms. Esther?" I yell down the stairs. "Are you alright?" She doesn't answer.

I move downstairs to find her door standing wide-open. I remember latching it behind me. "Ms. Esther?" I call inside the open door.

The room is empty. I call again, receiving the same response as earlier. Shit. Do I just walk in and look for her? There's a fine line between a wellness check and breaking and entering. "Fuck it," I mumble to no one. Moving inside the apartment, I turn her television off. The silence is overwhelming.

"Ms. Esther?" I call through the apartment, searching each room thoroughly. After a thorough check and not finding her anywhere, I close the door once more, checking three times to make sure it latched before heading back upstairs. I'm beginning to think the haunted sign wasn't a gimmick.

I spend the rest of the evening working on my thesis and manage to add three paragraphs before exhaustion sets in once more. At this rate, I should receive my doctorate by the time I'm fifty. I take a quick peek outside the balcony doors, finding the street mostly empty and no one staring toward the house tonight.

Ms. Esther's television has stayed quiet, and I resist the urge to check on her for the third time today. Instead, I crawl into bed and quiet my mind.

"Amelia," a voice whispers. Thinking I'm at the dorm, I awaken ready to reprimand whoever has snuck into my room. It takes a minute to remember I'm in my own apartment and not sharing a building with a hundred other hormonal teenagers. The streetlights fill the room with enough light to verify I'm alone and obviously having another weird dream. I fall back asleep easily before waking several hours later to the same voice. "Amelia," it whispers. That wasn't the imagination of an exhausted barista. That was real.

"Is someone here?" My voice sounds shaky.

"Amelia," the voice calls louder, this time from the kitchen. I jump out of bed and head straight to the source of the sound. "Amelia," the voice is directly behind me this time, whispering into my ear.

I turn, finding no one. "Leave me alone. This is my home, and you're not welcome." I heard something similar on a ghost show I watched once. I turn, hoping I've scared the ghost away when the image of a man appears across the room.

"Welcome home, my dear." He motions around the room. "It's quite lovely, isn't it?"

"This is the most vivid dream I've ever had. You almost look real." His hair is dark and slick to his scalp. Copper brown eyes glow in the faint light. He's dressed in clothes from the 1800s, wearing a black waistcoat, high-rise pants, and a perfectly creased white shirt. If I didn't know better, I'd swear I was looking at a vampire.

He moves faster than my eyes can track, straight toward me. I run to the bedroom closet, locking the door behind me. This is the most realistic dream I've ever had. I pinch my arm several times, hoping to wake up. "Amelia?" the man whispers inches from the door. "I can smell your blood. O negative, I believe. It's a delicacy for some."

Are you freaking serious? What the hell is happening? "I'm not tasty. I do drugs. *Lots* of drugs. You name it, I've done it. My blood is full of substances that would knock you for a loop. You wouldn't like it." A deep laugh echoes through the door. Looking around the closet, there is nothing to use for protection. My meager wardrobe and the ancient coffin are the only things in here besides me.

Fingernails scrape across the wooden doors. "I can help you, Amelia. You need to trust me." He's toying with me, leaving me no choice. Dream or no dream, I'm not going to stand here and wait for whatever is about to happen. The coffin door is heavy as I climb inside, closing it tightly behind me. I hear the closet door crash to the floor as it's ripped from the hinges.

"I guess this works, too," he laughs as he speaks.

The box smells like an old musical instrument that's been stored for fifty years in a moldy case. I can barely breathe over the stench. Seconds later, the box is shoved off the stand and moving through the apartment, taking me with it. The wood squeaks as it slides over the oak floors. I can only imagine the scratches being left in its wake. "This will make it easier anyway." He laughs as the box slides.

Part of me is still trying to process whether this is a

dream or really happening. Common sense says dream, but everything about it feels real. Either way, I need to get the hell out of here. I kick both feet on the end of the box, cracking the wood with my kick. I repeat the motion, and the wood cracks even more. My dream captor, or whatever he is, is still dragging the box through the apartment. I kick a third time, knocking a hole where my feet land. Light from the street below floods into the box. I kick once more, this time knocking the end of the box completely open just as he pushes the opposite end up, causing me to slide feet first out of the box and through the wide bars of the balcony's iron gate. I'm falling feet first toward Royal Street and the waiting concrete below.

Instinctively, I curl into a ball, prepping for the impact that's most likely going to end my life, when arms wrap around me and stop my fall. I open my eyes to see the familiar green eyes of Harrison Chamberlin looking down at me. "I've got you, Amelia."

"What happened to your accent?" The world goes black.

THREE

crazy house

THE FAMILIAR SMELL of ancient texts pulls me from my strange dream. Books have the same smell, no matter their age. I've always thought they should make a cologne or perfume to match the fragrance. Book lovers all over the world would make the bottler rich.

My eyes open to floor-to-ceiling shelves, covered in the very thing I smelled—books. The weight of the blanket covering me adds comfort to the bliss. This has to be another dream, although, this one is much better than the last. Moving toward the shelves, I run my fingers along the spines of the ancient contents. Most are titles I've never seen before. Each one begging to be opened and explored.

"Oh, good. You're awake," a voice says from the corner of the room. I freeze, not sure who's with me. A man steps from the shadows, making me more confused than before.

"Harrison? Why are you in my dream?"

He smiles the dimpled grin I remember from earlier. "You're certainly not dreaming." He steps in front of me. "What do you remember from your...dream?"

"Not much. A man in my kitchen told me I had O negative blood and chased me into my closet. You caught me before I hit the concrete." I rub my temples in confusion. Is this real? "How did I get here? Did you bring me here?" I'm so confused.

"You needed help."

"Where am I?" I look around the room for clues.

"My home."

I sit back on the couch. "That wasn't a dream, was it? There was some psychopath in my apartment trying to kidnap me, wasn't there?"

He moves closer still. "It wasn't a dream." He doesn't elaborate.

"Who was that man, and why would he want me?"

"May I?" He motions to the other end of the couch.

I nod, lowering my head into my hands as the memories come crashing down. "Why did he...?" God, how do I say this without sounding crazy? "He looked like a vampire." I laugh awkwardly. "That sounded even more dumb to say out loud." Harrison looks at me without answering. His silence speaks volumes. "That's impossible. Vampires only exist in mythology. I'm guessing you're telling me he's a cosplayer or some-thing. Maybe he dresses like that to scare drunk tourists."

"Vampires are very much real, and you are correct. He's a vampire."

I laugh loudly. "You don't seriously believe that man is a vampire?"

"I *know* he's a vampire," Harrison answers. "I've known him for more centuries than I'd care to count."

The reality of his words hits me like a load of bricks. "Oh, my God. Harrison, do you think you're a vampire?" He lowers his head.

"I am, but I promise you are not in any danger. You're safe here."

I jump to my feet, moving away from my lunatic rescuer. I scan the room quickly, locating the door. "This is insane. *You're* crazy, and I'm guessing whoever you hired to scare me last night is either crazy or stupid. I'm going home." I move toward double doors on the opposite wall, pulling with all my might. No matter how hard I pull, they're not budging.

Harrison raises his hands in surrender mode. "You can't go home, Amelia. Viktor will no doubt be waiting for your return."

I turn, finding Harrison hasn't moved from his spot on the couch. "Viktor...that's his name? You expect me to believe a vampire named Viktor tried to eat me last night?"

"I don't think eating was what he had in mind."

"Take me home," I demand. "Or better yet, I'll walk."

Harrison moves in front of the door before my eyes track any movement. "It's not safe for you right now."

"Fuck you, Harrison Chamberlin. Move out of my way."

"I'm afraid I can't do that." His eyes flash behind me just as an arm reaches around my chest from behind, and a vile of liquid is emptied into my arm. "Be gentle with her," Harrison says as the library fades to blackness.

I have no idea how much time has passed when my eyes open for the second time. The warmth of the library is replaced with four walls and an antique fireplace. My eyes have trouble focusing as I look around for clues to where I am. Soft bedding surrounds me, and I rub my eyes, trying to make sense of it all. It takes several minutes for details to fully come into view. I'm in a bedroom. Not an ordinary bedroom, but one that looks like a fancy picture from a *Homes of New Orleans* magazine. Ornate hand-carved crown molding lines the haint blue ceiling. The French Provincial mantle is finished in gold leaf and pale blue paint. Where the hell am I?

My head weighs fifty pounds as I lift it from the pillow. I'm still wearing the ratty pajamas that I had on when this whole nightmare started. I stumble through the room, exploring every corner for clues, finding nothing more than ornate decor and typical Victorian-era architecture. A large wardrobe in the corner is full of clothes, all of which are my size. Digging through, I run across three very familiar-looking shirts. Are these mine? That's weird.

I keep digging, finding a pair of jeans with a stain in the exact spot as my favorite pair. I dig through one of the pockets, finding a bubble gum wrapper of my favorite brand. These *are* my jeans. How the hell did they get here? Ignoring the new clothes, I slide into my jeans and a familiar shirt. I'm tired of this dream, or whatever it is, and ready for it to be over.

I sit in silence as the sun begins to set, casting dancing shadows throughout the room. The view through the small window is of a typical New Orleans courtyard, surrounded by buildings on all four sides. I turn the doorknob like I've done dozens of times previously, finding the same results as before. It's locked from the outside. "Let me out, please!" I yell through the tiny keyhole. I don't know how much time has passed since I've been locked in the room and have heard no sounds other than the ones I've made. "I won't tell anyone about you or this place," I yell with an awkward laugh. "Hell, it's New Orleans. No one would believe me anyway. I just want out of here! I'm sorry I laughed when you said you were a vampire. I wasn't making fun of you."

The sun has completely set, and I turn on the Tiffany lamp in the corner of the room. I've quit yelling. It's not doing any good. I sit on the plush bed in defeat.

A soft click at the door draws me to my feet. Grabbing a candlestick, I stand behind the door, not sure who or what's about to enter. The door creaks open as I raise the weapon high above my head. I'm just about to make whomever it is my victim when a woman comes into view. "Hello?" Her voice is soft and friendly. "Are you in here?" I lower my arms, backing away. "Of course, you're in here. Where else would you go?" She giggles at her words.

"Who are you?"

"Violet Du Four." She sticks her hand toward me, and I ignore it. She pulls it back quickly. "Harrison told me you might be a little upset." She nods to the candlestick. "Why don't you let me have this?" She takes the makeshift weapon from my hands. The woman in front of me looks to be in her early twenties, wearing low-cut jeans, military boots, and a camouflage jacket. Her short black hair looks like it was cut with a razor blade, making her the perfect combination of adorable and badass.

"Where am I?"

"You're in the French Quarter. I can't tell you any more information than that until Harrison gives permission."

"Gives permission? Is he your boss or something?"

"Or something," she answers. "I *can* tell you that you're safe."

"He thinks he's a vampire," I announce.

"Yeah, well, he is. So am I."

I've lived in New Orleans my entire life. I've lived around crazy my entire life, but this takes the cake. "Do you know how insane you both sound? Is this some sort of cult?"

Violet laughs. "To answer your questions, yes, I'm aware of how I sound, and no, this is not a cult. We're vampires, Amelia, and we're not the only ones."

"Viktor," I retort.

"Among others."

"How long...how long have you lived with Harrison?"

Violet shrugs. "I was turned somewhere around a hundred years ago. Been here ever since." She smiles warmly. "Harrison asked me to tell you dinner was ready if you're hungry."

"I'm not hungry." My stomach growls, betraying me.

"You sure about that?" She laughs. "Harrison and I are the only two in the house. Our cook has left for the day, and he left enough food to feed an army." A growl escapes my stomach once more. I have no idea how long it's been since I've eaten. "Harrison said he'd stay out of sight if it would help you feel more comfortable."

I don't feel comfortable, but this is my only way out. "Okay," I whisper. "If anyone tries to eat me, I'm not going to be happy."

Violet claps her hands. "Yay! Follow me." She leads me out of the room and down a narrow hallway lined with oversized portraits. The dim lighting makes it difficult to make out the details of the paintings, but it's obvious they're old and original.

"Are the people in these pictures vampires too?" My voice is laced with sarcasm.

She looks at the wall. "Most were." She points at one in particular. The man in the portrait is wearing clothes from the 1600s. I recognize the design style from my studies. "Look at his face closely." I stare into green eyes and black hair.

"He looks like Harrison. Must be a relative."

"Not a relative. That's a picture of Harrison. He's lived in this house, well, not this house exactly, the original burned, but in a house on this same spot for nearly three hundred years."

"That's not possible. This land was owned by natives until the French purchased it."

"Don't believe everything you read in history books." I follow Violet down a narrow set of stairs that into a grand foyer. The sitting room off of the foyer is filled with Victorian-era furniture that would rival any museum in the city. A portrait over the fireplace grabs my attention. It's been covered with black fabric, hiding the image behind it.

"Why is the picture covered?"

"You'll have to ask Harrison about that." She turns, leading me to the back of the house. "The kitchen is this way." We enter a kitchen that is the picture of modern conveniences. I feel like I've shifted timelines as we enter the stone countertops and modern appliance mecca of New Orleans. A large bar in the center of the room is covered in dishes, each holding more food than I've seen in a while.

"Is this all for me?"

"Thomas tends to go overboard. I told him you'd never be able to eat all of this, but he was excited about the opportunity to cook. Eat what you like. We'll donate the rest." I don't know why her words surprise me.

There's so much food, I have a hard time choosing what to eat. I add a small spoonful of everything, making my plate resemble a potluck dinner at church. "I'll be right outside if you need anything," Violet announces, moving toward the door.

"You're not staying?"

She stops walking. "I assumed you'd want to be alone. I'm happy to stay if you're sure I'm not going to eat you." She mocks my words from earlier.

I smile, weakly. "Please stay." The thought of being alone in a house full of people who think they're vampires is scarier than eating a possibly poisoned meal in front of one of them. The irony of my thoughts doesn't escape me.

"I miss food," she says, watching me take small bites from my plate. "What does that taste like? Can you describe it?" She points at the sweet potato souffle on my plate.

"Um, well, it's creamy, with a hint of cinnamon, and I think there's nutmeg mixed throughout. The pecan topping adds a little sweetness that counters the tartness of the potatoes." Violet covers her mouth with her hand.

"Oh, my God. I'm sorry," she mumbles from behind her palm. Her jaw wiggles, and she moves her hand away. I don't know what happened, and I don't want to know. It doesn't take long before I've had my fill. Sitting back in the seat, I resist the urge to pat my stomach.

"That was delicious. Thank you. My compliments to the chef."

"I think I enjoyed watching you eat it as much as you enjoyed eating it." Violet has an easy air about her, making me feel slightly more comfortable. Even if she is crazy.

"Are there more *vampires* in the city?"

She crosses her arms across her chest. "You do remember you live in New Orleans, right? This city is riddled with vampires and has been for centuries. Hell, I think vampires were here before humans. I can guarantee we're not the first ones you've come across in your lifetime." Thoughts of random faces I've seen on the streets flash into my mind. Could they have been vampires? What the hell? Why am I even considering this?

"Who is Harrison?"

She sits back in her chair. "That is a question for Harrison. His story is not mine to tell." She reaches across the bar, takes my plate from me, and sets it in the sink. "Do you mind helping me get the leftovers ready to take to the shelter?" She drags a few Ziploc bags out of a cabinet, along with several pieces of disposable plasticware. I help as we fill them with sliced ham, several kinds of casseroles, two loaves of homemade bread, and so many vegetables I lose count.

"Thomas did go a bit overboard." I smile.

"He always does, but it will go to good use." She bags the leftovers in grocery bags. "I hate to tell you this, but you have to go back into your room while I'm gone."

"That won't be necessary, Violet. I'll stay with her. In fact, why don't Amelia and I take the leftovers to the shelter?" Harrison is standing at the back door of the house. The jeans and Henley shirt he's wearing are so tight, I can see every muscle in his body.

"Sure, if Amelia's okay with that," Violet answers with a smile. "Are you okay with that?" she asks me.

"If I have to choose between being locked back in that room or hanging out with a supposed vampire, I'm going to choose the vampire."

"Good. Promise you won't try to run?"

"No," I answer truthfully.

"This should be interesting." He smiles, showing the dimples from earlier. "After you." He opens the back door wide, and I duck under his arm.

FOUR

vampires and beignets

I DON'T RECOGNIZE the street we're on. I've lived in New Orleans my entire life and thought I'd explored every inch of the Quarter, but this doesn't look familiar. "Where are we?"

"I think that's information for another time," he answers.

"If I run, I'll need to know where to come back to for my clothes." Harrison smirks at my answer, raising one side of his mouth higher than the other.

"You do have a good point. I believe you'll find your laptop in the wardrobe in your room. I brought everything I thought belonged to you."

I stop walking. "You went back to the apartment?"

"I did," he answers. "After the library, I went to retrieve your belongings."

"Was he there?"

"Viktor was gone. Your landlady was there."

I picture the white-haired woman. "Was she okay?"

"She was very much alive and well. You need to know something about vampires and your landlady." I resist the urge to roll my eyes. "She's not the sweet little old lady you thought she was. She was what we call a donneuse."

"A donor?" Three years of French are finally paying off.

"You speak French?"

"Enough to order in a restaurant, but not enough to sound intelligent. Why do you think she is a donor?" I persist.

"A donneuse or donor is a human that forms a contract with a vampire. Contracts can vary, but most are used for feeding."

I stop walking. "It's bad enough that you and Violet are trying to convince me that you and this Viktor person are vampires. Now you're telling me that my sweet little old lady landlord is in some contract to let a vampire feed from her?"

He ignores my jab and answers. "Most likely, however, it seems she's been finding other donors for him for the past few years." His answer makes this whole scenario sound perfectly normal.

I cross my arms across my chest. "I'm not saying I believe any of this, but if that's the case then she needs to be saved. Is that something the other pretend vampires do?"

He sighs. "A donneuse is bonded to their maître for life. She doesn't want to be saved."

"Master? You think Viktor is her master?"

"Most likely since she was young," he answers.

He continues walking, and I follow behind. Why? Because I couldn't outrun Ms. Esther if she was chasing me, let alone Harrison. Vampire or not, he's faster than I'll ever be. We approach a very familiar street in the Quarter, and crowds are slipping in and out of bars that line the road. "The shelter is on Bourbon Street?"

"It is." He opens a simple black door with a small window cut inside. "From the outside, it looks like nothing special. To the unsuspecting tourist, it's just another door to who knows where. To people who need a bite to eat, it's a place to get warm food and a welcoming smile."

"Harry!" a large woman exclaims as we enter a large room filled with cafeteria tables. People line the tables, filling nearly every seat. "Has Thomas sent more food for us?"

Harrison smiles, hugging the woman. "He has." He puts a hand on my shoulder, and I resist the urge to pull away. "Opie, this is Amelia. I'm giving her the five-dollar tour of the city."

Opie smiles. "There's not a better tour guide in the city, young lady. It's a pleasure to meet you, Amelia." She points to an apron and hairnet behind the counter. "We could use some help serving tonight. Would you two be willing?" Harrison looks at me for an answer.

I shrug. "Sure. What do we do?"

"Just fill their plates, baby. Most people just want a friendly smile and a warm meal. Just to know someone cares means more than you know." We tie on aprons, and I hide the laugh trying to form as Harrison slides a hairnet over his man bun.

"I look dumb, don't I?" he asks, mimicking my smile.

"No, not at all," I lie. We serve dinner to over forty people before the line begins to die down. All the food we brought is gone, and there's nothing much left to scoop onto the plates. "What about the rest of them?" I nod toward the remaining few in line. "There's not enough for them to eat."

He follows my line of sight. "I'll take care of it." He moves across the room, speaking to Opie and handing her something from his pocket. I don't know what he said, but she pulls him into a big hug, kissing his cheek before she lets go. "Ready to go?" he asks, back by my side.

"What did you give her?"

He shrugs. "A few dollars. It'll be enough to feed the rest of them." From the look on Opie's face, it's more than enough. We take off the aprons and hang them neatly behind the counter.

"Thank you, both. Amelia, it was a pleasure. Come back anytime." She blows Harrison a kiss as we exit the nondescript door, back into the craziness that is New Orleans nightlife.

"That was the last thing I expected after being locked up all day."

He looks at his feet. "I'm sorry about that. We couldn't take a chance on you running back to Viktor."

"Harrison, when are we going to end this charade? There are no such things as vampires. I don't know what part of the delusional truck you fell off of, but you're confused." I sigh. "I have a great therapist. I can talk to her about you if you're willing to go."

"Amelia," Harrison pulls me to the side of the street. "I appreciate the offer, but I am not delusional or confused. I am a vampire. Violet is a vampire. Viktor is a vampire. The city has many more, *most* of which are perfectly sane."

I sigh, feeling sorry for him. "Harrison, let me help you."

He backs me into an alley and against a brick wall. Bright green eyes stare into mine, making me feel uncomfortable. "You're not going to scream when I show you my teeth." His words echo through my mind several times before I repeat them back. "Good girl. I'm not going to hurt you."

"Good girl," I repeat. "I'm not going to hurt you."

Harrison smiles, bringing me back to the present. The smile I've seen for the past week is replaced with sharp teeth. He continues staring at me with vampire teeth hanging over his bottom lip, and I stare in complete confusion.

"Those are the most realistic costume teeth I've ever seen." My words are barely louder than a whisper.

His teeth disappear as quickly as they appeared. "They're not part of a costume. I am a vampire, Amelia." He laughs loudly. "I've never had to work this hard to convince someone of my true identity."

"Even if it is true, and I'm not saying it is, what would a vampire want with me? I'm a doctoral candidate with less than two dollars to my name. I don't have some mythological talent hidden in my bloodline. I can't fly or control the weather with nothing more than a thought. I'm just a regular, boring human, full of childhood trauma and student loans. A vampire rescuing me from my mundane life is the kind of thing fantasy books are written about."

Harrison laughs loudly. "Those books are full of vampires. I'll admit, I've read a few of them. I've been around a long time, and I have never seen a vampire *sparkle* in the sun." I laugh, knowing exactly which story he's referring to. "Don't even get me started on the hybrid baby and that werewolf. Werewolves act nothing like that."

The smile dissolves from my face. "Now you're telling me werewolves are real?"

"That's a subject for another day." I follow Harrison out of the alley just as a group of young women is moving toward us. It's clear from their strides and the looks on their faces that they're drunk.

"Well, hello, handsome," the leader of the pack

says. She steps between us and is inches from Harrison's face.

"Excuse me, please." He steps aside, trying to get away from her.

"Where do you think you're going?" Her words are slurred and hard to understand. She steps in front of him a second time. "You're really hot." She shoots a disapproving look at me. "I can treat you better than she ever could."

"Miss," his Southern Gentleman accent is back. "I do believe you're intoxicated and not making the best choices right now. Please excuse me and my friend as we make our way down the street."

"Damn, you have an accent, too." She runs her hands down his chest. "Oh, my God. What are you hiding under here." She tries to untuck his shirt.

"Please, don't touch me." Harrison's voice is calm, cool, and collected. The woman continues her assault, ignoring his plea. "Ma'am, I'm asking you nicely." She continues to run her hand down his body and slides her hands under his now untucked shirt.

I step between the two of them, pushing her back a few feet. "Bitch, back off. He doesn't want you. No, means no!" I've always been one to fight for the underdog. This woman is practically stripping him naked on Bourbon Street.

"I'm fine," Harrison says, moving forward. "Let's go, Amelia."

The drunk woman moves toward us again. This

time, something invisible pushes her back. Not hard enough to make her fall, but enough to push her far enough away that she can't touch either of us. We walk several blocks before I stop. "What the hell was that?"

"She clearly had too much to drink."

"I've been drunk before. I've seen drunk people before. That was more than drinking. It's like she was obsessed with you. You could've had sex with her in the middle of the street if you'd wanted to."

"Some humans are…" he searches for the right words, "unnaturally attracted to vampires."

"Harrison, you're not…" He disappears and returns seconds later holding a beignet.

I stare at him confused. "What's this?"

"I thought you might be hungry."

"That's a beignet. You didn't have it a second ago."

He hands me the ceramic plate. "I just went to get it."

"When exactly?"

He sighs. "I'm a vampire, Amelia. With that comes superhuman speed along with many other things."

"You ran to Café du Monde and got that beignet in less than a second?"

"Yes. I would've gotten two, but the lady took a bite just as I got there." He looks around the busy street. "I think it's best we get off the street. I'm likely to be approached again, and I'd hate for you to have to come to my rescue twice in one night." He smirks at his words. "We'll head back to the house now."

I look around at the crowds of people surrounding us. I could easily escape, blending into the crowd, and disappearing among the masses. Harrison is far enough away from me I could get away without much trouble. Should I run? Where would I go? All three of my outfits are at his home along with all my research. I look up at the so-called vampire walking next to me. The New Orleans humidity has made several strands escape his bun and stick out on the sides of his head. He looks like an extremely hot twenty-year-old, looking for a good time in the streets of the Big Easy, not the vampire he's working hard to convince me he is.

"You're staring at me," he says as we turn off the loud street.

"I'm trying to determine if you look like a vampire."

He laughs, showing his dimples. "What do vampires look like?"

"Well, for one they sparkle." He snorts a laugh at my words.

"We talked about that one." He continues to smile. "Seriously, what do vampires look like?"

"It's not an exact science, but from my doctoral research, I've built a mental image."

"I'd love to hear it," he admits.

"It sounds dumb now." I sigh. "Okay. Are you ready?"

"So ready," he answers with a smile. "Paint the visual image of a typical vampire for me."

"To start with, they're hot. Like really hot." He holds up a hand.

"Are you saying I'm not hot...?" He acts like his feelings are hurt.

"No interruptions, please. May I continue?"

"Of course. I apologize."

"So, they're superhot, tall and thin, dark black hair that ends in a widow's peak on their foreheads. Dark eyes with a shadow underneath. They usually wear a black suit and can blend into a crowd easily."

"Amelia, don't take this the wrong way, but you just described Boris Karloff."

"I don't have a clue who that is."

Harrison laughs. "He played Dracula in a movie from the '60s. Never mind, please continue."

"That was it. Did you know I'm writing my thesis on the history of mythological creatures in Europe?"

"How's that going?"

"To be honest, no matter how much research I do, I'm not finding overly helpful information. Most of the books and information I've found are based on the same information, just reworded to sound impressive." I sigh. "That's why it's taking so long to write my thesis."

"You have full access to my library if that helps." I think back to the room where I woke at his house for the first time. The room was filled from floor to ceiling with books.

"Seriously?"

"Of course," he answers. "There are texts well over a thousand years old inside. Since it's not safe to go back to your apartment, you're welcome to stay at my home with full access to the library and its contents."

"I'd have full access to the library?" I repeat his words.

"Of course."

"Then I accept."

"Perfect," he answers, smiling. "It's getting late. Nothing good happens in the Quarter this time of night." We walk in silence, allowing the sounds of the street to form our conversation. On the walk back, I notice him handing money to a few homeless people as we pass. Could Harrison be telling me the truth? Don't be dumb, Amelia.

FIVE

the makeover i never knew i needed

I WAKE the next morning as the sun rises high in the sky. Looking around the room, I take in the details of the design. To the right sits a small desk I hadn't even noticed yesterday. Personalized stationery sits on top, complete with ink and a feather pen. On a table beside the bed is a heavy book that wasn't there yesterday. I sit up, opening the ancient text to see the title written in French. "L'histoire des vampires en Europe," I read out loud. The French words sound strange to my ear. I flip through the pages, seeing pictures, drawings, and more information than I've seen on vampires in one text than all the other books I've already read. Oh, my God. I could write my entire thesis from this one book. Too bad that's frowned upon.

A knock on the door draws me from my book-induced trance. "Yes?"

"Good morning, Amelia. Breakfast is served if you're hungry."

"Thomas?"

"Yes, ma'am. That's me."

"I'll be right down." I search through the wardrobe, finding a pair of leggings and an oversized Loyola sweatshirt. I slip into the outfit and follow the path Violet led me through yesterday. A younger dark-skinned man is standing in front of the food-covered bar in the kitchen.

"Thomas?" I ask again.

"Yes, ma'am. It's a pleasure to meet you." He stares at me a moment, before setting a plate in front of me. "I sure hope you like to eat because I like to cook."

"I'm a fan," I answer with a smile.

"Do you mind if I eat with you?"

"I'd appreciate the company," I admit.

"Good, I was going to anyway." He sits across from me. "What brings you here?"

I shrug, not sure how to answer. "Just here for a bit, working on my thesis."

"Oh, you're in college?"

"Graduate school. I only have a few classes left and my thesis, then I'll have my Ph.D. in mythological studies of Europe."

Thomas stops eating. "Big market for that, huh?"

I snort a laugh. "Not really. Truthfully, I don't know what got me into it. I was a typical kid, fascinated by the unknown. As I got older, I guess I never lost that curiosity.

"You came to the right place." He smiles, filling my plate with more food.

"I couldn't eat anything else. Thank you for a wonderful breakfast."

Thomas smiles, showing a mouthful of perfect teeth. "My pleasure, Amelia. It's nice to have someone around here that eats."

"Don't tell me you are in on it, too?"

He stands, clearing the plates. "There's nothing to be in on. Harrison and Violet are vampires. I've known Harrison for over ten years. He found me on the street and offered me a job here, as a cook. I've been here ever since. Although, I'll admit, I don't know why a vampire needed a cook."

"You believe them?"

"Yes, ma'am. Why wouldn't I?"

I stare at the man in front of me. "Because there are no such things as vampires."

Thomas laughs deeply. "Girl, I don't know who told you that, but they were lying to you. You can't live in New Orleans and not believe in vampires. Where I grew up, they were everywhere."

"Are you a donneuse?" I ask, remembering Harrison's explanation from yesterday. I can't believe I'm actually questioning whether or not it's true.

"Since I don't know what that means, I'm going to say no."

"Can I help you clean up?" He shoos me away. "Goodness, no. I need something to do."

"In that case, can you point me in the direction of the library?"

"Of course. Go back into the living room, and turn right off the foyer. It's a few rooms back." I follow his directions, stopping in the sitting room. The large covered portrait grabs my attention. Why, out of all the paintings in the house, is this one covered? I make a mental note to ask Harrison the next time I see him.

I find the library right where Thomas directed. The smell of the texts lifts my spirits. I may actually get this thesis written after all. On a table in the middle of the room is a laptop with a bright pink bow on top. Being the nosey person I am, I read the card attached. *Hope this helps with your research. Harrison.*

Oh, my God. This is for me? I expected it to be a gift to Harrison not *from* him. I open the MacBook to find it already loaded with research software and a card catalog of his entire library. This is the nicest thing anyone has ever done for me. I realize how sad that statement is the moment I think it, but sadly, it's true.

Growing up in what is commonly called "the projects" of New Orleans, I wasn't given anything other than a roof over my head. My mother was my only source of family, and she wasn't there most of the time. If I had food, it was because I found it. She stopped coming home when I was twelve. The day I moved to college was the last time I saw that apartment, and I've never looked back. I fight the sadness those memories bring, putting them in their safety basket in the back of my mind and opening the online card catalog.

Three books pull up with my search, and I set off to find them. Each is full of information on vampires and, hopefully, holds the answer to what the hell is going on in this house. Several hours later, I find a list of names of men who were rumored to be vampires. I type each name into the Google search bar, finding nothing substantial. It's not until I'm nearly through the list that I find something interesting. Typing the name Luquire into the search, an old black-and-white photo of the man that was in my apartment pulls up.

"What the hell?" I ask out loud. The article accompanying the picture is nothing more than a quick snip about a donation made to the city of New Orleans, nearly seventy-five years ago.

"Amelia?" Violet's voice makes me jump, causing me to nearly drop the new laptop.

"I'm here," I answer.

"Oh, good. You were so quiet, Thomas decided you were asleep."

I snort. "No, just engulfed in research. I can't thank you enough for letting me stay here. This library is the answer to prayers."

"Hmm, this is like the third time I've even been in this room. It smells weird to me. But I'm glad you found what you needed!" She shows fake enthusiasm. "Harrison thought you might like to go with me to get out of the house for a bit."

"Yes!" I close the laptop, hiding the photograph. "Where are we going?"

"Shopping!" she exclaims.

"I don't have shopping money."

"Nonsense. We have plastic money and a trust fund. Let's go." She takes my hand into hers, pulling me from my chair.

"Violet, I don't own plastic money. Every last penny I had went to pay for an apartment I can't live in anymore. I literally have less than two dollars in my bank account. I can't even afford to shop at Dollar Tree."

"I'm not taking no for an answer. Let's go. I'll drive." I follow her out the back door, into the courtyard. A door lifts, revealing a garage full of expensive cars. Against the back wall is my ancient Nissan.

"Is that my car?"

"It is. Harrison brought it here for you. He thought you might want it." She pushes a key fob in her hand and a bright red BMW roars to life.

"Is that yours?"

"One of them." She slides into the driver's seat and pushes a button on the dashboard. A second hidden door slides open, this one leading to the street. She pulls onto the street in a move straight out of F1. I grab the "oh, shit" bar and hang on as she weaves in and out of traffic, passing anyone going slower than forty. "Where do you like to shop?"

"I don't. Shopping is miserable when you don't have money to spend," I answer, still holding on for dear life.

"Then we'll go to my favorite place." What should be a fifteen-minute drive is completed in five. I don't know how she magically bypassed the traffic lights and pedestrians without issues.

We enter the mostly empty mall, and she heads straight for a store I've only seen on television. The rich smell of leather fills my nose the moment we enter. A saleswoman practically runs to our side, offering to help us find items we might like. She offers Violet a handful of bags, hoping to draw her attention and her money. I step away from the show and toward a dark brown backpack. The leather is so soft, it feels like butter.

"Gorgeous, isn't it?" a new saleswoman asks.

"It is."

"Shall I wrap it up for you?" She unhooks the bag from its theft deterrent system.

"Oh, no. I'm just looking. My friend," I point to Violet, who looks bored with the bags she's being shown, "is the one with the money. I'm just along for the ride."

"We'll take it," Violet says, coming up behind me.

"I can't afford..."

"Hush," she interrupts. "We'll take it. Wrap it up, and charge it to my account."

"Yes, Miss Du Four," the first saleswoman answers. Violet ushers me out of the store toward one across the building with a familiar blue color.

"Violet, I can't afford that bag, and you don't need to buy it for me. It was over three thousand dollars. That's more than my car cost."

We stop walking, and Violet turns me toward her. "Let me do this for you. It's not about the money. I have more money than I could ever spend in a hundred lifetimes. I want to buy you these things. It'd be an honor for me, really."

"How is spending thousands of dollars on me an honor?" We clearly grew up in different worlds.

"Because you're my only friend."

"Okay," I relent. "This doesn't make me your donneuse, does it?" I ask teasingly. Violet laughs loudly.

"No. Besides, Harrison would stake me for something like that." I don't question her choice of words as we enter the next store, and she leads us straight to the jewelry department. "That's gorgeous." She points at a diamond cross necklace. "We'd like to see that, please," she tells the anxious salesman.

"Violet," I whisper. "Can you touch that?"

She genuinely looks confused. "Touch what? The glass cases?"

"No, the cross." The man sets it in her hand, draping it across her wrist.

She doesn't bother flipping the price tag over before declaring it sold. She opens the clasp, placing it around my neck.

"It looks stunning with her...sweatshirt," the salesman clearly disapproves of my clothing choice.

"Yes, it does. Put it on my account," she says, pulling me out of the store.

"Of course, Miss Du Four," the man calls after us.

"Does everyone in this mall know you by name?" I ask, following her through the empty hall.

"No, but they know my money." She smiles, making me smile with her. "To answer your question, yes, I can touch crosses. Contrary to what you've read in books, we are not demonic creatures. Yes, we can die, but a cross won't do the trick." She stops in front of a high-end salon. "Here's our final destination."

"Miss Du Four," the woman at the front desk greets us. "I didn't realize you were coming in today. I would have cleared our schedule."

"Today is for my friend. She would like the works please." The woman smiles, and I swear dollar signs fill her pupils.

"Of course, this way please." She motions me to the back of the building as Violet sits in the waiting room, reading magazines. "Please put your feet in the tub. Let me know if the temperature is to your liking."

"It's perfect," I lie. The sensation of my skin being scorched from my body the instant the water touches my feet is hard to hide. A younger woman sits at my feet and scrapes, clips, and moisturizes my feet in ways I've never felt before. Thirty minutes later, my toes are sparkly red and don't look like they belong on my body.

"This way, please." The woman from earlier leads me to a seat in front of a mirror. I sit as she wraps a black gown over me, velcroing it around my neck. "What are we doing with your hair today?"

I pull the ponytail holder free, letting my red curls fall into place. "All I've ever done is wear it in either a bun or ponytail. I don't know how to style it."

"Such beautiful hair. It's a shame to hide it." She pulls the sides of my hair down, checking the length. "If we trim off the dead ends and add some long layers, you should be able to style your hair easily. You have a natural curl that is begging to not be hidden any longer. All you need are a few products and some education."

"I can't afford..."

"Whatever you use to style her hair, we'll take four of them with us." Violet has magically popped in behind me.

"Violet, that's too much." She glares at me from behind, squinting her eyes in the mirror.

"She's right, you have beautiful hair. Let it down a little." She laughs at her own joke, heading back to her chair in the front.

The stylist takes me to the back where she washes and conditions my hair using more product than I've used in my entire life before wrapping a towel around my head and leading me back to the swiveling chair.

She spends the next hour carefully cutting my hair, making sure it's even on both sides and giving me sweeping bangs, as she called them. Finally happy with the cut, she adds more product to my hair before diffusing the curls until they're dry. After the cut, she turned me away from the mirror, wanting to make a big reveal. Everyone, including Violet, is standing in front of me, admiring their creation.

"I was right. She is beautiful," the woman who's painstakingly been working on me for the past few hours says. I swear a tear is streaming down her cheek.

"I'll do the honors," Violet says, turning my chair toward the mirror. I'm in shock at the image looking back at me. Long spiral curls hang past my shoulders and are perfectly curled, with no frizz. I've had frizzy hair my entire life.

"Is that my hair?" I'm legitimately confused.

"That's all you, my dear," the stylist answers. "People pay thousands of dollars for curl like that."

"You look beautiful," Violet says. "I feel like this is a proud mom moment."

I look back at the girl staring at me. Her bright blue eyes are more tired than I've seen before, but she's the same girl. A small spattering of freckles is displayed across her nose and cheeks, and her skin is so white it resembles porcelain. That girl is me.

a night on the town

THE NEXT FEW days pass uneventfully, with the same routine of eating a huge breakfast and research filling the rest of my day. I haven't seen Harrison since the first night, and I'm a little curious about his whereabouts. No, I'm nosey. I'm nosey about his whereabouts. The first morning I came downstairs after my hair makeover, Thomas made such a big deal about my hair that he boosted my self-esteem by several degrees

On more than one occasion, I've caught him staring at me when he thinks I'm not looking. It's not the creepy guy kind of staring but more of a curious glance. I pretended not to notice, not wanting to make the energy between us awkward.

I've spent the majority of my time in the library researching information for my thesis while searching for information to disprove their claims to be vampires. Not surprisingly, I find nothing.

My back is stiff, my eyes are crossed, and I've read through several priceless books on mythology. There are no clocks in the library, and I have no idea what time it is. From the shadows dancing throughout the room and the growls of my stomach, I'm guessing it's time for dinner. I put away the books from today and make a stack to read tomorrow before leaving the silent room and heading toward the kitchen.

To my surprise, there aren't ten dishes of food waiting for me on the bar. "Thomas?" I step into the courtyard. "Thomas? Violet?" No one answers. "Hello?" I close the door, heading back into the living area. How did this change from locking me in my bedroom to leaving me alone in the huge house? Moving back into the sitting room, the fabric-covered picture grabs my attention, and I make a mental note to ask someone why it's covered.

On the other side of the stairs is a room I've never explored. Usually, the door is closed, but today the pocket door is cracked open. "Hello?" I whisper, with no response. I enter what must be Harrison's office. The cedar-lined walls are home to framed university degrees and newspaper articles, some dating back as far as the nineteenth century. Running my finger across each, I'm surprised to see Harrison's name neatly printed on them all.

The largest piece of furniture, an antique wooden desk, sits directly across from a fireplace while bookshelves cover the wall behind. This room reminds me of something from a movie set. Every detail is perfect, down to the arrangement of books by spine color on the shelves behind. I run my fingers along the intricately carved details on the edge of the desk, admiring the craftsmanship that went into its creation.

The bookshelf in this room is different from the library. The titles that line the shelves are academic in nature and cover everything from rock and minerals to the production of oil in the United States. This is Harrison's personal collection. My stomach growls loudly, echoing off the wooden walls, reminding me that I haven't eaten since breakfast. Sliding the pocket door back in place, I head toward the kitchen in hopes of finding something to eat.

Opening the industrial-sized refrigerator, I find a plate, covered with foil and a note attached. *I had to leave early, please enjoy your meal. ~Thomas*

Thank God for Thomas. I haven't been here long, but I'm already spoiled with his cooking. I'm taking a bite of Alfredo when movement in the courtyard catches my eye. I continue eating my creamy deliciousness when I see it again. Am I being paranoid? It's a courtyard. No one can get inside unless they know how to fly. It's then that I see the source. In the corner are Harrison and Violet. In their hands, they each hold one of Thomas's wrists and they're...biting him. Oh, my God. They're drinking his blood.

I back away from the window, stumbling over one of the barstools, making it crash to the tile floor. Shit! I run full speed up the stairs and close my bedroom door behind me. Dumb move, Amelia. You just did what every victim in a horror movie does. I slide the antique desk in front of the door, deluding myself into thinking that could keep Harrison or Violet from coming right through.

My heart is pounding as I listen for any sounds throughout the house. I don't know how much time has passed before a gentle knock on my door pulls me from the corner I've been crouched in. "Amelia?" Harrison's voice is soft. "I'm so sorry you had to see that." I don't answer. He's quiet for so long, I'm beginning to think he's no longer at the door. "I'm still here," he says as if he can hear my thoughts. "I understand if you don't want to open the door, but I hope you won't mind if I try to explain."

"It's true, isn't it? You're...vampires."

"Yes," he whispers. "You're safe here."

"You two were feeding on Thomas. Is that what you're going to do to me?"

"No," he answers quickly. "I would never feed from you. Neither would Violet."

"Is Thomas your donneuse?"

"No, he's not." Harrison sighs before continuing. "I made a choice, centuries ago, not to hunt and feed on humans."

"Seems like you may have broken that." My words are laced with venom.

"I know it looked that way, but that's not what was happening. Thomas offered his blood."

"How is that different from hunting and feeding?"

"I'm sustained through the blood of animals. Goat and deer mostly. Drinking their blood sustains me but doesn't give me the strength that human blood does. With everything going on, I need to be stronger." I picture him sitting on the hallway floor with his back against my door.

"What do you mean by everything going on? What are you not telling me?"

"It's nothing to concern yourself with. Thomas is a willing donor who offers his blood when we need it. We don't hunt him, nor do we take more than we should." His head hits the other side of the door. "I know seeing that was scary. I can assure you that you're not in any danger. You're much safer in this house than in the streets of New Orleans."

"Why?" I persist.

I hear movement from the other side of the door as he sighs. "Violet and I are leaving for the night. I don't want you to feel unsafe. If you want to leave, you have free rein to do so." He pauses. "I hope you don't." His footsteps soften as he moves away from my door. I spend the night hiding between the wardrobe and the wall. Ever since being a child and listening to Tammy make money for rent, it's the only place I feel safe. I spent many nights, alone, hiding in my closet, and any small spaces I could find.

Through nothing short of magical pixie dust, I manage to sleep a few hours, waking as the sun shines a brain-piercing beam straight into my eyeball. The room looks the same as before, and I'm still in one piece with no fang holes.

I spend way too much time in the bathroom, scrubbing my body from head to toe. I emerge an hour later with bright pink skin and shriveled fingers and toes. The sunshine brings a dose of reality into my brain. Harrison and Violet have never done anything to scare me or make me feel like I'm in danger. Maybe I overreacted?

I slip into a pair of leggings and an oversized hoodie and make my way down the stairs. To my surprise, Thomas is in the kitchen as the door swings open. "You're still here! Good. I made breakfast."

I slide on top of one of the barstools. "What was that?" He continues stirring whatever is in the skillet, ignoring me. "Thomas? What did I see yesterday?"

He stops stirring. "Amelia, you saw something that has only happened a few times in the years I've been here. I provide food to humans and others. It was nothing to be frightened of, and it was my choice to help them."

"Does it hurt?"

"At first, yes, but their saliva takes away any pain." He continues stirring whatever's in the skillet.

"Thomas, you have to know that's not normal."

Turning his back to the stove, he faces me. "You want to know what's not normal? Not normal is being kicked out of your home at the age of thirteen because your grandmother thinks you're a 'queer.'" He uses finger quotes. "Not normal is having to work on the streets, in every sense of the word, just to have food for a day." He pauses. "I did what I had to do to survive, Amelia...in the *normal* world. I'd much rather be here, in this world than out there in that one. Mr. Chamberlin and Miss Du Four have never made me feel unsafe, used me, or asked me for anything. He provides a warm bed, a safe place to call home, and friendship. If this isn't *normal*, then sign me the hell up." He turns and continues stirring his creation on the stove. "Hungry?" he turns with a smile.

"I'm sorry. I just assumed..."

"Girl, has anyone ever told you what happens when you assume? Don't assume anything. I'm fine. I'm healthy, I'm happy, and I'm hungry. Let's eat." He dishes what turned out to be scrambled eggs on my plate along with a few pieces of bacon. We eat in silence as the reality of his words comes crashing down into my soul.

I spend the rest of the day in my usual spot, the library. I've managed to complete several chapters of my thesis, which is more than I've ever done before. I haven't seen anyone other than Thomas all day. I need to apologize to Harrison. My brain misconstrued what I saw in the courtyard with the information I've seen in movies and read in fantasy novels. I need to apologize for my naivety. Closing up my writing spot for the night, I head out to find someone, anyone.

The kitchen is empty, and Thomas is nowhere in sight. I don't know why that surprises me. I guess part of me expects that he sleeps in here when he's not cooking. I open the refrigerator, hoping to find a plate of food, and find nothing.

My phone vibrates in my pocket, scaring me. On the screen is a text from an unknown number.

> Meet me in the garage in thirty minutes. We're going out tonight.

I've seen too many movies with this same scene. I ignore the text and continue rummaging through the refrigerator.

> Close the fridge door, you're going to let all the cold out. I'm taking you to dinner.

I turn around, not sure what I'm expecting to see.

> Harrison?

> Sorry, I should've told you it's me. I forgot my number is unlisted.

> I want to apologize for yesterday. I jumped to conclusions, and I was wrong.

> Can you be ready in thirty minutes? Wear something nice.

> What makes you so sure I won't run away?

> Twenty-nine minutes.

I rush to my room, looking through the wardrobe for anything that would classify as "dressy." Apparently, Violet snuck a few items in here when I wasn't around. I find a black wide-legged pantsuit that I've never seen before. It fits like it was made for me and hemmed to match my short legs. I spritz a little product into my curls, springing them back to life, and add powder, mascara, and lip gloss. "I look pretty damn good," I say out loud to no one. I throw my cell into the overpriced bag Violet bought and head downstairs to the garage. According to my phone, it's only been twenty-five minutes. "Ha, I beat your deadline, Harry."

"You did." Harrison is standing by the back of the room, staring at me. "You look amazing."

I feel my cheeks turn red instantly. "Thank you. I want to apologize for yesterday and also for not believing you. I realized today you were telling me the truth. I'm sorry for that."

He holds up his hands, stopping me. "It's not necessary." He moves closer, and I realize he's wearing a suit. His hair is out of its usual bun and hangs past his shoulders. His green eyes shine in the moonlight, and for some reason, butterflies take flight in my stomach. For God's sake, Amelia. He's a vampire.

A car on the other side of the garage roars to life. Harrison is in front of me before I register movement. "Shall we?" He holds his hand to me. I take it, letting him lead me to the silver sports car. He closes the door behind me as I settle into the rich leather of whatever kind of car this is.

"Where are we going?"

"My favorite restaurant," he answers, with a smirk.

"But you don't eat."

"I eat, just not what you eat." I try not to think about what his words imply. We drive through the streets of New Orleans toward the river, stopping at what looks like an abandoned dock. "We're here."

"Where? There's nothing here." Out of nowhere, a man appears at Harrison's window.

"Good evening, Mr. Chamberlin. May I park your car for you?"

"Yes, thank you." Harrison is at my door in the blink of an eye, opening it for me. His smile is warm as he takes my hand into his. "Are you ready?"

"Harrison, am I about to *be* dinner?"

He smiles, trying to hide his humor. "No. I assure you this is a real restaurant with real food. Human food." He wraps my arm through his, leading us into what looks like an abandoned shipping container.

"If I die, I'm going to haunt the hell out of you."

"Good evening, Mr. Chamberlin, Miss Lockhart. Your table is ready." He leads us to an elevator and to the tenth floor of a building I never realized we entered. The doors open, revealing the New Orleans skyline and a single table with a million-dollar view.

"Is this for us?" I whisper. Harrison pulls my chair out before taking his seat across from me. "This is beautiful."

"Yes, it is." He's staring right at me.

"Do you come here often?"

"I try to come every couple of months or so. Sometimes I forget how beautiful this city is. I come here when I need reminders." The server sets a covered plate in front of me and a glass of red liquid in front of Harrison. "It's goat blood," he says after the server is out of earshot. I don't know why his words surprise me. I didn't imagine him drinking the blood of virgins, but goat blood seems strange.

Pulling the cover off my plate, I find a beautifully cut filet. I've never had steak like this before. Growing up, the only steaks I ate were made from hamburger meat. "This looks perfect." I have no clue if it's perfect or not.

"Let me know if it's not to your liking." The server says before disappearing into the shadows of the rooftop once again.

"How long have you lived in New Orleans?" I ask after eating half the steak.

"Since I can remember. My family settled here from France." I don't push for more information. "How about you?"

"My entire life. I grew up in the Calliope Projects, downtown. I didn't have the greatest childhood. My mom was absent for most of it, jumping from man to man and drug to drug. The minute I turned eighteen, I left."

"I'm sorry."

"I'm not. Some people aren't meant to be mothers. I lost the mother raffle somehow and ended up with a Karen. That wasn't her actual name. Her real name was Tammy, but Karen fits her better." I take another bite of steak.

"Why did you choose your course of study?"

"You mean, European Mythology?" I mimic his moves, sipping my actual wine slowly. "When I started the program, they were offering huge scholarships through a study abroad program for European studies. I was faced with finding a mediocre job, barely paying the bills with my undergrad, or pursuing more education and changing majors. I chose to change majors."

Our server returns, this time carrying a giant piece of chocolate cake, covered with ice cream. "Your desert, ma'am."

"Dinner was delicious. Please tell the chef, I thoroughly enjoyed it." I hand him my nearly empty plate.

"I will, thank you."

"So, long story short. Now I'm working on my doctoral degree, still barely paying the bills, and have yet to study abroad." I laugh at the irony. "Seems I didn't make it very far."

"You made it much further than you realize." His words are seductive and low.

"Are you doing some sort of hypnosis on me?"

Harrison laughs, setting his drink on the table. "That's another false rumor. I cannot force you to do anything you don't want to do." I slide back in my chair. "I can, however, put suggestive thoughts into your mind."

"I have more questions."

"I'm ready." He laces his fingers together, resting them on the table.

"Can you run fast?"

"That's one thing they almost got right. I don't run, as much as move before being seen."

"That was as clear as mud." I smile, looking down awkwardly just as hands brush across my shoulders from behind. I turn, seeing Harrison standing behind my chair. "What the hell?"

"See, I didn't run. I just moved quickly."

"Move quickly back to your seat, please." He laughs, sitting back across from me. "Next question. How old are you?"

"Twenty." The look on my face must mirror my inner disbelief, making him smile. "I was twenty when I was turned, making me eternally twenty years old. To answer your question, I was born in the year 1315."

"Holy shit." I stare at the vampire across from me with newfound curiosity. I can't imagine the things he's seen, the things he's lived through.

"What are you thinking?" he asks, searching my face for answers.

"I'm thinking you could write my thesis for me."

He laughs. "I could. I have earned many degrees over the years."

"You experienced things I've only read about in books. I can't imagine seeing the world through your eyes."

"It's not as exciting as you'd think. Along with it comes the pain of watching mankind repeat the mistakes of the past and not being able to do anything to stop them."

I've never thought of it that way. I look over the city below. From here everything looks happy and healthy. From here you don't see homeless people, sleeping on the street, or prostitutes trying to earn enough money to survive. All you see is beauty. "From here, everything is beautiful. It's why this is your favorite spot, isn't it?"

"Yes," his voice sounds sad. "Thank you for coming with me. I wanted to share it with you."

"I'm glad you did. Thank you." We walk to the railing, overlooking the river with the lights of the city behind. For a brief moment, I allow myself to disappear into his world. The world of immortality and the freedom to do whatever I wanted.

The drive back to the house is quiet as we move through the same city, we overlooked hours earlier. From down here, I see the pain on their faces. The pain they wear is my pain. The pain of humanity.

"A penny for your thoughts," he says as the garage door slides open.

"Nothing in particular. I guess my brain is on overload thinking of the life—the lives you've lived. You lived through what I study."

"I'm not sure living is the right word. Most of it has just been surviving." He closes my door behind me, escorting me inside the house. A small charcuterie board is on the counter, featuring meats and cheeses from around the world.

"I swear, Thomas is going to make me gain fifty pounds before this thesis is complete." Harrison laughs.

"He does like to cook. I have something for you. I'll be right back." He disappears, leaving me alone with the collection of cheeses. I sneak a few as he comes back, carrying a wrapped present.

"Harrison, you didn't have to buy me anything."

"I know. I saw this in a bookstore while I was out of town, and it made me think of you." He hands me the brown paper package. "If you don't like it, I can return it."

I carefully tear the edges of the tape apart, trying

not to tear the paper. Inside is a leather-bound book with gold inlay edges.

"It's a journal," his voice is no louder than a whisper. "You spend so much time reading other people's writing, I thought you could do a little of your own."

"This is beautiful." I hug the book close. "Thank you." I can't remember the last time someone gave me a gift. Most holidays and birthdays are spent alone, and I've been okay with that. Somehow receiving this book brings the loneliness of those days to the surface, and I fight the tears threatening to fall. "This is the most thoughtful gift I've ever received."

"We'll have to change that." His eyes haven't left mine since he gave me the journal.

"Good night, Harrison."

"Good night, Amelia."

......

I awaken to the sound of piano overtones, echoing through the halls. I recognize the piece instantly. *Lent et douloureux* by Erik Satie, *Gymnopédies*. Thank you, Music Appreciation 101. I follow the music to the bottom floor of the house. Harrison is sitting at the keyboard of the grand piano, the source of the music. I sit on the stairs, hoping to stay out of sight and listen as the music sings to my soul. I've known this piece for years, but hearing it played live is nearly an out-of-body experience. He finishes the piece and sits in silence. I don't know whether to applaud or sneak back up the stairs.

"Any requests?" he says from behind the piano. I don't answer. "Amelia?"

"I'm sorry. I didn't mean to interrupt." I stand, moving from the shadows. "You play beautifully."

"Thank you. Erik wrote that piece after reading a poem he was particularly fond of." He stands, moving toward the staircase.

> "Slanting and shadow cutting a bursting
>   stream
> Trickled in gusts of gold on the shiny
>   flagstone
> Where the amber atoms in the fire
>   gleaming
> Mingled their Sarabande with the
>   Gymnopaedia."

"That's beautiful. You were friends with Satie?"

"I was." Harrison takes his phone from his pocket. "Excuse me," he says, answering a call. "Yes?... Where?... I'll be right there."

"Everything okay?"

"It's Viktor. He's been spotted."

"Viktor? My Viktor? I want to go."

"That's not the best idea right now. Viktor isn't like me. He'd rather kill you than look at you."

"Where is he?" I ask.

"Violet spotted him in the Quarter."

"Give me five minutes. I want to come with you. I *need* to come with you."

Harrison moves toward the door. "No, I won't lose you. Not again." He disappears into the night with barely the blink of an eye.

SEVEN

a new perspective of new orleans

I BARELY SLEEP the rest of the night. My mind flashes through the millions of possible outcomes of Harrison and Viktor's meeting. What did Harrison mean by losing me again? Did he misspeak? My mind won't let go and shut down. I finally give up trying to sleep and head down to find a snack. Knowing Thomas, there will be several to choose from. Opening the refrigerator, I'm right. There's an entire collection of tiny sandwiches waiting for me to devour. I eat my weight in chicken salad before heading back to my room.

I could get some work done. I sigh, thinking of the amount of work that's still left with my thesis, and decide against it. Over the past week, I've learned more about vampires and mythological creatures than in the two years I've been researching. Having access to a priceless library has helped tremendously.

Passing through the sitting room, the covered

painting grabs my attention. I move in front of it, willing the cloth to fall off magically. "Who are you?" I whisper.

"Would you like to see?" Harrison's voice provides the jump scare I didn't need. "I'm sorry. I didn't mean to scare you. I thought you heard me come in."

"Nope, didn't hear you, and yes, I would love to see what's behind the fabric." He moves to my side. "Please, sit down."

"I'd rather stand."

"Very well." He pulls the corner of the velvet, uncovering the portrait of a woman. Soft red curls sit high on top of her head while piercing blue eyes and porcelain white skin complete the rest of her look. She's dressed in clothing from the eighteenth century, and I can't take my eyes off her. If I didn't know better, I'd swear that the painting was of me.

"Who is she?"

"She was my wife." He stares lovingly at the painting. "Her name was Penelope."

"Was she...was she a vampire?"

Harrison sighs before answering. "Yes, a very powerful one."

I lower myself onto the sofa. "What happened to her?"

"She was taken from me." He moves to the other end of the sofa.

"Why do I look like her?"

"Not only do you look like her, but you also act like

her, smell like her, and if I didn't know better, I'd swear you were her." He wipes a tear from his cheek.

"Is that why I'm here? Because you think I'm some reincarnation of your dead wife?" I stand, moving away from him.

"No," his words are gentle, unlike mine. "Unfortunately, the belief that vampires don't have souls is real. She didn't have a soul; therefore, she cannot be reincarnated."

"Are you trying to turn me into her?"

"Amelia, I would never do that. You are your own person. I'll admit when I first saw you, I was enamored with the similarities, but the more I watched you and learned about you, I saw that you weren't Penelope."

"Harrison, what are you telling me without telling me? Did you...did you stalk me?"

"Did I watch you? Yes. Stalk you? No." He pauses in thought. "The first time I saw you, you were very young."

"Oh, my God. This is getting worse by the second."

"I know how this sounds..."

"Do you?" I interrupt. "Because I don't think you do."

"Please, let me finish." I nod, giving him permission. "You couldn't have been older than twelve or thirteen. You were walking down Chartres Street, alone. Your clothes were filthy, and I could tell you hadn't had a meal in a few days. There was something about you that called me. I could sense your strength just from watching you." I circle my hands, trying to speed him up. He sighs. "I followed you to those horrible buildings."

"The projects," I answer for him. "They're called projects. It's where people like me live."

"I followed you to the projects and watched you pass prostitutes, dealers, and druggies like it was nothing. I couldn't imagine someone so young being so desensitized to the dangers around them. That night, I brought a bag of food and set it outside your door."

His words trigger a core memory. "That was you?" I remember finding a bag full of canned goods. I ate from that bag for two weeks.

"It was. I watched you from afar, never getting close enough to be seen, but always checking to make sure you were safe."

"Safe? I spent days hiding, terrified for my life in that place. I was never safe."

"You were safer than you realized. Humans will do anything for money." I think back to the insanity of my childhood, and despite all the dangers of that place, I was ignored. He's right. I witnessed horrible scenes, but no one ever bothered me, no one. Did he pay people to leave me alone? I don't know how to process his words. I sit back on the couch, not sure what to say.

"I've checked on you over the years, never interfering, just keeping track. When I discovered you'd rented an apartment in Viktor's building, I knew my time of staying in the background was over."

"That's why you showed up in my class."

"Yes."

"How did you know he'd come for me?" Harrison pauses, looking at the portrait of his wife.

"Because he's the one responsible for her death." I stare at him, not sure what to say. Viktor killed Penelope and tried to kill me.

"Is she the reason he came after me?" I nod toward the portrait.

"That's a question for Viktor. I've learned through the years that he's unpredictable and crazy, which is a lethal combination." He pauses. "You should know that Ms. Esther is safe, and I've closed the building down to renters."

"What?"

"I called in a few favors. Ms. Esther is living in a small apartment away from the city."

"Won't that just piss him off?"

Harrison smiles. "Probably, but we have a long history of pissing each other off. Losing a donneuse and one of his many buildings closing is nothing in the grand scheme of things."

"Did you find him earlier?"

"No," he answers softly. "Would you like to get out of the house?" He completely changes the subject.

"Okay, we just took a full one-eighty." Outside, darkness is giving way to daylight as peaks of light begin cresting over the horizon. "The sun is coming out."

"You'd think with all that research you've been doing you'd know we can venture out during the day. Direct sunlight is more like a light sunburn, but I can stay in the shade as long as I like."

"I'll have you know the study of mythological creatures is about more than just vampires. At least the books are correct about vampires and their arrogance." I head toward the stairs. "I'll be down in thirty minutes." I swear I hear him laugh behind me. I take a shower, thinking over his revelations. The fact that I look like his dead wife is beyond creepy. No wonder I catch Thomas staring at me on occasion. He's probably as confused as I am.

Finding out that Harrison has watched me since I was a kid is a new level of creepy, and I'm unsure how to feel about it. Not only did he save me from Viktor, but now I've discovered he made sure I had food and was safe as a kid.

Thirty minutes later, I'm dressed in my new uniform of leggings and an oversized sweatshirt. I don't know where Harrison plans on taking me, but after his revelation of seeing me as a kid, I'm not up for anything romantic. Hell, today may be the day I take off. I stuff extra clothes into my overpriced backpack along with the flash drive holding my thesis, just in case, and head downstairs. I'm surprised to see Penelope's portrait is missing from its home above the fireplace.

"You are not Penelope and making you look at her portrait every day is not what I want for you while you're here," Harrison answers my unasked question. He exits the kitchen, wearing blue jeans and a black form-fitting t-shirt.

"Thank you," I respond.

He holds up a wicker picnic basket. "Thomas packed lunch." Knowing Thomas, there's probably a full five-course meal inside, complete with appetizers and dessert.

"Are we driving?"

"No, I thought we'd go for a walk and have a picnic in Jackson Square."

That doesn't sound too creepy. "Sounds like a plan," I say, trying to erase some of the snarkiness in my tone. He opens the door, waiting for me to exit before following. We walk through the Garden District and enter the Quarter. The noises of the Quarter are familiar and strangely comforting. The walk is not a short one, and it's not until we're far into the Quarter that Harrison says more than a few words at a time.

"Do you see that building?" He points at the remains of a dilapidated brick building compacted between two remodeled ones.

"I do."

"That was owned by Viktor. He used it much the same way as the one you lived in shortly. One of his donneuse would rent an apartment to an unsuspecting young man or woman, and he would visit them in the night."

"Oh, my God." I stare at the building with newfound respect. "Is that something he does often?"

"We've discovered a few of them around the city. I'd imagine there are more waiting to be discovered."

"Who owns it now?"

"Violet," he answers and continues walking.

As we walk, groups of unsuspecting humans pass us in the streets. I wonder if they know they're passing a vampire. Some smile seductively, while others walk a wide trek around him, but one thing they all have in common is, they notice him.

The steeple on top of Jackson Cathedral comes into view as we approach the historic center of New Orleans. Vendors are setting up their art around the wrought iron fence that surrounds the grassy square, preparing for a day of tourists and sales.

"I've always loved coming here," Harrison says as we stop at several vendor booths. Most of the artwork is pictures of the cathedral or other landmarks around the city. One particular picture catches my eye.

"Is this the apartment building from Royal Street?" He takes the painting from me.

"Possibly, not recent though." I scan through more of the artist's pictures, all of them are older buildings in the Quarter.

"Beautiful, isn't it?" an older woman asks from behind.

"Yes, it is. Are you the artist?"

"I am! Most of them were painted when I was

younger and were homes or apartments that I lived in throughout the Quarter. Each house has a history, and I tried to paint that into the pictures." I turn, looking fully at the woman. Dark circles outline her faded blue eyes. Evidence of once dark hair is intermixed with white. She smiles a warm smile before taking the picture from me. Her eyes land on Harrison, and her energy changes in an instant. "These aren't for sale." She turns her back to us, pretending to straighten perfectly displayed art.

"That was weird," I whisper as we move toward the next vendor.

"Some people have abilities and don't realize it." I stop walking.

"Did that woman know you are a vampire?"

He looks at the woman, who is now busy with new customers. "She may not know what I am but knows I'm something."

I laugh. "That's a skill that could be useful in this town."

Harrison opens the gate, leading us inside the grassy square. He chooses a quiet spot in the corner and away from a touch football game several preteens have started on the other side. "Is this okay?" I plop on the grass, answering his question.

Harrison spreads the red and white checked tablecloth onto the grass and spreads a mixture of sandwiches, fruit, and fried chicken. This is the iconic Southern picnic that's depicted in movies. "There is no way I can eat all of this." I laugh. The items keep coming from the bottomless basket, and it's almost embarrassing looking at the spread between us.

"Tell me about her," I say, biting into a piece of fried chicken.

"Who, Violet?" Harrison asks, taking a sip from his "wine."

"No, Penelope." He sets his glass down. "I'm sorry. I understand if you don't want to talk about her."

He pulls his legs closer to his chest. "She was wonderful." His eyes look away, lost in thought. "She was feisty, brilliant, demanding, loving, and the perfect mate. She was the one that turned me."

"Turned you? She's the reason you're a vampire?"

He looks at his feet. "Yes. Viktor too." I set the piece of chicken I'm working on down and settle in for what I hope is a story. "We grew up together, the three of us, in a small French village. All three of us were poorer than poor. Weeks without food, living in filth, it wasn't the life you see depicted in your fantasy books or movies."

"I'm sorry." I don't know why I'm apologizing.

"I was seventeen when the Black Plague made its way to our village. History says it was never in France, but history has it wrong." His eyes seem to be far away as he continues. "Half of our village was dead within a year, and most of the others were sick." He pauses. "Penelope was the first of us to get sick. Two of her brothers had already passed from the sickness, and it was only a matter of time before she would. We couldn't let that happen."

"We? You and Viktor?" He nods before continuing.

"There was a woman that lived in the mountains. Rumors of her draining the blood from livestock and kidnapping young children were prevalent throughout the area."

"A vampire?" I fill in the blank.

"Yes. We were young and naive and didn't understand the true implications of what she truly was. We'd heard rumors that people were being healed after visiting her, so we decided to take Penelope to her." He pauses, trapped in a memory. "I still remember her screams as her blood was drained, replaced with the vampire's own." He takes a drink from his glass.

"Viktor and I remained healthy for the next few years, while most of our families perished. Penelope lived in the mountains with her...her maker for several years after her change. We visited on occasion, but she wasn't the same. She wasn't Penelope. She was young and hungry without much control. Viktor was the next to get sick. We thought we were immune to the plague after being surrounded by it for so long without either of us getting ill. We were wrong."

"You took Viktor to Penelope when he was dying?" I ask, knowing the answer.

"I begged her to change me too. I had nothing left. I couldn't bear living alone." His voice is sad. "At first, she refused." He pulls his shirt sleeve up, revealing a three-inch scar down his forearm. "I didn't give her a choice." Oh, my God. He forced her to turn him to save his life. "For the next three hundred years, the three of us were inseparable and grew very rich. We owned nearly half of France and hunted not only to survive but for fun. We were cruel and evil." He pauses while tourists take pictures next to our picnic spot. I'm on pins and needles, waiting for them to leave. They wander away, and he continues.

"In the 1700s, I grew tired of the game, of killing innocent humans for sport. I wanted out. It took years, but I convinced Penelope to come with me, and we sailed here, to New Orleans." He looks around the square. "These were the first streets carved into the land. It was called the Old Square at that time and was the beginning of the French and Spanish hold on this land."

"Did Viktor come with you?"

"Not at first. He wasn't interested in changing his ways. He enjoyed the hunt, enjoyed killing. Penelope and I married after arriving here and set up our home. She agreed with me about hunting, and we worked for years to overcome the need to feed and kill. When Viktor found us, he didn't agree with our lifestyle and was jealous of our marriage."

"You don't have to continue." I hear the pain in his voice.

"You deserve to know the truth." He takes a deep breath. "He tried for many years to convince us to return to our earlier ways, but by that time, we'd lived our lifestyle for nearly a hundred years and knew this was the way we wanted to exist." He looks me in the eyes. "When we refused, Viktor went mad, killing anyone he could find. We tried to stop him." He awkwardly scratches his head before continuing. "He was stronger than we were, because of the human blood and our naivety. He killed her." A tear streams down his cheek, and I don't push for more details.

"Harrison, I'm so sorry. I don't know what to say."

"You don't have to say anything. Just being here is enough." He smiles weakly before finishing his "wine" and clearing his throat. "Would you like to tour the cathedral?" he asks after helping me pack the leftovers into the basket.

"Sure." I shrug. I've been inside more times than I can count, but being with someone who witnessed its construction should be fun.

"Good afternoon, Mr. Chamberlin," a middle-aged woman greets us as we enter the heavy wooden door. "Would you like a candle?"

"No, thank you, Judith. We're just taking a quick tour."

"Of course. Please let me know if you need anything." She smiles, moving to the guests behind us.

"You're on a first-name basis with the tour guides?"

He smiles. "It's amazing how many people know your name when you contribute large amounts of money around the city." I follow him past a group of tourists to the front of the sanctuary. "This pulpit isn't original."

I stare at the large piece of furniture. "Every tour I've been through in this building says it is."

"It's not," he says with a smirk. "And the painting on the ceiling wasn't added until a hundred years ago." I stare at the pictures of the disciples, each one meticulously painted above our heads.

"You are full of information." I laugh.

"If you only knew," he says, leading us down the aisle and out the other door. The minute we step outside, I feel it. There are no words to describe it, other than when a dog raises his hackles and goes on alert. Harrison stops feet from the door.

"What is it?" I ask, scanning the square for anything out of the ordinary.

"We're not alone." He takes my hand, pulling me to a narrow alley behind the cathedral. The smell of trash is nearly overwhelming as we weave through the bags of rubbish. From the corner of my eye, I see the source. A tall dark-haired man, wearing a waistcoat.

"Is that?"

Harrison turns me to face him. "Amelia, I need you to get in a cab and go straight to the house. Don't stop for anyone or anything. Don't stop until you're safely inside." I stare at him blankly. "Amelia, go now."

EIGHT

there's no place like home

I FLAG down the first yellow cab I see, jumping inside before it comes to a complete stop. "Where to, miss?"

"The Garden District and hurry." He slips in and out of traffic without wasting time. "This is it, stop here." I slide to the edge of the seat and open the door.

"That'll be seventeen dollars and thirty-two cents." Shit. I don't have a penny to my name.

"Wait here," I instruct, running to the front door.

"Miss!" I hear him call from behind. "Dammit!"

I ring the bell methodically, begging someone to open it quickly. "I'm coming," Thomas's voice echoes through the door. I continue pushing, trying to get inside. "Push that button one more damn time," he says as he opens the door. I run inside as soon as the handle turns. "Amelia? What the hell?"

"Viktor," I answer.

He doesn't question me. "Get inside." He looks at the cab parked in front. "Do I need to pay the driver?"

"Yes, please."

"You're safe inside. Viktor can't get onto the property or through this door. I'll be right back." He steps out, walking the short path to the parked cab. The two men talk for a few minutes before Thomas hands him cash. He waves as the cab drives away and turns back toward the door.

Something moving faster than my eyes can track, picks Thomas off the ground, carrying him high above the roofline. "Thomas!" I scream toward the spot where he stood moments earlier. Oh, my God. He's gone. "Violet!"

A loud thump on the walkway grabs my attention as the reality of what I'm seeing registers in my mind. Thomas, the strong man from seconds earlier is now lying in quickly pooling blood.

I stumble backward, bumping into a table in the foyer and knocking it over with a loud crash. "Violet!" The scream that leaves my throat is guttural. "Violet!" I scream again. She's next to me in an instant.

"What?" She turns me to face her. "What's going on?"

"Thomas." I point to the lifeless corpse lying in the middle of the walkway. "Something grabbed him."

She leaves my side and returns faster than I can blink. I close the door behind them, positioning the antique locks in place. "Where's Harrison?" she asks, laying Thomas on the foyer floor.

"I don't know. We had a picnic at the square and Viktor showed up and..."

"Viktor?" she interrupts. "What did he do?"

"Harrison sent me here and stayed. Did Viktor do this to Thomas?" For the first time, I look down at the man who's become my friend.

"No, I don't think so." She looks at what's left of the man between us. "I can save him."

"Do it! Do whatever you have to do."

"Not without his permission. That choice was taken from me. I won't do it to him."

"Thomas!" I shake his shoulder. "I'm so sorry, Thomas. Can you hear me?" He grunts, forcing blood to spurt from his neck.

"Violet!"

"Amelia, go into your room."

"Why?" I sound like an insolent child, even to myself.

"Amelia, please. Every second I wait is one less he has before he dies." I run upstairs and straight into my room, locking the door behind me, unsure if we saved Thomas or cursed him. I don't know what I expected to hear, but silence isn't it. I slide between the heavy wardrobe and the corner of the room, with my back against the wall. I just want to crawl into a hole and hide.

I don't know how much time has passed when a

soft knock on my door brings me back to reality and the present. "Amelia, it's Harrison." His voice is soft. "May I come in?"

"How's Thomas?"

"He'll be asleep for a few days. Until then, we won't know anything else."

"He died for me."

"He's not dead. He's reborn." I move to the door, turning the ancient key. Harrison's still wearing the same clothes as earlier. His t-shirt and jeans are torn and now covered in mud.

"Can I see him?"

"That's not a good idea right now." I step forward, laying my forehead on his chest. I don't know what I expect from him, but I have never needed a hug more in my life. "Amelia?"

"I'm sorry. I know it's inappropriate, but I need to feel that you're real. That you're really here." He wraps his arms around my shoulders, offering comfort. His arms feel stiff, as they flank each side of my shoulders. "Thank you, I whisper." His arms soften slightly with my words.

......

I spend the next few days pouring myself into my thesis. With five chapters completed, I'm more than halfway finished with something I couldn't care less about completing. I haven't seen Violet or Harrison since that day, and to be honest, I'm okay with that. My time has been spent between the library and my bedroom with quick stops in the kitchen. Disturbing Thomas's space seems wrong. I've lived off sandwiches and canned goods. Anything I can find that's quick.

Opening my second can of soup for the day, I realize there's a chirping sound coming from one of the drawers in the kitchen. I search until finding the source —Thomas's phone. The contact that's calling reads, "Boo Thang," and there are ten missed calls from the same number. Shit. Thomas has a significant other.

"Hello?" I push the bright green button.

"Oh, my God. Thomas! Do you know how worried I've been? What the hell's going on? You better have been close to death, or I'm going to kick your ass when I see you."

"Uh, this isn't Thomas. He left his phone here."

"What? Who is this?"

I think fast on my feet. "Rodney's Burgers and More on Bourbon. Someone turned this phone in a few days ago after it was left at a booth," I lie.

"Well, shit. He would lose his head if it weren't attached. I'll come by tonight. Can you hold it for me?"

"Of course." I hit the end button before any more lies can be spread and set the phone back in the drawer before I realize Violet is hiding in the shadows of the corner.

"How long have you been there?"

"A while," she answers. Her face is pinker than

before, and her eyes are more defined. The look on her face reminds me of a hungry child in a buffet line.

"Violet, is everything okay?"

Harrison steps between us. "Violet, I think you need to go to your room." She frowns before heading up the back staircase.

"Is she okay?"

"She will be. To turn Thomas, she had to drain what was left of his blood. It's the first time in a long while that she's had that much human blood flowing through her veins. It'll take her a while to come down off of it.

I didn't even think of that. "She looked like she wanted to eat me." He doesn't respond.

"Thomas is awake."

"Can I see him?"

He nods. "You can't get too close. He'll be unstable for a while." I follow Harrison into the courtyard and through a door on the other side. We enter what used to be the stables and head up an ancient set of stairs. The apartment at the top is decorated with bright colors and mixtures of antique and modern furniture. Thomas is lying in the middle of a king-size bed. His wounds are healed, and he looks five years younger.

"Thomas?" his eyes open wide.

"I can smell you," he whispers. Harrison steps in between us.

"I'm so sorry, Thomas. It was my fault. I shouldn't have let you go outside to pay..."

"I can smell you," he repeats. This time his voice is louder.

"It's time to leave, Amelia." Harrison remains between the two of us until we're out of the apartment and back in the courtyard.

"How long will he be like that?"

"It depends on the person. Some just a few days and some a few months. He's not safe to be around at the moment."

"This whole thing sucks. Thomas didn't do anything to deserve what happened to him. Now he has to live with it for the rest of his eternal life." I give up trying to fight tears and let them stream down my cheeks. "I didn't want this. I didn't want any of this. Why couldn't you and Viktor just leave me the hell alone?"

"I'm sorry, Amelia."

"I just want to go home." The minute the words leave my mouth I realize how dumb they sound. I don't have a home. The garage door lifts to the right of where we're standing. Inside, a horn beeps, and lights flash.

"Let's go."

"Where...where are we going?"

"Home," he answers, moving into the garage. He opens the door to a large black SUV, closing it behind me.

He hasn't spoken a word the entire time we've been weaving in and out of traffic. The moment we turn onto Royal Street, I know where we're going. We come to a stop in front of the apartment building that started this entire shit show. He pulls the skeleton key from his pocket, clicking the front door open. Ms. Esther's door is standing open. I'm surprised to find her small apartment still furnished and looks just like it did when I was here.

We move upstairs to what was my apartment. The inside looks the same as the only week I spent here. The closet is empty, and someone made the bed. "Why did you bring me here?"

"Because this was your home, Amelia. This apartment you slept in for barely a week and nearly died in was your home. Is this where you want to go? Perhaps we can go visit the projects where you spent most days and nights hiding in the closet?" His voice sounds angry.

"What the hell are you trying to say?"

He takes a deep breath. "I'm trying to say that your home is with us, with me. It's where you belong."

"I knew you wanted me to be her. You want me to be Penelope. What kind of sick joke is this?" I turn, slamming the main door to the apartment behind me, and stomp down the stairs. I have no clue where I'm going, but wherever it is, Harrison Chamberlin isn't there. I open the front door of the building to find him standing there, waiting.

"Dammit, move."

"Where are you going?"

"Somewhere you're not. Get the hell out of my

way." I push my body weight into him, he doesn't budge. "Move, Harrison."

"You don't get it, do you?"

"Enlighten me, please." I cross my arms over my chest.

"Viktor planned all of this. He made sure you would find this apartment, he made sure you would be desperate enough to take it without question, and the worst part is, he made sure you would grow up alone."

"What does that mean?"

"It means your mother was his donneuse, and he convinced her to abandon you before killing her. You think I'm the stalker? The truth is, I'm the one that kept you safe. I'm the one that saved you. He wanted you dead."

"Why?" My voice is full of emotion.

"Because he wants something he was never able to have—Penelope."

"Dammit, I'm not Penelope!" My voice echoes off the front of the building. I bypass him, stomping my way toward the black SUV, leaving Harrison alone on the front porch. In an instant, I'm swept off my feet and flying through the clouds without a clue of how I got here or what's happening. A pair of copper-colored eyes and a black waistcoat are the last things I see before the world goes black.

vampires, werewolves, and witches. oh, my!

I'VE READ throughout countless books that hearing and smell are the last senses you lose when you die. I can account that they're also the first to return when regaining consciousness. The overwhelming smell of mold fills my sinuses instantly, along with soft shuffles from the other side of the room. My eyes open, revealing the room around me. Broken glass covers the wooden floors along with years of trash and debris. Where the hell am I? I try to sit up, but my head feels like an elephant has taken up residence on top of it.

"You're awake," a deep voice echoes through the empty brick walls.

"Harrison?"

"I'm afraid he's not here right now." The voice moves closer as a shadow stands between me and the light from the broken window. I recognize the man in front of me as the same man from my apartment. "Hello, Penelope." A deep smile covers his face.

"I'm not Penelope, you sick freak. My name is Amelia Lockhart, and I demand you let me go."

Viktor looks around the abandoned room. "I'm afraid you are in no position to demand anything, my dear."

"Fuck you."

"Tsk, tsk, tsk. Such foul language for such a pretty little thing. Of course, you were always the one for flare."

"What do you want from me?"

"You're safe with me, whether you believe it or not." He steps closer.

"You were ready to suck me dry a few days ago, now you want to be with me? You're a psychopath."

"I can assure you I had no intentions of sucking you dry. I'm perfectly sane. No doubt your precious Harrison has filled your head with lies and deceit."

"He's not *my* precious anything," I retort.

"Trouble in paradise?" He laughs. I don't respond. Arguing my point is a waste of time. "Back to the original topic." He pauses, making sure I'm listening. "My intentions were never to kill you." He moves close enough that I can smell his cologne. "No, my intentions were to protect you and turn you."

"Turn me? What happened to free will and all that?"

Viktor laughs loudly. "I'm afraid you've gotten me

confused with God. He's the one into free will, not me. I do understand your confusion, however."

He grabs my arm, pulling me next to him. "Don't confuse the fact that you're still alive with the fact that you may talk to me in any tone you wish. I will be respected, and you will learn that one way or another." His words send chills down my spine. Any bravery I once felt leaves in an instant. Viktor leads me down several flights of broken stairs to an awaiting car. "Slip that on, please." He points to a blindfold, sitting on the seat. I do as he says, sliding against the opposite door as far as possible. He crowds next to me.

We drive for several minutes before I lose count of the turns. The car comes to a stop, and my arm is tugged from the other side. "We're here, mon amour." I cringe at his words. We enter another building, this one not as echoey as the first.

"Where are we?" I ask.

"You'll find out soon enough." He leads me up several flights of stairs only taking the blindfold off after unlocking a door and ushering me inside. My eyes squint at the light. "This will be your room." He turns, leaving me locked inside.

What the hell? I scan the room, looking for clues to where I am. Unlike Harrison's house, which was built during the nineteenth century, this one resembles a picture from *Modern Architecture* magazine. The walls, floors, and ceilings are stark white with a large platform bed in the middle of the room. The bedding is black and contrasts with the overwhelmingly large amounts of white. "This is hideous," I say out loud, hoping he hears me.

Instead of hiding in my corner, I scream at the top of my lungs through the door. I don't know when the transition from being scared Amelia and being crazy, annoying Amelia happened, but I'm okay with it. The only person I can depend on is me. That means the only person that's going to get me out of here is me, myself, and I.

I search every nook and cranny of the room, finding nothing that will help me get out of here. A knock on the doors makes me jump. "Miss Penelope?" a soft voice calls through the door.

"She's not here right now," I answer sarcastically. "My name is Amelia."

The woman ignores my correction. "You'll find clean clothes in the closet and towels in the bathroom. Mr. Luquire has requested you shower before dinner." I resist the urge to laugh out loud. I don't bother changing or taking a shower.

Thirty minutes later, she returns with a soft knock on the door. The door unlocks and a small woman enters. She makes me look tall, which is a feat. Snow-white hair is neatly stacked on top of her head in a large bun. Her outfit is opposite the decor of the room. She's wearing a form-fitted top with a corset underneath and a large hoopskirt. "Oh, dear. This will never do. Did the clothing not fit?"

"It was all too small," I lie.

"Oh, dear. Mr. Luquire will have my head." She wrings her hands together.

"You'll get in trouble if I don't wear appropriate clothing?"

"Are you sure it was all too small?" The woman is visibly shaking. Whatever Viktor will do to her outweighs my stubbornness.

"One of them was close to fitting." I grab something from the wardrobe and head into the bathroom to change. No matter how rebellious I feel, I refuse to let him harm someone because of me. I slip on the white pantsuit, which fits perfectly, pull my hair into a loose bun, and wash my hands and face before exiting.

"Thank you, Amelia." She hands me the blindfold from earlier. "I'm going to have to ask you to put this on. I'll lead you to the dining room."

"Is he always this controlling, or is this something special for me?"

She smiles, without answering. I slide the blindfold on as she wraps my arm through hers. "This way, please." I count each of the twenty-six steps as we descend to the bottom floor of the house. The woman leads me to what feels like a chair before pulling the blindfold off.

"Don't you look lovely," Viktor says from the far end of the table. It takes a minute for my eyes to acclimate to the light. The room we're in is furnished from a different century than the bedroom I'm supposed to call my own. A large mahogany table takes up space in the middle of the room, surrounded by ten crimson velvet chairs. An open fireplace covers one wall, while a large sideboard covers the opposite. Two men stand at either side of the sideboard, ready to serve.

He snaps his fingers and the man closest to him jumps to service. "What are you waiting on?" he demands. "Her plate is empty." Both men rush toward me, carrying bowls of food I've never seen before. They scoop several spoonfuls of items I don't recognize onto my plate.

"That's plenty." I cover my plate, preventing them from adding more.

"Bring me the blonde," Viktor demands from the other end of the table. One of the men disappears, returning quickly with a young woman in tow. Oh, my God. He's going to "eat" from the girl.

The girl whimpers and begs while being dragged into the room. He sticks a gag in her mouth, stopping her from making noise. Tears stream down her cheeks, as she's forced to her knees in front of Viktor. "No," I whisper. He smirks, raising one side of his mouth higher than the other.

"Penelope is displeased," he tells the server. "I'll eat later." I watch as the woman is taken out of the room and fight the tears threatening to fall. "By all means, eat *your* dinner while I watch." His voice is full of sarcasm. Narcissistic asshole. I move food around on my plate and pretend to eat the mush that covers it.

"I'm full." I push the plate away, feeling sick to my stomach. "I'm ready to go back to my room now."

Viktor nods, and the woman from before appears out of nowhere, covering my eyes with the blindfold and leading me from the table. "Good night, mon amour," he calls after me. I hold onto the tiny woman's arm tightly as we climb the twenty-six stairs to my room.

She stays quiet until we're safely inside my room. "You'll find pajamas and undergarments in the closet. You did well." She pulls the blindfold off, closing the door behind her.

My mind races through a thousand possible scenarios of my escape, none of which end with me actually surviving. I have to get out of here. I lock the bathroom door behind me and hang the cross Violet purchased on the doorknob. It doesn't bother Violet, but maybe it'll keep Viktor away.

I turn the shower to scalding and step in quickly. I feel vulnerable standing here naked and wash all the important parts before sprinting to the clothes I brought from the closet. I slide down the bathroom door, feeling the sting of cold tile on my bare thighs. For the first time in a long time, I feel out of control. There's no hero ready to swoop in and save me. Harrison is probably pissed at me and has every right to be. Violet would accidentally eat me on the way back to the house and Thomas... I don't even know. I'm trapped with Viktor. I cry until there are no tears left to fall.

"Amelia?" a soft voice whispers through the bathroom door. "Are you in there?" I open my eyes to white bathroom tile. I spent the night on the floor.

"I'm here," I answer.

"Mr. Luquire requests your attendance for breakfast."

"We just ate dinner."

"That was twelve hours ago. Let me help you get dressed." I pull the door open, revealing the small woman from yesterday. "Oh, my. We have some work to do." I glance in the mirror, seeing an imprint of tile grout across my cheek. "Come," she pulls me into the bedroom, sitting me at a makeup table. My hair is a mixture of frizz, more frizz, and sticking straight up on my head.

"If you brush it, it'll be worse." She puts the brush she's holding down. I grab a few products from the table and work on reviving my curls. I stare at her reflection in the mirror, looking for any clues of who she used to be. "What's your name?"

"Sara," she answers with a smile. "My name is Sara."

"Thank you, Sara." The rest of the time is spent in silence while getting presentable for whatever's waiting for us downstairs. She hands me a soft pink lip gloss to finish off my makeup before declaring we're ready for breakfast.

Sara stops at the bedroom door. "Amelia, don't react, stay calm."

"What do you mean?"

She clears her throat. "I mean, whatever you see, don't react. Remain calm. It's your only way out of here."

"Why are you helping me?"

"Because I wish someone would have helped me." She slides the blindfold into place, leading me through the door and down the twenty-six stairs.

"Is that bacon?" I whisper on the way down. Sara squeezes my arm. I know without asking, she's telling me to stay quiet. I resist the urge to cover my nose. The further we go, the stronger the burning smell permeates my sinuses. Sara leads me to the table, pushing the chair under me as I sit before pulling the blindfold off.

I hold in the scream that begs to leave my lips. In the middle of the table is a human head. Splotches of blonde hair are scattered among the small amount of burnt flesh that remains. Her eyes are open, and her mouth is frozen in a perpetual scream. *Don't react. Remain calm.* Sara's words echo through my mind. That's what he wants. Viktor wants me to have a reaction. He's trying to shock me. "Good morning, mon amour. I trust you slept well."

I do everything I can to avoid looking at the head. I nod, afraid my voice will betray me if I try to speak. I move what looks like scrambled eggs around on my plate, refusing to eat. Something tells me this isn't scrambled eggs. "I thought we might go for a walk this morning, or even take a tour of one of the old cemeteries in the city." Viktor makes plans like we're a couple that's been together for years.

Getting outside could be my chance to escape. "I'd like that," I answer quickly. Viktor smiles.

"Whatever Penelope wants, Penelope gets." I look around the room, finding Sara hiding in the shadows of the room. Viktor isn't eating this morning, and I'm grateful. He watches my every move as he drinks from a wine glass. "You need to eat, my dear. It will keep you strong."

"I just don't seem to be hungry. Maybe I'll be hungrier after our walk." If I survive this whole thing, I'm signing up for acting classes. I'm almost convincing myself.

"Very well. Shall we go?" He's in front of me in a split second, offering me his arm. Sara slides the blindfold back into place before we exit the house. It takes thirty-seven steps before I feel the texture of grass squish beneath my feet. My body suddenly feels weightless as I'm shifted to a different area. Losing my sense of sight confuses the rest of my senses. I have no idea which way is up or where we are until Viktor pulls off the blindfold. We're next to the river in what looks like a park, but I don't recognize our exact location.

He takes a deep breath. "I loathe the smell of New Orleans in the morning. It's a mixture of human excrement and garbage. God, I miss the French countryside."

"Tell me about your life there." Maybe if I can get

him talking, he'll say something that will help me escape. Viktor smirks.

"My life in France isn't something I want to talk about right now. What I want to talk about is you." We continue walking along the river, the only two people in sight.

"There's not much to tell. I grew up a typical traumatized kid in the streets of New Orleans." I remember what Harrison told me about my mother being one of Viktor's donneuse and decide to use that knowledge to my advantage. "My mother wasn't there much when I was growing up." I'm curious how he'll respond.

"How sad." His voice is emotionless as he fakes compassion for my childhood.

"Why do you think I'm Penelope?" I pull the band-aid straight off without warning.

We stop walking as he turns his nose high in the air. "We're about to have a visitor. Stay calm and don't speak."

"Who?" I ask as a large man appears out of nowhere. He's at least a foot and a half taller than me.

"Viktor," he nods, looking me up and down. "Who's this?"

"None of your concern. What do you want, Edon?"

"Is that any way to treat an old friend?" the man answers.

"It would be if we were old friends. You're disturbing our walk."

Edon smells the air around me. "She smells like Chamberlin."

Viktor laughs. "We'll just have to change that, won't we? Whatever you need to tell me can wait. I'll find you later." He dismisses the man with his words.

"Two o'clock at the bridge."

"If you insist," Viktor answers.

"I do." Edon disappears as quickly as he arrived.

"Who was that?" I ask, not sure where the bravery is coming from.

"Just your average, run-of-the-mill werewolf. Unfortunately, they're quite prolific. You can barely throw a rock in the Quarter without hitting one." That man was a werewolf? I stare in shock at the spot where he stood moments earlier.

TEN

an asshole and a friend

AFTER OUR "WALK," Viktor returns me to the
house as quickly as we left. It's not until I'm back in the
white bedroom that the blindfold comes off. I sit on the
edge of the bed and let the tears flow. I've cried more in
the last two days than I've cried in my entire life.

"Amelia?" Sara whispers through the door.

"Come in," I answer, wiping the tears from my
cheeks. She closes the door behind her, making as little
noise as possible.

"Come with me." I watch as the petite woman
walks into my closet. I follow her inside, confused
about what we're doing. "This is the only place without
a camera." She closes the door behind us before
handing me an envelope sealed with a wax stamp of
the letter "C."

"What's this?" I whisper.

"It's a letter from Mr. Chamberlin." I stare at the

seal, unsure of what to think. "Only open it in this room. There are cameras everywhere else."

"There are cameras in the bathroom?" Asshole.

She nods. "Mr. Luquire hasn't returned from his meeting yet, so I expect dinner will be later tonight." She hands me a white napkin. "Eat this." I pull back the edges to find a peanut butter and jelly sandwich. "I hope you're not allergic."

"I'm not, thank you." I devour the sandwich in three bites. It hits every taste bud on the way down, and I resist rolling my eyes from the ecstasy of flavor.

"I'll be back as soon as I have a meal time. You need to exit the closet wearing different clothing than you entered with." She exits the bedroom door before I register any movement. I change into a soft pink dress that looks straight out of a '50s sitcom. With one glance in the mirror, I'm surprised that it's actually cute. Carefully lifting the wax seal, I open the letter Sara brought.

Amelia,

I'm sorry for allowing this to happen. The bastard caught me when my guard was down.

There are no excuses, but rest easy knowing we will get to you. No matter what he says about me, don't believe him.

Harrison

I fold the letter, placing it neatly inside the envelope. I don't know what to think. "Amelia," Sara knocks on the door. I place the envelope deep inside a tall boot before opening the closet door. "Mr. Luquire has arrived and has brought company. Dinner will be served in thirty minutes."

Twenty-four, twenty-five, twenty-six, I count silently as we move from the stairs into the dining room. The bacon smell has been replaced with the smell of copper which can only mean one thing—blood. Sara squeezes my elbow, warning me not to react before pulling the blindfold off. At the large table sits Viktor and Edon, the werewolf from this morning. Next to him sits a second man. He's nearly the same size as Edon, and I know without asking he's a werewolf.

"There she is," Edon says, standing. "I'm afraid we weren't properly introduced this morning." He glares at my captor. "Edon St. James." He reaches a large palm toward me.

"Amelia Lockhart," I answer, shaking his hand. Something about his eyes relaxes me.

"Jeremiah DeWitt," the second man says, standing next to Edon.

"Mon amour, please have a seat." Viktor sits at the head of the table. I choose a seat closer to the wolves. The two butlers from yesterday enter the room with platters full of raw meat. Both men smile as a platter is placed in front of them. "Not quite as fresh as catching it yourself, but fresh nonetheless," Viktor says to his guests.

"Raw venison," Edon answers. "A personal favorite of mine." One of the butlers brings me a platter full of fresh fruit. This actually looks edible. I catch a glimpse of Sara behind Jeremiah. She ever so slightly shakes her head, telling me not to eat what looks like sliced apples, pineapple, and grapes. I don't question her. Instead, I move the fruit around before pushing the plate away.

"You're not eating, Viktor?" Jeremiah asks, finishing the last few pieces of meat on his platter.

"Penelope frowns on my *eating* at the table," he answers.

"I thought you said your name was Amelia?" Jeremiah is looking straight at me.

"I believe that's enough dinner conversation, gentlemen." Viktor stands, finishing off his glass of red liquid. "Please give my regards to our mutual contact, and report what you've been sent to look for." He waves his hand in my direction. "As you can see, she's well cared for and happy. This meal is over."

The two wolves stand, covering what remains of their food with a napkin. Edon turns to me. "It was a pleasure to officially meet you, Miss Lockhart." He shoves his chair under the table. "No matter what this asshole says, you are free to leave here if you choose. All you have to do is say the words."

"How dare you come into my home and insult me, Edon. I thought better of you."

Edon faces Viktor. The two men are equal in height. "I don't care how important you *think* you are, Viktor. When you're in New Orleans you follow *my* rules and my rules only. As Alpha of Orleans Parish, which includes the very land we're standing on at the moment, you are under my authority and guidelines. My predecessor may have turned a blind eye, but I can assure you I will not." He turns back to me. "Now, *Amelia*," he stresses my real name. "Would you like to leave?"

"Yes, I would." Jeremiah reaches for me and what happens next is a scene straight from a movie. Viktor is behind Jeremiah in a split second, ripping the younger wolf's head clean from his shoulders. Edon explodes into a gigantic wolf and pushes Viktor backward against the fireplace. I can't fully grasp the reality of what just happened. Jeremiah's head falls to the blood-stained wooden floor a moment before his body.

Edon and Viktor move quicker than my eyes can track. Furniture and priceless antiques are thrown around the house as their fight rages through each room. "Amelia!" Sara screams inches from my face. "We have to go."

"Go, where? He's...he's dead." I stare at the remains of someone who was breathing and eating minutes earlier.

"Amelia!" she screams again. "You have to stay focused if you want to survive." I nod, allowing her to drag me from the chaos that has ensued. We run through a large kitchen and into an ancient courtyard, moving across the beautifully landscaped grass to an open garage door. Inside the garage is a small collection of sports cars and small SUVs. She pushes a button on a key fob, and a small red sports car flashes its lights. "Go!" she says, staying next to the door.

"I can't outrun him, Sara. He can fly for shit's sake."

"I'll keep him here. Go. Harrison is waiting just outside of the parimeter." The fight breaks through the backdoor into the courtyard. Edon is still in wolf form, and Viktor has lost his human form, looking more like a black streak of energy.

"I won't leave you here!"

Sara turns to me, and her face is completely transformed. Where the kind, older woman was earlier, now stands a vampire. Her eyes are faded, and her skin is wrinkled, but she's a vampire. "You will leave me, and you will leave now." She flashes her fangs. "If you want to live, go!"

I jump into the car and push the button. Thank God I know how to drive a stick. I throw the car into first gear and pop the clutch. I push the door opener, sliding it open moments before I exit the garage. Oh, my God. This is going to work. My excitement is fleeting as Viktor lands in front of the car, holding the crumpled body of Sara. I slam on the brakes, stopping inches in front of him. He drops her body on the hood, cracking the fiberglass where she hits. Oh, my God. Her eyes are open wide, and blood drips from her nose and mouth.

"Don't worry, mon amour. She'll be fine. It may take a few hours to recover, but she is a vampire, after all." He slings the small woman over his shoulder before grabbing my arm and jerking me from the sportscar. "You weren't trying to leave without saying goodbye, were you?" I feel myself losing control. Sara's words play through my head. *Don't react, Amelia. Don't react.*

He drags me back into the house, handing me over to a younger woman I've never seen before. "Get her cleaned up, and make sure she's secure in the room."

"Yes, sir." The woman wraps her arms through mine, pulling me up the stairs. "You shouldn't have done that," she says once we're on the second floor. "Mr. Luquire will be angry."

"I don't give a rat's ass if he's happy, sad, or angry. He's an asshole." She opens the door to my room, following me inside.

"Change your clothes, now," she demands.

"Fuck you, bitch." The girl slaps me, knocking me back a few feet. What the hell?

"Change your clothes, now," she repeats. Her tone is monotone and flat, almost robotic. I refuse to rub the burning spot on my cheek as I enter the bathroom. My face looks like it feels. The woman staring back at me looks exhausted. Dark circles have formed under her eyes, and her cheeks look sunken in. I scream a guttural scream, punching the glass in the mirror as hard as possible. Glass shatters, throwing shards around me as blood drips down my knuckles. The vampire girl slams into the bathroom door. "I smell you." She sniffs through the cracks like a dog chasing a bone. "Why don't you come out to play?" This is just great.

I hear the door to my room slam shut and the heavy sniffing stops. "Hello?" There's no response. I peek through the bathroom door, finding the room empty and my door standing open. I slam it shut and run into the closet.

Pulling out Harrison's letter, I read over his words several more times. I was wrong. I do have someone trying to rescue me. Not caring what the cameras show, I spend the rest of the night in the closet, making a pallet on the floor and curling as far into the corner as possible. The next morning comes and goes, along with lunch and dinner. No one has come to my room, and my stomach is growling louder than I knew possible.

Everything about this moment reminds me of my childhood, and those memories come crashing down. Years spent alone, with no food or comfort. It's all repeating itself. My mind pulls even further out of my situation, and I feel my body rocking but don't have control over the movements. I remember learning about disassociation in psychology class sophomore year. Is that what I'm doing?

Two days have passed since anyone came to check on me. I should've never answered Edon's question. What if he's dead? Did Viktor kill him? My mind wanders in and out of reality and delusion as I continue rocking back and forth. My stomach has stopped growling and my clothes are baggier than they were a few days ago. I haven't even needed to go to the bathroom for a day. Not eating or drinking has that effect.

"Penelope, mon amour?" Am I dreaming? I struggle to sit up, still hiding in the corner of the closet. "Why are you hiding in that small room when you have a bed and anything you could possibly need out here?" I open my mouth to speak, but nothing comes out. Light floods the tiny room as he opens the door wide. Viktor's wearing a three-piece suit and a top hat. "Oh, my. Smells like someone could use a shower." He snaps his fingers, and a man comes from behind him. "Get her cleaned up. We can't have any more of this. I want her healthy when I return."

"Yes, sir." Viktor leaves the room, and the man moves into my makeshift safety square. "Nothing personal, but he's right. You could use a shower."

"Who are you?" I whisper.

He smiles warmly. "Colby."

"Are you, are you..."

"Handsome?" he answers. "Yes. Thank you for noticing." He moves closer. "Do you mind if I help you up?" His accent reminds me of Harrison the first day we met in class. I don't have any fight left in me. I nod as he wraps one arm behind my shoulders and the other under my knees, lifting me like I weigh nothing. "I'm going to take you straight to the bathroom so you can do your thing. Do you think you can stand long enough to take a shower?"

I nod. "Will you stay in there with me?"

"That's a little forward, don't you think?" He smiles. "How about I sit on the bed while you take a shower? When you're ready to come out, I'll turn my back." I nod, grateful for the interaction. "Get on in there and hand me those clothes when you're under the water. I'll fetch some clean ones from the closet."

I wash my hair, lathering it three times before bubbles actually form. The hot water breathes new life into my exhausted bones and helps ground me back to reality, no matter how shitty it is.

I hear the door to the bathroom open and close as Colby leaves a clean set of clothes. "You alright in there? Need me to come and take my place on the throne?" he calls through the closed door.

"No, I'm coming out."

I dress quickly in the pair of sweatpants and hoodie he left for me. The elastic waistband on the pants isn't stretched at all, and they threaten to fall as I move. I run a brush through tangled curls, pulling out a small handful of loose hair with the brush. The rest of the massive amount of hair remaining is rolled into a bun and plopped on top of my head.

"There she is," Colby says as I exit the bathroom. "I got you something to eat and drink." He hands me a bottle of water and a sandwich. Pulling the bread apart, I inspect the contents.

"What is it?"

"A personal creation. I call it a fluffernutter." He

laughs. "You never ate a marshmallow fluff and peanut butter sandwich when you were a kid?"

"I rarely ate as a kid." I take a bite of the sticky creation. The sugar instantly hits my stomach. "This is delicious."

"See, I told you. My mom used to make them all the time." His energy is light and comfortable, and I'm grateful. I drink the entire bottle of water in one gulp. "I should have brought more with me. I'll get you some in a bit."

"Where did you come from?"

"New Orleans," he answers with a smirk.

"Do you work for Viktor?"

"I'm not a vampire if that's what you're asking."

"Are you anything?" I ask, not sure I can handle an answer.

"Other than an amazing sandwich maker? Yes, I'm Lycan."

"Werewolf?" I whisper.

"Edon sent me to keep you safe."

"What if...what if Viktor kills you?" My mind flashes back to Jeremiah's head leaving his torso.

"He'd have to catch me first."

ELEVEN

a library makes everything better

THE NEXT FEW days are almost bearable. Colby makes sure I have edible food, and my attendance hasn't been required in the dining room since the "incident." Colby even brought a few books to keep me occupied. Surprisingly, they're not about vampires or werewolves.

The chair next to the window has become my favorite reading spot, and I'm deeply enthralled in a fairytale retelling in which the main character is forced to work in a brothel, servicing the dwarves to pay for her doctoral degree. I laugh out loud at her brilliance. "Miss Honey White, you are a genius. I should've done that. Forget all this vampire shit."

"What was that?" Colby says, entering my room.

"Oh, nothing. Just a missed opportunity." I hold the book in the air, showing him the cover.

"Why is the man on the cover gray?" he asks, taking the book from me.

"He's a dwarf." I snatch the book from his hand. "You're the one who brought it to me."

He smiles a wicked smile. "It's one of my favorites. Eindride is hot and could hire me anytime—if you know what I mean." He wiggles his eyebrows, making me laugh. "Don't you want to know why I'm here?"

"I figured it was my amazing personality that just keeps drawing you in."

"Well, that, but I come bearing good news and bad news."

I close the book at his words. "Bad first." I'd rather get it over with. Rip off the band-aid.

Colby sits on the edge of my bed. "Your attendance is requested for dinner tonight."

I jump to my feet. "Oh, hell no. I'm just getting over the trauma from the last dinner party. I'm not up for another."

"I don't blame you, but are you ready for the good news?" I nod. "I'm joining you and will make sure this is a non-traumatizing meal."

"How is that good news?" He pretends to be stabbed by my words.

"Get in there and wash the stink off. I'm not letting you go down those stairs without looking anything but fierce." He snaps his fingers, making me laugh again. "Let's pick out something from the closet." I stay in my chair waiting for him to show me his selections. "You coming? I mean I could model them for you, but that would be weird."

I sigh. "Fine." Once inside the closet, he holds a finger to his lips, pulling out a small notebook and pencil.

I'm going to say random things while we're in here. There are microphones hidden throughout the room.

I nod.

"This would look amazing on you. Whoever picks out your clothes has great taste." He moves a few hangers around, clanking them together before motioning for me to speak.

"This doesn't leave much to the imagination. I like showing off my girls, but not exposing them to the whole world." He gives me a thumbs up.

There will be a guest tonight for dinner. I need you to act like you don't know him.

I take the pencil away, scribbling underneath his note.

Do I know them?

"This is the one, Amelia. This will look beautiful on you and won't make the girls too much of a spectacle."

Out of time.

He opens the closet door, leaving me alone. "I'll be back in a little while. Remember, fierce." I hear the door to the room close behind him. I follow instructions, fixing my hair and makeup the best I can. The color has returned to my cheeks, and the black circles have disappeared.

"Fierce," I whisper to the image staring back at me. Colby doesn't bother knocking. He enters the room, wearing a pair of khaki pants that are skintight and a button-down plaid shirt. Unlike the other two were-wolves I've met, Colby's face is clean-shaven, and his pale blonde hair is perfectly trimmed. He looks more like a model than a lycanthrope.

"Damn," he stops in his tracks. "You clean up pretty well. Shall we?" He holds an arm toward me.

"No, but okay." I wrap my arm through his, holding on for life rather than support. Since my failed attempt at escape, I haven't had to wear the blindfold. However, this is the first time I've been down the hall since it happened. I'm surprised at how normal everything looks. The hallway doesn't match the bedroom in its modern design but looks more appropriate for an authentic New Orleans home. The stairs are lined with painted portraits, similar to the ones hung at Harrison's house. The wooden staircase is original to the house and features a stained glass depiction of the crucifixion on the landing. Colby unwraps my arm from his as we round the corner into the dining room.

I stop dead in my tracks. The guest Colby warned me about *is* very familiar. It's Thomas. "Good evening, mon amour." Viktor and Thomas stand as I enter the room. "Penelope, this is Thomas Overstreet. Thomas, this is my lovely companion, Penelope."

"It's a pleasure to meet you, Penelope. Viktor failed to tell me how beautiful you are." Colby moves to Thomas's side, wrapping his arm around him. I stumble for words looking at the man I witnessed die not long ago. His dark skin is flawless, with high cheek-bones and a chiseled jawline. He's wearing khaki pants, similar to Colby's, and a pale green sweater that is the perfect contrast against his skin.

"Thomas and I are a thing," Colby says, lifting their joined hands to his lips. Oh, my God. Is Colby, "boo thang"? I snap back to reality.

"Welcome, Thomas." I smile as one of the butlers rushes to my side, pulling a chair out for me. "It's a pleasure to meet you."

"Colby requested his friend meet you." It's clear from his tone, Viktor is not overly happy about our present company.

"Actually, Viktor. I believe the request came from Edon."

Viktor ignores him, shaking his napkin out before

placing it on his lap. "I imagine it's a rarity for a vampire and a werewolf to be a couple. It's my pleasure to host such an oddity." I cringe at his choice of words. Homophobic asshole.

Viktor snaps his fingers, beckoning the food to be brought from the kitchen. To my surprise, I'm given a pre-made plate of food I recognize instantly. I fight the tears at spotting Thomas's cooking. "I hope you like chicken casserole and turnip greens. It's one of my specialties," Thomas says from across the table. "Colby told me you might enjoy one of my world-famous home-cooked meals."

"He was right, thank you." I swear Viktor rolls his eyes.

"Is my food not good enough for you?" he asks, glaring into my soul.

I ignore his narcissistic jab. "Thank you again, Thomas." I take a few bites, praying Viktor doesn't pursue the issue or worse, punish Thomas for my enjoyment.

"Edon asked me to review the treaty with you," Colby says, drawing Viktor's attention away from me. "As his liaison, now is as good a time as any."

"Part of that *treaty* was allowing you to be here, to watch over Penelope. It has nothing to do with discussing matters of business at my dinner table. Please make an appointment if you wish to pursue a conversation about anything other than the weather or the night life of New Orleans." Viktor slides his chair back from the table and crosses his legs at the knees.

He turns to Thomas. "Who's your maker? You smell familiar."

"It seems that discussing who my maker is would be a conversation other than the weather or night life. I'll keep that to myself." He takes a sip from his wine glass.

Viktor toasts the air in front of him. "Touché, Mr. Overstreet."

"Penelope?" Thomas turns to me. "Perhaps you would enjoy meeting me for lunch tomorrow? I know a place in the Quarter that..."

"Penelope will not be meeting anyone for lunch." Viktor stands from the table. "I believe our meal is finished." My heart sinks at his words. Thomas and Colby stand, mimicking Viktor's energy.

"I'll meet you later," Colby says, rubbing the top of Thomas's arm. Thomas moves in front of me.

"Penelope, it was a pleasure to meet you. I hope you don't mind, but I'm a hugger." Before I can react, his hands are wrapped around my shoulders, and he squeezes tightly. I want to scream for help. I want him to tell Harrison to rescue me, instead, I hug him back silently.

He pulls away, keeping my hand inside of his, and slides a folded piece of paper into my palm. I keep my face even, not reacting to the exchange. "Anytime you want a day on the town, let me know." He smiles, turning away quickly. He steps in front of Viktor. "Thank you for the meal and the company."

Viktor looks bored with his acknowledgment. "We'll walk you out," Colby says, gently nudging me toward the front foyer.

"That's far enough, wolf," Viktor warns.

"It's fine, boo. I can walk myself out." Thomas turns, leaving me in Viktor's house. The sharp point of the paper he passed me, cuts into my palm.

"Well, wasn't that fun?" Viktor slams his glass on the table. "Penelope, care to join me?" My heart jumps into my chest. No, I don't care to join you.

"I was hoping Colby could show me where the library is." I make the first excuse that comes to mind. "I've missed reading since being here." Colby knows I'm lying.

"Nonsense. If you want to see the library, I'll take you there," Viktor announces as Colby squeezes my elbow, moving away from my side.

"Of course, thank you." Viktor is at my side in an instant with my arm wrapped through his before I caught his movement. We wander through the narrow hallways, past several sitting rooms, closed doors, and finally to the library. I smell the books before I see them.

"Here we are, my dear." He pushes an antique button on the wall, and the room glows. We've switched decorating timelines again, and this room reminds me of a dark academia-designed university library. Dark leather couches form a reading nook in the center of the room, while floor-to-ceiling shelves line the walls.

"This is beautiful." For the first time, Viktor smiles.

"I'm glad you approve." I let go of his arm, running my hand along the spines of the books.

"Is there a catalog of some sort?"

"I wouldn't know. I'm never in here."

"I'd love to organize and record them for you." Having a purpose would make my life here easier.

Viktor shrugs, "If you enjoy that sort of thing, of course." For the first time since being here, my spirits lift. "Despite what you and that wolf may think, my goal isn't to make your life miserable." I don't answer, but I'm smart enough to stop dreaming over the books, and I turn to face him. He smiles, taking another drink. "You're even more beautiful than I remember." He walks to one of the leather couches and sits.

"Viktor?" He raises his head from whatever memory he's reliving. "Tell me about her."

He's quiet for so long, I decide he's not going to answer and continue exploring the shelves. "She was the most beautiful soul I've ever known. Not only on the outside but inside as well. I was only a child, but I fell madly in love with her." He takes a drink, sets his glass on a table close to the couch, and stands. "I believe that's enough reminiscing for one night. Stay as long you like." Viktor is gone in the blink of an eye. I slowly exhale, not sure if he's actually left me alone.

"Viktor?" I ask into the stillness. The room is silent.

I turn, facing the bookshelves, and pretend to sort through a few of the hardback books. I unfold the paper Thomas passed me, careful not to make any sounds. I move to another shelf, pretending to flip through a particularly large book and place the paper inside of one of the pages.

We have a plan.
T

What the hell is that supposed to mean? I glance behind me, expecting Viktor to be reading over my shoulder. Thankfully, the room is still empty. I leave the note inside the book, slide it back onto the shelf, and continue exploring the room. I'm not interested in a plan. I am interested in action.

Three hours later, I'm still alone in the library. Curiosity gets the best of me, and I turn the knob on the library door. Surprisingly, it turns, and the door opens. He left me in an unlocked room, alone? This is a test. I can't explain how I know, but I do. I close the door, step back into the library, and choose a particularly inter-esting read to occupy my time. With no idea how much time has passed, I lose the battle to keep my eyes open.

I wake to stark white walls and black bedding. How did I get here? I'm back in my room. Throwing the covers back, I'm relieved to see I'm dressed in the same clothes I wore to dinner last night.

A stack of notebooks, pens, pencils, and index cards sits on the stand next to the bed. A note is tied to the bright red bow on top.

Hope this helps with the library.
Viktor

TWELVE
the death of amelia lockhart

HAVING A PURPOSE, even something as menial as organizing a library lifts my spirits. I'm up and dressed when Colby enters my room.

"You're up early," he says, looking me up and down. "Going somewhere?"

"Yes, the library." Colby wrinkles his forehead.

"Viktor's going to let you out of the house?"

I laugh. "No, I wish. The library in the house. It's almost as exciting."

"Forgive me if I don't share in your enthusiasm." He stretches his arm toward me as I gather my gifts from Viktor. "May I escort you to the library, miss?"

"Why, yes, I'd like that, kind sir." He stays silent as we descend two flights of stairs and into the main living area of the house. I stop in place when a familiar face is in the corner of the room, dusting an antique lamp. "Sara?"

The woman jumps at my voice and moves out of the room instantly. "Maybe she's not a fan of Lycans?" Colby tries to lighten the mood.

"Most likely not a fan of the punishment she'll receive if she's caught speaking to me."

"Was she the one that tried to help you?" I nod, wiping a tear. I can't fathom the punishment she must have endured because of it. We stand still, staring in the direction of her movement for longer than normal. "Come on," Colby says, pulling me toward the library.

We enter the dark room, and the smell of books welcomes me into its bowels. I flick the switch Viktor used yesterday and the room comes to life. "I don't know where to start." I stand, staring at the overwhelming number of books on the shelves.

"What exactly are we doing in here?"

"We're categorizing and organizing them into sections. You know, like a library."

Colby laughs. "I wouldn't know."

"Oh, come on. You've been in a library before, right?"

"Nope, never."

I turn, staring at the werewolf. "Are you shitting me?"

He laughs. "Speaking of shitting, do they all smell like this?"

"Libraries? Yes. I love it."

"Seriously? It smells like a mixture of poo and dust."

"Now, I'm offended." I pretend to slap him on the

shoulder. "Here's what I'm thinking. We go one shelf at a time, making a list of the titles and categories for each book. Then we make stacks on the couches of each category and group them together."

"Does that involve reading?"

"I'm afraid so." I hand him a notebook and pencil. "I'll start on the bottom shelf if you want to start on the top."

Colby sighs. "I'm still trying to figure out when this became a 'we' project." I ignore him and pull the first book from the shelf. It doesn't take long before I have a stack of index cards and several rows of books started on the couches. The next book on the shelf is the hiding place of Thomas's note. I pull it out, adding more to the bottom.

What's the plan?

"Colby, this is a book you might like. It's about lycanthropes." He takes the book, opening it directly to the note.

"This can't be right," he laughs. "We don't run around in the woods on a full moon." He writes on the bottom of the note, handing it back to me. "I'll let you organize this one."

I pull the paper out, pretending to write the category and title, trying to decipher his writing.

Witch-Harrison-Potion-be patient.

136

This answers nothing. Be patient. Seriously? I slam the cover shut, stacking it with the group of mythological stories on the couch. I've been nothing but patient. I've lost track of time, being patient in this damn house. I miss my life. I miss not being under constant surveillance in everything I do. I miss me.

We finish the first shelf, moving on to the second one when my stomach growls loudly. "Hungry?"

"Very. Thomas's food has worn off."

"Will you be okay if I leave you in alone to see what I can come up with in the kitchen?"

"Can I come?" I ask.

"I think it best you stay here. Keep working on this shelf, and I'll see what I can find." I cross my arms, like the insolent child trapped deep inside.

When Colby leaves, I move to an old desk in the corner of the room. My fingers glide over the intricately carved woodwork that has worn through time. Roses and birds in flight are scattered throughout the ivy outlining the edges. I open a few of the drawers, finding them empty. My eyes are drawn to the center of the desk and what looks like hinges with no obvious opening. Rubbing my fingers along the hinges, I look for a way to open a hidden door. I run my hands along the side of the drawer, feeling a small lever.

Sliding it over, the drawer pops open. I try not to show my excitement as I slowly pull the hidden drawer and the one next to it open at the same time. Inside the hidden drawer is a bundle of letters, each sealed with a wax seal and tied together with a pink hair ribbon. I pretend to lay my head on the desk, covering the hidden drawer and my findings from the center of the room and from, most likely, cameras. Gently sliding the top letter from the stack, I slip it into my pocket before closing the hidden drawer and sitting up.

"Prepare to be astonished," Colby announces as he comes back into the room. I try to hide the fact that he scared the shit out of me, but I'm not very successful. "I'm sorry, did I wake you?"

"No, I was just sitting here, trying not to get overwhelmed with the amount of work we have ahead of us."

"There you go using the word 'we' again." He sets what looks like a burnt grilled cheese sandwich and potato chips in front of me. "I made this myself. It may or may not be the first grilled cheese I've ever made."

"Really? I would've never guessed this is the first one you've ever made."

"I'm detecting sarcasm."

"Thank you, it's perfect." It's not too burnt and hits the hunger spot perfectly.

"Thomas gave me some pointers."

"Speaking of Thomas, how did you two meet?" I finish my sandwich and chips, collecting both of our plates.

It's hard not to miss the smile that forms on his lips at the mention of Thomas's name. "We met in the Quarter. You know how Bourbon Street can be?"

"Enough said. I can tell this conversation is going to be way too much information for me." I set the plates on a table next to the door. "Ready to get back to work?"

"No," he answers, joining me at the bookshelf. We continue the same system, making it through five bookshelves before the sun begins to set. "Those couches are going to be full by tomorrow. You might want to brainstorm a way to organize them tonight."

"Done." I point to a set of shelves on the other side of the room. "Those are going to be non-fiction." I point to the empty shelves behind me. "These will be fiction. I figure we'll separate them by those two categories, then expand more as the days pass."

"Sounds like a solid plan. I'm tired of smelling poodust." I laugh at his description. "Can we continue tomorrow?"

"Sure. Thank you for your help and the company."

"My pleasure." I'm relieved to find the dining room empty and Viktor nowhere in sight as Colby escorts me up the two flights of stairs.

"Can you help me choose something to wear?" Colby wrinkles his forehead but follows me into the closet. I hand him the letter I found hidden inside the desk. His eyes open wide.

"*What?*" he mouths. I shrug, pointing at the letter. On the outside, in beautiful script handwriting is written a name I don't expect to see in Viktor's home.

Harrison

Colby's eyes are as large as saucers as he points to his watch. "This is my favorite of all that you showed me," he says loudly, pretending for the cameras. "I don't believe there is a meal tonight. I'll bring something to your room." *"Read it and tell me what it says,"* he mouths, leaving me alone in the closet. I change clothes, slipping into a pair of yoga pants and a long-sleeved t-shirt, and hide the letter along with the one I received from Harrison inside of my boot.

If I stay in the closet too long, it will draw the attention of whoever's assigned to watch me. I move to my reading chair and pretend to read my smut from earlier. No matter how hard I try to focus, I keep thinking of the letter hidden inside the boot. I pick up a glass of water, spilling it purposefully down the front of my clothes, soaking them completely.

"Damn," I say loudly. "My clothes are soaked." I head into the closet, close the door behind me, and pull the letter from its hiding spot. I move the back corner, shrinking behind several long dresses before opening the letter.

My Dearest Harrison,
I've lost track of our time apart. Every moment away from you feels like a lifetime of pieces ripped from my soul. You'll never see these letters but writing them feels like we're speaking, and I will write to you

until I can write no more. Viktor has weakened me to the point of no return. I've had no food for months, and I feel my life force draining daily.

Don't hold anger toward him. Inside, he's the same scared little boy from when we were young. However, his delusions have taken over and his thoughts are consumed with my unrequited love. He blames you for his being alone and is convinced you took me from him. His delusional mind believes that when I die, I'll return to him.

Even as I write, I feel my life fading. However, my love for you will never fade. I love you, my darling. Now and forevermore.

With Undying Love,
Penelope

I don't try to stop the tears. Harrison told me Viktor killed Penelope, but reading it in her own pen, makes it come to life. He kept her hidden and starved until she died with the insane delusion that she'd come back and be his. What the hell? That's a new level of insanity. I fold the letter and hide it in my boot before wiping my tears and exiting the closet. I don't even care that I forgot to change clothes.

I step into the bathroom, drying my face and willing the redness that comes with crying to leave when I hear Colby come through my door. "Amelia?"

"In here," I answer, taking a deep breath. "I'll be out in a minute."

I exit, finding a bowl of soup and crackers sitting on the desk. "I didn't make this but supervised as it was being made. It's vegetable soup. I hope you're okay with that."

"It's a close second to burnt grilled cheese." I smile, trying to hide the sadness from the letter. "To be honest, I'm not very hungry."

Colby turns me to look at him. "Amelia. It's very important that you eat all of this soup. It was made especially for you." His eyes beg me to follow directions. "You need to keep up your strength," he continues.

I don't know what he's trying to tell me, but I don't question him. When it comes to trusting the men I'm surrounded with, Colby wins. "Okay, okay!" I retort. "I'll eat every bite."

While I eat, Colby picks up my *Honey White* book, reading the seedy scenes out loud, bringing redness to my cheeks. My stomach suddenly cramps, forcing me to bend slightly. A pain hits my forehead in an instant and the room spins a little. "Colby, I don't feel well."

He puts the book down. "What do you feel like?"

"My stomach and head hurt. Did you poison me?" I laugh.

He moves to my side. "Let me help you." He pulls me toward the bed as I fight to stay upright. "Lie down. See if that helps a little."

The room spins even more, and I fight the urge to cry out from the twisting pains in my stomach. What the hell is happening? Did he poison me? My heart is racing, I'm sweating profusely, and my skin is on fire. "Oh, my God! Colby? What did you do to me?" I scream in pain. The door to the room crashes open as Viktor literally flies in.

"What's happening?" he asks, moving to my side. "Amelia, what's wrong?" My stomach empties, sending the contents to the foot of my bed. "Dammit, Colby what's going on?" He sits on the edge of the bed, pulling me into his lap.

"If she dies, you can't change her," Colby's words are the last thing I hear as the world goes black, and my heart stops beating.

THIRTEEN

home...maybe

"GIVE HER TIME," a voice says a few feet away. "Her body's been through a lot. She's not going to sit up and start talking." The voice feels familiar but not at the same time.

"That damn witch better not have lied," a deeper voice adds.

"She didn't. Her body just died. Give her time to recover."

Died? Are they talking about me? Did I die? My head hurts too badly to think. No matter how hard I try to force my eyes open, nothing happens. Dammit, eyes. Open! I fall back into the blackness of death or survival. I'm not sure what this is.

I wake to a voice next to me. It sounds like they're reading. I can't place the text but recognize the prose. The voice is deep and songlike and relaxes the confusion swirling through my head. I will my eyes open, and this time they follow instructions. In front of me is a blur of light, and I'm unable to focus on anything specific.

"Amelia?" the reader stops. "Amelia? Are you awake?" I turn in the direction of the voice, still not able to see any details. The dark spot moves closer, and I feel the bed lower from its weight. Someone on the other side slides a warm cloth over my eyes, helping to clear the haze.

The dark spot moves close enough to see—Violet. Her hair is dyed a different color from the last time I saw her, but it's definitely Violet. She leans down, pulling me toward her. "Oh, my God. I thought you were a goner."

"What happened?" I manage to whisper through cracked lips.

"You died," a voice on the other side of me answers. I turn my head to see Sara flashing a warm smile.

"Sara?"

"I'm here," she answers.

"Sara works for us," Violet answers my unasked question.

"Spy?" I whisper. My voice still isn't working.

"Something like that," Sara answers. "Get some rest."

"Colby?" I ask, trying to keep my eyes from closing.

"He's alive." Violet's words are the last thing I hear before falling back into the world of darkness.

I awaken hours, days, weeks... I don't know how

much time later. This time there's a new voice in my room. I recognize it instantly. I open my eyes to see Harrison sitting in a chair next to the window. "Harrison?" He's at my bedside in an instant.

"Amelia? You're awake." He takes my hand into his, sitting on the edge of the mattress. "I'm so sorry." I raise my hand, stopping his words.

"It's not your fault." My voice sounds weak, but more like me than before. "I'm alive... I think."

He smiles. "You're very much alive."

"Okay, just checking. How long have I been asleep?"

"Two weeks." I try to sit up without much luck.

"Two weeks," I repeat. "Are you sure?"

"Definitely, two weeks." With my eyes clear, I look around the room and realize I'm at Harrison's house.

"I'm at your house?" He nods as a soft knock on the door draws our attention.

"Come in," I croak toward the door.

"You're awake?" Colby asks, walking into the room.

He looks like he's been in a fight, but he's alive. "You killed me."

"I can't take all the credit. It was really Ophelia." I scan through a list of names in my head.

"The woman from the shelter?" I ask Harrison.

He nods. "She's a powerful witch and owed me a favor."

"Colby really did kill me?"

"In my defense, I told you there was a witch with a

potion and to be patient." I think back to the note he passed me in Viktor's library.

"A potion killed me?"

"And brought you back," Harrison adds.

"Damn." I look at the bruises covering Colby's face. "What happened after?"

Colby looks at the ground. "While Viktor tried to kill me, Sara and Thomas got you out of the house and brought you back here."

"Did he do that to your face?"

"It was an epic fight and would've been worse if I wasn't so fast." I remember him telling me Viktor was going to have to catch him to kill him.

"Viktor's going to be angry."

"He doesn't know you're alive," Harrison says, still holding my hand.

"Does he think I magically disappeared from the room?"

"I don't know or care what he thinks."

"He thinks I'm Penelope. He kept calling me by her name."

Harrison drops my hand, moving toward a window. "He's been in love with her since we were children. When she chose me over him, he never got over it."

"He wanted to turn me into a vampire so that I'd be his, forever."

"He thinks you're Penelope, returned to him." My mind flashes back to the letter I found in the library.

"He killed her for the same reason."

Harrison turns back toward me. "He's delusional and a psychopath."

"He didn't kill her because he couldn't have her. He killed her so she would come back and be with him."

"How do you know?" He moves back to the side of the bed.

"I found letters that she wrote. They were hidden in a desk in the library." Harrison looks hurt by my words. "I was able to get one of them and read it." I look down, not sure how much I should share with a room full of people.

"What did it say?" Harrison's words are no louder than a whisper.

"Penelope...she hadn't eaten for months. She said she could feel her life force draining and for you not to be angry at Viktor for it."

"Go on," Harrison urges.

"She said he believed when she died, she would be his and his alone." A tear streams down Harrison's cheek. "I read the letter on the top of the stack. I think it was her last. I'm sorry."

He stands, heading toward the door. "Please, excuse me." Colby takes his place next to my bed, and I watch Harrison leave the room. The overly confident Southern Gentleman is replaced by slumped shoulders and sadness.

"He'll be okay." He looks at the door. "More importantly, you're alive, well, and safe."

"Someone told me there was a request for potato

soup in here. Is this true?" Thomas says, walking into the room.

"Thomas." I smile. "Thank you."

He sits on the edge of my bed. "Do you know how hard it was to not jerk you out of that house when I was there? It took everything I had."

"He would've killed you before you laid a hand on her," Colby says from the other side of the bed. "Viktor and Harrison are the two strongest vampires in the city. You're a baby vampire who wouldn't have stood a chance."

"Whatever," he answers. "Feel like eating?"

"Is it poisoned?"

Colby smiles. "I can guarantee it's not poisoned." Thomas feeds me a few spoonfuls. I taste every spice as it slides down my throat.

"This is delicious."

"I know," he answers. "You think I waste my time making food that's boring?"

"Thank you, but I can't eat any more right now." I push the next spoonful away.

"Get some rest," Thomas says. "There's always more soup." On command, my eyes close, and I'm pulled into a world of dreams. Dreams full of vampires, werewolves, and witches, oh, my.

The next few days pass in a blur of sleep and visitors. I feel stronger each time I wake and decide to venture to the shower for the first time in who knows how long. The water clears my head even more as the reality of what my life has become comes crashing down. I've gone from a doctoral student to nothing more than a plaything being passed around the vampire community. Is there a vampire community? It takes five washes to clean the buildup from my hair. I don't know what kind of water heater Harrison has, but I've been in here long enough that every toe and finger have shriveled to prune status, yet the water is still scorching.

"Amelia?" Sara's voice calls through the door. "Are you okay in there?"

"I'm good, thanks. I'm coming out."

"Your professor is here."

"What? My professor? Which one?"

"I didn't catch a name, but he's a hottie. Late 50s, with salt-and-pepper hair and a cute little smile." A smile sounds through her words.

"Oh, my God. That's Dr. Cavish. He's my advisor." I shut the water off. "Tell him I'll be right down."

I throw on a pair of leggings and a sweatshirt and throw my hair into a bun. How the hell did he find me? Is he a vampire, too? I head downstairs, stopping every few steps to catch my breath. "Amelia," Dr. Cavish greets me as I reach the bottom of the stairs. "How are you doing?"

"Um, I'm good." I have no idea what he's been told about my absence from the program.

"That's good to hear. Mr. Chamberlin alerted the university to your accident. Don't worry about the classes you've missed. I met with the board on your behalf, and they agreed unanimously to give you an extension of your thesis and defense." He shifts awkwardly from one foot to the other. "I will say, for being in such a horrible accident, you look better than I expected."

"Thank you. It's been a long road to recovery. I'm feeling more like myself every day. Can I ask you something?"

"Of course," he answers.

"How did you know where to find me?"

"Harrison told me you'd rented a room from someone at this address." He looks around the lavishly decorated foyer. "I've studied homes in the Garden District extensively but never been in this home. It's beautiful."

"Thank you. I'll let the homeowner know. Can I walk you to the door?"

"That won't be necessary. Get well soon, Amelia. Let me know when you're feeling up to coming back." He heads toward the heavy doors.

"Thank you, Dr. Cavish. Hopefully, it will be soon." He closes the door behind him, leaving what has to be our strangest conversation ever. Something felt off about him.

"I told him you were in a horrible car accident," Harrison says, walking around the corner. "I hope I didn't overstep."

"No, thank you for doing that. He just seemed...weird."

"He may be like the vendor in Jackson Square. He may be able to sense me but doesn't understand what he senses. The most important part is you have an extension. I would hate to see all the work you've done go to waste."

"Agreed. Speaking of my work, is my computer still here?"

"It's in your room." He moves closer. "I've heard a rumor that breakfast is being served in the courtyard. Feel like eating anything?" My stomach growls on command.

"I'd like that." Harrison offers his arm and leads me slowly through the dining room into the kitchen.

"There she is!" Thomas is in front of me in an instant. "You're a sight for sore eyes."

"You need to get those sore eyes back to work," Sara says, stirring something on the stove. "If you think I'm not going to burn this, you're wrong."

Thomas gives me a quick hug before taking the wooden spoon away from Sara. "Girl, we talked about this. We're folding the eggs, folding...not beating the shit out of them."

Sara turns and winks. "Thomas is teaching me how to cook. You'd think at my age I would be halfway decent."

"You'd think," Thomas mumbles from the stove. He

turns, facing us. "Please, have a seat in the courtyard. Breakfast will be served momentarily."

New Orleans doesn't experience four seasons in the true sense of seasons. It's hot most of the year with a few weeks of bone-chilling cold. Today is neither too hot nor too cold. It's the perfect temperature and feels amazing on my skin. Harrison moves to the shade quickly, while I bask in the sun, soaking up every ounce of vitamin D possible. Being a redhead, the sun isn't my best friend, but a few minutes of direct sunlight, hopefully, won't turn me into a tomato.

"I'm sorry I left your room after you awoke. Hearing about Penelope's letters," he pauses. "I wasn't prepared to hear that she'd written me while she was with him."

I stare at the vampire across from me. His eyes look more tired than I remember, and his normally smooth hair is frizzed on the sides. "Feel like talking about it?"

"Here ya go!" Thomas bursts through the back door with a tray full of food. "I hope you're hungry, Amelia." He sets a glass of red "wine" in front of Harrison, while the rest is all for me. By the time he's done, I have every breakfast food possible, sitting in front of me.

"This looks great, thank you."

"You'll have to tell me if it's edible. Human food doesn't taste good to me anymore." He pauses in thought. "I miss it."

"I have no doubt it will be perfect." Thomas smiles, heading back into the house. I've eaten my fill when Harrison answers my question.

"Penelope died in 1829." I set my fork on the table, not sure I heard correctly. That was nearly two hundred years ago. I don't know why, but I assumed she died relatively recently. I don't speak, scared he'll stop. He looks down before continuing. "I told you earlier about Viktor's anger at our choice to change our way." I nod, remembering the conversation from before. "I found out later it wasn't me he wanted to change. It was Penelope. He tried relentlessly to win her over, make her choose between the two of us, love him more than she loved me. When he wasn't successful, he took her."

"Took her? You mean he kidnapped her?" My mind flashes back to being swept into the sky in an instant.

He nods. "When he took you..." he doesn't finish his thought. "He kept her out of my reach for years. I tracked them throughout the world, yet he managed to stay one step ahead of me." He takes a drink from his glass. "Penelope was strong, but Viktor was stronger."

"Wasn't she his maker?"

He nods. "However, human blood makes us stronger. Her diet weakened her."

"Years passed as we played the same cat and mouse game. He was always one step ahead and seemed to know my thoughts before I thought them, keeping her just out of reach." He laces his fingers together. "When he realized she was never going to relent to his desires, he killed her. Confirmation through that letter hit me harder than I expected. I knew all along that was his reasoning, but to hear it from someone else affected me more than it should've. I apologize for leaving you alone up there."

"You don't owe me an apology. You saved my life. You, Thomas, Colby, Violet, and Sara. I wouldn't be here if it weren't for all of you." I close my eyes realizing I have something I've never had before—a family.

FOURTEEN

laissez les bon temps rouler

AFTER BREAKFAST, I venture to my room, find my laptop, and open my completed thesis chapters. The writing seems foreign and immature as I read through what I was so proud of only weeks earlier. A soft knock on the door draws me back to the present. "You awake in there?" Colby says through the door.

"I am, come in."

"What are you working on?" I close my laptop, embarrassed at the level of incompetency on the screen.

"My doctoral thesis. Reading through it has me questioning my life choices." He flops on the bed, taking my laptop from me.

"Oh, come on. It can't be that bad." He opens the computer and begins reading. I fight the urge to hide underneath the chair from embarrassment. "It's good!" he says several minutes later. "Although, you need to work on your information on Lycan."

"You can't tell me you read it that quickly."

"Just the werewolf parts." He smiles. "I can answer any questions you might have."

"Seriously? Like an interview?"

"Sure." He lays back on my bed, stretching his long legs to the footboard. "What would you like to know?"

I grab a notebook and pen, ready to take notes. "Okay. I read in multiple books that werewolves need a full moon to change into wolf form. But when Edon and Viktor were fighting, he was in wolf form, and it wasn't a full moon night."

"You've read too many fantasy books and seen too many sparkly vampire movies. The full moon affects our change but does not demand it. It's ultimately up to the wolf whether they change into their true form. Edon is Alpha. He can do any damn thing he wants."

I write his answers, before asking another. "I know the alpha is the strongest of the pack and the others are required to follow him, but how is the alpha chosen?"

"Most alphas are made, not born. Some take over the pack when their father dies, others fight their way to the top and earn the position." I set my pen down.

"How did Edon become alpha?"

"He's the exception to the rule." He pauses. "Edon is the strongest lycanthrope in the southeast, and being alpha is something he never wanted. Our pack has been ripped apart over the years, and he was the only leader able to pull it together and keep it together." I think back to the bearded man at Viktor's house. "Why didn't he want to be alpha?"

"Being alpha is a hard job." He looks up. "My mother died because he was alpha."

I'm confused. "What are you saying?"

"Edon's my father." I stare at the young werewolf in front of me, not sure what to say.

"Are you the next alpha?"

"Girl, you've met me. I'm not alpha material. No, my oldest brother has been groomed since birth to be the next in line. He's nearly as large as Edon and will be larger by the time he's ready to take over. No one will question his leadership." He slaps his thighs. "Ask me more questions. This is fun."

"Does he want to be alpha?"

Colby laughs. "He doesn't have a choice."

"Do you eat human food or just raw meat?"

"Raw meat is gross unless I'm in wolf form. Some Lycan eat raw meat as a diet, but I eat whatever I want." He crosses his arms across his chest. "Next question."

"Are Viktor and Edon friends?"

Colby laughs. "No. Viktor's not friends with anyone. Edon keeps the peace between vampire and werewolf, nothing more than that."

"Okay, one more question. How many are in your pack?"

He takes a deep breath. "Honestly, I'm not sure of the exact number, but last I heard, there were over one hundred living in the Quarter."

"One hundred werewolves living in the Quarter, in this small area? That means you're not the first I've met."

Colby laughs. "Definitely not." He turns his head toward me. "I have an idea. Would you like to go to a Mardi Gras party with Thomas and me?"

"Mardi Gras?" I thought it was still January. "I don't know. I'm not the partying type."

"Come on, Amelia. Let's show off those legs you keep hidden. Get out there and dance a little." He jumps off my bed, pulling me up and spinning me under his arm. "See, you've got skills."

"Somehow, I don't think spinning is a skill." He opens the closet door, laying three formal gowns on the bed. "Choose one."

My bed looks like a fabric store threw up on it. "What if Viktor's there?"

"He won't be. Choose."

"How do you know?" I persist.

"If you don't choose, I'll choose for you."

"God, you're annoying." My eyes are drawn to the dark green gown first. "This one."

"Good choice." He holds it in front of me and heads back into the closet. "Here." He hands me a pair of three-inch heels. "You'll need these."

"I'm thinking you've never met me before. I won't even make it down the stairs before I fall in these things."

"It's two o'clock. The party starts at six. Can you be

ready by then?"

My inner voice is screaming as social anxiety kicks in. "I can try," I answer. What am I doing? Just say no, Amelia.

"Meet us downstairs at five-thirty." The door latches behind him, and I instantly regret agreeing. I finally break down and take a shower at three o'clock, procrastinating as long as possible. I took one earlier but feel the need to rewet my hair. I shave every possible spot on my body before exiting and beginning the primping process. I've never been to a formal party, prom, dance, or anything of the sort. A small part of me is excited, while the rest of me is experiencing an introvert breakdown.

Sorting through the piles of makeup, I find the colors that match the dress and my skin tone the best and follow a tutorial video for application. By the time I'm finished, I don't look anything like myself. My eyes are shadowed in different shades of green, matching the dress perfectly, and my hair is the perfect combination of curls and body. I decided against pulling it back and let it hang halfway down my back in long red waves. I slide my feet through the top of the dress, pulling it up around me. The strapless top fits perfectly as I zip it into place. I slip on the heels and look at myself in the mirror. Holy shit. Who is that woman staring back at me?

One look at my phone tells me I need to get my butt downstairs. I pray each stair won't be the last all the way to the bottom. "Excuse me, ma'am. I think you're at the wrong house." Thomas greets me at the landing.

"Damn..." Colby whistles from behind him. "I knew you chose the right dress when you picked that color, but you look hot. If I were into girls, I'd be all over you."

Thomas turns toward Colby. "Don't make it weird, boo."

"Too much?" Colby laughs. "It's true, though." He wiggles his eyebrows.

Harrison steps into the foyer from seemingly out of nowhere. He's wearing a custom-cut black tuxedo. His hair is out of his usual bun, laying perfectly smooth against his broad shoulders. The way he looks at me sends shivers down my spine.

"I didn't realize you were going with us." I move closer to him.

"Me either, but apparently my attendance was requested by Edon."

I turn to Colby. "Is this a lycanthrope Mardi Gras party?

"Totally. *Krew of the Fanged Tooth.*" He laughs at his words.

"You just made that up, didn't you."

"No, believe it or not. It's a real thing." He wraps Thomas's arm through his and heads to the door. Harrison steps in front of me, offering me his arm.

"You look beautiful," he whispers for my ears only, sending the shivers once more. We follow Thomas and Colby to a waiting limousine, sliding into the seats across from them. A few minutes later we stop and Harrison steps out, offering me his hand. It doesn't take long to realize we're in the middle of the warehouse district with no other cars in sight.

"Are you sure we're in the right place?"

"We are," Harrison answers. The limo pulls away, leaving us in the middle of nowhere.

"This way." Colby leads us around the back side of the building. We follow him to a door hidden from the view of the road. Just like a scene from a movie, Colby knocks three times before a small door opens at the top.

"Colby? Is that you?"

"Yeah, dude. It's me. Open the door." The rusty metal door creaks open, revealing a tall bearded man. He's wearing a tuxedo with cutout sleeves, displaying muscles that were obviously too large to fit into the arms of the jacket.

"My man," the guy says, patting Colby on the back. He stops, looking at the rest of our party. "They with you?"

"They are. I can vouch for them."

"We don't want any trouble." The man looks Harrison up and down.

"Neither do we. We're merely here as guests of Edon." Those are the magic words. The door opens wide, and we enter into a world of glitz, glamour, and rock 'n' roll.

I hang onto Harrison's arm a little tighter as we enter a

room full of men and women dressed similarly to us. Howls of excitement can be heard echoing through the room as most of the guests are in the middle of the dance floor, jumping with the beat. This feels more like a rave than a Mardi Gras party. In their defense, I've never been to either so I'm not the best judge. Thomas and Colby disappear into the crowd, leaving me alone with Harrison.

"Let's get a table." He leads me to the edge of the room and away from the crowd, where several large tables are set up. "Care for a drink?"

"Vodka?"

"I'll be right back. You'll be okay on your own?"

"Maybe?" I smile. "I'll just hit them with the heel of my shoe."

Harrison laughs, disappearing in a blink. Thankfully, he returns less than a minute later, setting a fruity drink in front of me. "They didn't have vodka, so I got you this blue fruity thing."

"It's perfect, thank you." I take a few sips and realize it's mostly alcohol with a hint of fruit. "A couple of these, and I'll be out on the dance floor."

"Let me know when you're ready," Harrison says with a smirk.

"You're a dancer?"

"I'm not sure dancer is the right word. However, I can wiggle with the best of them." His choice of words makes me laugh.

"Harrison," a tall man I recognize from Viktor's

house says, walking to our table. "Thank you for coming."

"Of course, Edon. Thank you for the invitation." He turns to me.

"Amelia? Colby has kept me up-to-date on your health. I'm glad to see you looking well."

"Thanks to Colby. He kept me alive when I was at my worst." Edon nods his head, while Harrison looks down.

"He's one of the best. If you need anything, please don't hesitate to ask." He turns back to Harrison, exchanging a silent warning. I'm not sure why, but I don't question them.

Several blue fruity drinks in, Harrison is a man of his word and escorts me to the dance floor. While the crowd around us bumps, grinds, and gyrates to the music, Harrison pulls me close, wrapping his arm around my back. He leads me around the dance floor, guiding my every step as we weave through the mass of Lycan with grace and style. Dancing with him feels easy, normal, and intimate. I'm not sure if it's the fruity drink talking, but I'm having a good time. Sea green eyes stare into mine as we glide our way across the floor and away from the crowd.

"You're much more than a wiggler," I say with a smile.

"I've had many years to perfect my wiggles." He returns the smile. The song changes from loud and bumpy to slow and romantic, and the energy of the room shifts with it. Everyone around us couples up, moving slowly with the beat. "This is better." He pulls me closer until only inches separate us.

"Yes, it is." I lay my head on his chest as we sway, matching tempos with the couples nearby. The silence between us isn't awkward, instead, it's strangely comforting.

"May I have this dance?" a large man I don't recognize says, tapping Harrison on the shoulder. What is this, eighth grade?

Harrison looks at me for an answer. I nod, not sure what the protocol is. "I'll be at our table." The large man steps between us, pulling me to his front.

"I saw you come in," he says, slobbering over me. "You're hot."

"Thank you?"

"You want to get out of here?"

I stop dancing, trying to pull away. He refuses to let go of my arms. "Let me go, please."

"Our dance isn't over." He slings me around, before pulling me tight against him again.

"You're wrong about that, wolf. The lady asked you to let her go. I suggest you do so." Harrison has returned and is standing next to my new dance partner.

"Shut up, vampire. You have no power here."

"Let me go, asshole." I kick him in the shin with the heel of my shoe. "Do you know who he is?"

The lycanthrope grabs me around the wrists, pulling me away from Harrison. "I don't care who he is.

He's a vampire, that's all I need to know." Harrison is between the two of us before I know what happened. He pushes the large man back, separating him from me.

"You have exactly two seconds to get away from her before either I or your alpha disposes of you. You are either too drunk or too dumb to be in the same room as she is. I suggest you leave while you're still in control of your bowels."

"How dare you threaten me, vampire." The wolf raises a hand toward Harrison before something hits him in the back, knocking him to the ground. Behind him stands Edon, his Alpha.

"You should learn to listen, Drew. Go home before you single-handedly break a treaty with no skills except your stupidity."

"Creep," I say, kicking Drew on the leg. "I wouldn't go anywhere with you if you were the last mythological creature on earth."

The werewolf scurries to his feet, breathing hard. "Edon, I was just trying..."

"I don't care what you were *trying* to do," Edon interrupts. "Next time use your manners, and for God's sake, don't pick a fight with the oldest vampire in the city." Drew turns back to Harrison, assessing him from head to toe. Clearly, he's not convinced. "Apologize and go home. You're lucky you're still breathing."

"Apologies," he spews.

"I believe that is owed to the lady, not me." Harrison stands his ground.

The giant bearded man turns to me. "Forgive me, miss. I've had a bit too much to drink tonight." The look in his eyes doesn't match his words, and I don't respond. Harrison slides his arm around my back as Drew is escorted by two men larger than he from the building.

"I'm sorry about that," Harrison says once the trio is out of sight.

"That had nothing to do with you and everything to do with the fact he's an asshole," Edon offers his apologies before leaving our side.

"Very true. I've only met a handful of Lycan that weren't assholes. Would you like to stay or go for a walk?"

I look through the room of gyrating, intoxicated werewolves. "Walk, please." He offers me his arm, and we leave the party behind.

FIFTEEN

reincarnation?

CRISP NIGHT AIR fills my lungs and clears my head the moment we step outside. Normally, the warehouse district isn't an area I would walk through, especially at night. Ironically, on the arm of a vampire, I feel safe.

"Thank you for coming to my rescue back there."

"It was my pleasure, Miss Lockhart," he answers, using the strong Southern accent I remember from the first time we met. God, that feels like a million years ago.

"Can I ask you something?"

"Anything," he answers.

"Why have you stayed here, in New Orleans? I mean after Penelope, why stay?"

He takes a deep breath before answering. "I've left many times, but something about the city calls me back." We stop walking, overlooking the river below.

"I've lived here longer than I've lived anywhere before. It's my home. It was *our* home."

"I'm sorry I told you about her letters." He turns toward me.

"I'm not. Hearing her words from you somehow provided me with the closure I didn't realize I needed. It was a gift, and I'm grateful." I turn back to the water, not sure how to feel about his admission.

"Thank you," I whisper.

"For what?"

"For saving me from Viktor...twice. For giving me a place to live. For ensuring my safety as a child. For talking to Dr. Cavish—for everything. I've never thanked you, for any of it."

"My pleasure, ma'am." The Southern drawl has returned, and I can't hide my smile. He wraps my arm back through his, and we continue walking toward the Quarter. The closer we get, the more people we pass. Most are wearing brightly colored beads they caught during one of the many parades through the city and are stumbling as they walk.

"I used to hate living in the Quarter during Mardi Gras. I can't tell you how many times drunk and confused tourists would wander into the school dorms."

Harrison laughs. "I can only imagine. This season is prime for vampires." I stop walking and turn toward him. "Drunk, confused people make for easy prey. Most of them won't even remember what happened to them."

"Are there many vampires here?"

"We're far outnumbered by the wolves, but there are more than you'd expect."

"At the party, Edon said you were the oldest. Is that true?"

"Viktor and I are the oldest."

"What does that mean?"

"Being the oldest makes us the strongest. Does that scare you?"

I look into the green eyes staring down at me. "Not at all." Harrison's smile is warm as we continue walking.

"Got any money?" a man says from a few feet away. He's leaning against the side of a brick wall and from his torn and dirty clothing, I can tell he's most likely homeless. "Hey!" he yells louder. "Money. Got any?" I watch Harrison slip a group of bills into the man's hand as we keep walking. "Thank you, sir." His demeanor changes as he pulls out the wad of cash. "Thank you!"

"Aren't you afraid he'll just buy drugs or alcohol with that?"

"The way I see it, it's my job to help others. What that man chooses to do with the money is up to him. God blesses the giver, not the gift."

"Do you believe in God?"

He pauses before answering. "I believe in helping others and showing love even when it's not returned. I believe love is the center of the universe, and our job while being here is to show others love, no matter how much it may hurt. I believe that's what God is: Love."

I stop walking, pulling him to a stop beside me. "That was beautiful."

He laughs. "Don't tease me."

"I'm not teasing you. I've been trying to explain my feelings for years without adequate words. You expressed them perfectly. Thank you." Something passes between us, setting butterflies loose in my stomach. I stare into his eyes, not sure what, if anything, is happening.

"Do you feel that?" Harrison whispers.

I nod, not trusting my voice. The look in his eyes mirrors the emotions swimming through my mind. I lean forward, wrapping my arms around his waist, pulling him as close as possible. We stand, wrapped in each other's arms, not nearly long enough. "What's going on?" I ask, pulling away.

"I don't know, but I know someone who might." Long fingers wrap through mine as we leave the river, heading into the heart of the Quarter. The streets are crowded with leftover people from the earlier parade. He leads me into a small shop, not far off Jackson Square. A familiar woman stands as we enter.

"Harry!" she claps her hands together. "You brought Amelia to see me." She rushes around the counter, throwing her short arms around me. "Girl, you're a sight for sore eyes."

"Thank you, Ms. Ophelia. Your potion saved me."

"You're welcome, dear one. Call me Opie, please. Ophelia is an old woman's name. What do I owe the pleasure of your visit tonight? I'm surprised to see you out in the middle of this craziness."

A group of tourists walks in, shuffling through a big spell book displayed in the window. "I'm going to do this on you!" one of them says, pointing at something in the book. They all laugh and exit the store, leaving the three of us alone.

"I don't know how to put this," Harrison shifts from foot to foot. "Earlier, Amelia and I were talking, and something passed between the two of us. Something familiar." He sighs. "I don't know what I'm asking."

"It's like I knew him," I add. "Not in a cordial kind of way but *knew* him and have known him my entire life."

Ophelia smiles. "I've never seen you so...human. I like this side of you, Harry." He laughs, wrapping his fingers through mine. His touch brings comfort. Opie looks at our joined hands. "Come with me." She locks the front door and leads us to a room behind a curtain. "Sit." She points at a table in the middle of the room. "I'm not only a witch. I'm also a medium."

"Like a psychic?"

"No. Psychics and mediums are two different things. I can speak to the dead, not see into the future."

"I don't know about this," Harrison says, sliding away from the table.

"You're a goddamn vampire. How is *this* weird?" He

slides forward and the three of us join hands. "I can feel your connection. I felt it the first night we met at the shelter. Although, it's much stronger now." Harrison squeezes my fingers.

"Clear your minds and relax. I'm going to take a look through the veil." Opie is quiet for a long time. What feels like hours later, she opens her eyes, turning to me. "I have seen."

"The reason you feel connected is that you are." She pauses. "You have known him in a previous life. You are Penelope."

Harrison stands from the table, knocking over his chair. "How is that possible? Vampires don't have a soul."

"When I crossed the veil, I was met by several guides. They showed me your and Penelope's love and her eventual death. They also showed me Amelia's birth. They are one and the same."

"That can't be." Harrison turns to look at me. "She can't be Penelope, can she?"

"I only know what I'm shown. The guides told me she's returned, and then showed me Amelia."

I don't know what to say. "Is that why I look like her?"

Opie pulls her hands away from the two of us. "Reincarnation isn't something I've studied much about. I can tell you that a reincarnated soul can share characteristics throughout each life, but as far as looking the same, I don't know."

"Thank you, Ophelia." Harrison stands, and his energy changes. "Amelia, I'll walk you home." We walk through the crowds, pushing our way through the drunk partiers, moving away from the Quarter and toward the Garden District. Harrison hasn't said a word since leaving Opie's shop, and the energy streaming from him is darker than earlier.

"Harrison?" He doesn't answer. "Please talk to me." The crowd is beginning to thin out, making it easier to walk. "Harrison?"

"Not here." He keeps his arm around my waist, leading us closer to home. We round the corner where his house sits, and I stop walking.

"How about here?" I plant my feet.

"Amelia, I don't know if I'm ready to talk about it. I don't know how to feel about any of this. If you are Penelope and I..." He wipes a tear. "I could've saved you from a life of misery, but I didn't. I left you there, alone without anyone to take care of you."

I reach up, touching the side of his face with my palm. "You did save me."

"I made sure you were protected, that's not saving you." For the first time since leaving Opie's, he looks me in the eyes. "I'm so sorry. I never meant for any of this to happen." Harrison runs his free hand through my curls, lifting them to his nose and inhaling. "We're going to do this right." He steps away. "I will not force myself on you, ever. If you choose to be with me, it will be your choice. Amelia's choice. Not a choice based on Opie's words."

"Okay," I whisper. "Amelia's choice." He wraps my arm through his, leading us to the front door of his home. The house is silent as we enter the darkened foyer.

"Good night, Amelia. I enjoyed our dance tonight." He bows at the waist.

"Good night, Harrison. I enjoyed dancing with you as well." I curtsey the best I can before heading to my room. I feel his eyes on me the entire way up the stairs.

I spend a sleepless night, tossing and turning, thinking through possible outcomes of falling in love with a vampire. Is that what this is? Am I falling in love with Harrison? I wonder if he's able to sleep. Does he sleep? Is there a coffin somewhere he sleeps in? My mind is on a crazy ride of insanity when the sun peeks through the window. I don't waste a minute getting up and getting ready for the day. I spend longer than normal in the shower with my brain in overdrive and extra time on my hair and makeup. I don't know what I expect to happen, but I want to look as nice as possible. Dressed in a nice pair of jeans and a white ruffled shirt, I head downstairs to what I hope will be breakfast with Harrison.

"Good morning, sunshine!" Sara says as I enter the kitchen. "You look nice this morning. Going somewhere?"

"No, just felt like cleaning up a little."

"You might want to find a nice little restaurant to eat breakfast in. Thomas isn't here, and I'm the one in charge of cooking. I'm warning you now."

"I'm willing to risk it." I laugh. "Has anyone else come to eat?"

"I saw Violet in the courtyard earlier. Other than her, no." I peek out the door to see Violet dressed in yoga clothes in a pose I don't recognize.

"Thank you. Let me know if you need any help." Sara smiles, and I head into the courtyard.

"Is that downward dog?"

"Hell, I don't know. I just do what feels good." She stands up. "I'm sorry I didn't visit you much after you returned. I was afraid that I might be a danger to you after Thomas. It takes a while to come down off of a high like that."

"Don't apologize. I understand." I laugh awkwardly. "I'd rather you take your time than eat me."

Violet laughs out loud. "We agree on that." She waves her finger up and down. "What's with all this?"

"What do you mean?

"I mean, when you first came here you looked like a college professor, I mean no offense...and now, you look snatched." I laugh at her usage of slang.

"Thank you, I think."

"Snatched is good." She resumes her yoga pose. "Care to join me?"

"Oh, I'm not really dressed for yoga. Have you seen Harrison?" Violet jumps from her position.

"Is that what this is about? Harrison?" She smiles deeply. "Girl, spill the tea."

"There is no tea to spill. I just hoped he might be around for breakfast." On cue, Harrison exits the house, stepping into the courtyard. He's wearing a pair of khaki pants that are rolled up at the ankles and a pale green shirt. The color brings out the green of his eyes.

"Speak of the devil," Violet says, resuming her position.

"I presume I'm the devil you speak of," he says, moving to my side.

"If the shoe fits." Violet smiles at her words.

"I thought you might enjoy going for a drive."

I can't contain my smile. "I'd like that."

"Oh, my God," Violet exclaims from her yoga mat while pretending to gag herself. I wrap my arm through Harrison's as we head to the garage and an awaiting royal blue convertible.

"There's a scarf in the glove box if you want it for your hair." Pulling my curls into a bun, I hide them under the scarf, tying it tightly around my head. "Hang on," he warns, pulling onto the busy street.

"Where are we going?"

"I don't know." He smiles. "I just want to spend the day with you."

SIXTEEN

powdered sugar and vampires

WE DRIVE out of the Garden District and head north toward the lake. I'm not sure where we're going, but like Harrison, I don't care. I just want to spend the day with him. I catch myself staring at the vampire in the driver's seat. His hair is pulled back in a tight bun, and the dark glasses he's wearing somehow make him look even hotter. The smirk on his face tells me he knows I'm staring.

We pull into a spot in a park I recognize immediately. "St. John Park?"

"Yeah, this is where we landed when we arrived in New Orleans." I exit the car, looking at the remains with newfound respect. I've been here many times, but never really paid attention to the history. We walk across the grassy park to what's left of the fort. "Back then, the only way into the city was through this fort. We took a small boat across Lake Pontchartrain and landed not far from here." We stand next to what looks like the remains of a fireplace. "We lived a few miles away before the city began building up, and we were able to build a house."

"What did you do for money?"

Harrison smiles. "I was a farmer."

I laugh. "I can't picture you as a farmer."

"We brought plenty of money with us from France, but neither of us wanted to draw attention to ourselves. We wanted to fit in and be one of them. I chose to farm. It provided food for the people in the parish and added to our wealth." He looks out into the lake. "I think the people knew we were different, but with the massive amount of food we provided, no one questioned us."

"I'm still trying to wrap my head around the fact that you were one of the first ones in New Orleans."

"When the Spanish arrived, we stayed. Times were harder, but like before, I provided enough food to feed the soldiers, and we were allowed to remain." He takes my hand into his, and we walk along the edge of the lake.

"Thank you for sharing this with me." I stop walking. "Can I share something with you?"

He shrugs, "Sure." I lead him back to the car and give him turn-by-turn directions to the heart of the Quarter. "Park here." I point to a spot along the street. In front of us are the remains of the Calliope Projects. The place where I grew up.

"This is where you lived."

"Yes. This is where you saved me." I take his hand into mine.

"Amelia..."

"No, this is my turn." I motion to the empty buildings. "This is where the poor little girl with no family, who slept in the closet every night, lived. This is where she learned to be strong. This is where she learned to fight for what she wanted. This is the place where she was the strongest." He leans against his car, and I move next to him, resting my head on his shoulder before running back to my side of the car. "Come on, there's another place I want to show you."

I lead him across town to the university. He parks along the main road. We stand on the side of the busy thoroughfare, staring at the dorms I once called home. "This is the place where I discovered who I am. This is where that little girl turned into a woman. It's where she realized she was strong and capable of anything she put her mind to."

He turns toward me. "Why are you showing me this?"

"Because you think I grew up without anything. I'm showing you I didn't. What I had wasn't the American dream, but I had a roof over my head and a place that taught me to be the person I am today." He moves inches in front of me, glancing down at my lips. Kiss me, Harrison. My soul begs for our lips to touch. Instead of kissing me, he lays his forehead against mine. The intimacy shared with our touch makes my body tingle from head to toe and in all the right places.

"Thank you," he whispers.

"You're welcome. You know, I would kill for a beignet right now."

Harrison laughs. "No need for violence. We can make that happen."

"Let's walk." I lace my fingers through his, and we walk the few blocks over to the most famous beignet restaurant in New Orleans. Luckily, it's early in the morning, and most of the tourists are still in bed or hung over from last night's party. We find a table quickly and place our order. Harrison orders his signature black coffee, reminding me of his visit to the coffee shop. Minutes later, I'm covered in powdered sugar, and Harrison's taken one sip of his steaming drink.

"I think you're wearing more than you ate," he teases.

"That's the best part." Thankfully, I chose to wear white this morning. I wipe what remains of the sugar onto the concrete.

"I used to hunt here."

I wrinkle my forehead. "I thought you had stopped hunting by the time you came to New Orleans."

"I did. After Penelope died, that changed." I set my apple juice down, not sure where this conversation is going. "I spiraled after her death. I spent the next hundred years in that downhill spiral."

"You started hunting again." He nods.

"I couldn't handle the pain of her death. I was weak. Penelope was always the strong one."

"What made you stop again?"

"Violet." He looks around the café. "This is where I found her."

"Found Violet?"

He nods. "She was with a group of young women the same age as she was. They were laughing, having a good time, and I didn't like that. The love of my life was gone, how dare anyone else have a good time." I haven't seen this side of Harrison. Hearing him talk about himself like this feels different. "I followed them, determined one of them would be my next meal. I wasn't picky. They all were the same." He looks lost in a memory. "Violet was the lucky recipient of my anger."

"You turned her?"

"That wasn't my intention. I intended to drain her, leave her to die like I had many others before."

"What changed?"

"She did." He pauses. "She begged me not to kill her. I'd heard that so many times before, it didn't faze me. But something about Violet did. She knew what I was and what I was doing. She begged me to change her, that she was going to end her life tonight anyway."

I stare at the vampire across the table from me. "She planned to take her own life?"

"Yes. The night out with her friends was to be her last before completing the deed. She said I was her angel, her savior, and she begged me to turn her into the creature I was."

"And you did." He nods, lost in thought.

"She was the last. I came to my senses and haven't hunted since." I slide my hand on top of his.

"Thank you."

"For what? Being a killer?"

"No, for feeling comfortable enough to tell me."

"Well, you're still here. I guess that's a good sign." He smirks.

"It's a very good sign." I stand, and a pile of sugar falls to the ground. "I think you're right about wearing more than I ate." A small group of people, led by an older man dressed in colonial clothing, passes by us. "Is that a ghost tour?"

"Most likely. Want to go?"

"Yes. I've lived my entire life in this town and never once taken a ghost tour." He grabs my hand, pulling me toward the group. It doesn't take long to catch up.

"Hello there!" the guide says. "You're welcome to join us. Tours cost twenty dollars with an extra five for the cemetery tour. Harrison hands the man a large bill, telling him to keep the change. "Yes, sir." Our small group consists of a family of four, an older couple, and us.

We stop at a small building not far from the café. "This is one of the oldest hotels in the Quarter. It dates back to the year 1785, and most of what you see in front of you is original. The first building burned down in the early eighteen hundreds, but parts still remain. Legend says it's inhabited by vampires still to this day." I turn to Harrison for confirmation. He nods, with a smirk. The tour guide continues with a story of lost love, death, and vampire legends that surround the structure. "Today you can stay here for a little over two hundred dollars a night. Guests are often awoken by ghostly visitors and leave with stories of horror and fright."

The tour continues for the next half hour with stories of ghosts and legends, culminating with St. Louis Cemetery, No. 1. "This is by far our most frightening experience on the tour. I won't even come inside after dark," the guide continues. "The most famous ghost inside the walls is that of Marie Laveau, otherwise known as the Voodoo Queen."

"Did you know her?" I whisper.

"Yes, she was terrifying. Come with me." While the group moves to a new spot in the cemetery, Harrison leads me to a grave several rows away. He stops, staring at the stone grave.

I read the name etched into the stone, *Penelope Chamberlin*. "This is her grave?"

He nods. "It is. This is the first time I've been back since."

"I'm so sorry. We shouldn't have come here."

"No, it's alright. I need to be here, with you." He takes my hand into his. I stare at her name, not sure what I expect to happen.

"I see you've found the grave of what many think is the first vampire in New Orleans." The tour group joins us. "Legend says Penelope Chamberlin was a powerful vampire who ruled for many years over the weaker ones she created. It's said she hunted the streets of New Orleans, killing hundreds and leaving a trail of corpses in her wake."

I feel the anger rolling off of Harrison. "Legend is wrong. She was the kindest, most gentle spirit that ever lived."

"I beg to differ. I have a few books you might be interested in reading about the subject."

Harrison steps closer to the man. "I'm not interested in books. Your stories are wrong, and I'd appreciate it if you stop spreading lies and factless rumors." I beg the man to shut up with my eyes.

"Okay, the tour is over. If you'd like, you can follow me back to the store and gift shop where we have books on each of the locations we covered today." The guide turns, leading the small group away from us.

"I'm sorry, Amelia. I let my anger get the best of me."

"Don't apologize. You were protecting your wife. He was wrong and deserved to be called out on it." I take his hand into mine. "I'm kind of ready to get out of here, anyway. This place gives me the heebie-jeebies."

"Agreed." We walk the three blocks back to the café, and his energy lightens slowly. "How about a tour of the French Market?"

"I'd like that. My mom would never take me when I was a kid, and after she left, I couldn't afford to go. Not that we could afford to go when she was around, either." We walk around the aisles, looking at the mixture of homemade and resell items on display. I find a table of handmade jewelry, my eye landing on a particularly beautiful jade necklace.

"She'll take it," he says before I realize what he's done.

"Oh, no. You don't have to buy it for me." He hands the woman cash before I finish my protest. He clasps it behind my neck, and it's the perfect length to hang in front of my shirt. "It's beautiful, thank you."

By the time we finish our trek around the market, I've collected a necklace, a bracelet, a Baja jacket, and a shell headband. "This is the strangest haul I've ever made." He laughs at my mish-mosh of items. "Thank you."

"Anytime." Harrison's demeanor changes in an instant. He looks around the open-air market, checking every booth.

"What is it?" I ask.

"You need to hide, now."

"Hide? From what?"

In an instant, a black streak stops in front of us. "Well, look what the cat dragged in. And here, I thought you were dead." Viktor turns to Harrison. "Should've known you and that baby wolf were up to something."

"Leave, Viktor. Amelia is not an item that you can *steal* when you like. If you lay one finger on her..."

"What, Harrison? More of your mindless threats?"

"Leave me alone. I don't want to be with you," I spew.

"Of course, you don't, but you will. He's not what he pretends to be, Amelia. You're not safe. He's trying to turn you into his Penelope." He moves so quickly I don't detect movement. Harrison has a scratch on his cheek.

"You're delusional. That's your agenda, not Harrison's. Penelope didn't love you, Viktor. Accept it and get over it. She loved Harrison, and your jealousy won't change that."

"Jealousy? Is that what you think this is, jealousy? Any number of women would beg for my company."

"Then you should go do that," I urge. "Get one that wants you because this one doesn't."

Harrison keeps moving, keeping me protectively behind him. "Everything okay over there?" a vendor from the market calls to our group.

"We're fine, thanks." I smile, trying to reassure the small group staring at us.

"Leave, Viktor, or I will make you leave."

"Such humor. Some things never change. Nearly one thousand years later, you still think you're better than me. The truth will be revealed, sooner rather than later." Viktor looks around at the small number of humans that have stopped to watch the spectacle.

"This isn't over," he says, disappearing as fast as he arrived.

"We have to go." Harrison wraps his arms around me, and within a second, we're in the courtyard of his house.

"What the hell? What about the car?"

"I'll get it later. Your safety is my priority."

SEVENTEEN

i volunteer as tribute

INSTEAD OF BEING TERRIFIED, as most normal women would be, I'm pissed. I don't know who I'm pissed at, but I'm pissed. Both of them, maybe? "Is this how it's going to be for the rest of my life? On the run from Viktor, always trying to stay one step ahead or hiding in the shadows, hoping he won't discover me? Or trapped in the confines of this courtyard and house?" I ask the moment he sets me down in the courtyard.

"What's going on?" Violet comes from inside.

"Viktor. He's what's going on." I cross my arms in front of my chest.

"What happened?" She looks at Harrison.

"He found us and knows she's alive."

Violet laughs. "Did you think she'd get to live the rest of her life without Viktor realizing she's alive? It was only a matter of time. He has spies everywhere."

"So, you agree?" I turn my anger toward Violet. "You think I should be locked inside a tower somewhere?"

"That's not what I said." Her voice is as calm as mine is angry. "We all knew he'd discover you were alive, sooner or later. Now, we have a choice of what to do about it."

"Violet," Harrison warns.

"What? He's not going to rest until he has her. He's been pining over her for nearly a thousand years. You think he's just going to magically forget about her now?"

"What do you suggest we do?" Harrison asks.

"You know what to do." I watch from afar as the two vampires have a silent conversation I'm not privy to.

"Any chance one of you could share this with me?"

"We can leave," Harrison says.

"Sure, you can. That might work for a year or two, but what will you do when he finds you?" Violet is relentless and absolutely correct.

"I don't know if I can." Harrison's voice is softer.

"If you want Amelia to survive, you don't have a choice."

I look back and forth between the two of them. "What the hell are you two talking about?"

"Harrison has to kill Viktor. In order to be strong enough, he has to drink human blood. He has to hunt."

"Does hunt mean to kill?"

"Sometimes," he answers.

I move to a park bench underneath a blooming cherry tree. "I won't do that. I won't sacrifice innocent lives so that I can live."

"Amelia..."

"No. Absolutely not. What kind of person does that make me?"

"There are alternatives." Harrison moves behind me.

"Will they make you as strong?" He doesn't answer.

"No," Violet answers for him. "Warm human blood provides us with the most strength. Even with animal blood, Harrison is stronger than every other vampire."

"Except, Viktor," I add before she can. She nods.

"Use me." My voice is no louder than a whisper.

"No."

I turn, looking at the vampire behind me. "Why not? You don't have to drain me. The human body takes twenty-four hours to replenish its blood volume. I wrote a paper on it one time."

"Amelia, I won't hear any of this." He turns, heading toward the door.

"I'd rather it be you." I wipe a stray tear from my cheek. "I'd rather it be you."

"I'm not listening to this. You know how I feel." Violet walks back inside the house, leaving the two of us alone, staring at each other.

"Do you know what you're asking?"

"Honestly, no. But if I'm going to be sucked on by anyone, I'd rather it be you." That didn't come out quite the way it was intended, and I resist the urge to laugh. "I trust you, Harrison."

"What if I take too much?"

"You won't," I interrupt. "You didn't hurt Thomas when I saw the two of you drinking from him."

"That was different."

"How was drinking his blood any different from drinking mine?"

"Because it was."

"How, Harrison? Explain it to me!"

"Because I don't feel the same for Thomas as I do for you." He pauses, deep in thought. "Drinking your blood would be intimate, sexual, and I don't know..." he trails off. "I don't know if I could control the emotions that come with that." I step close enough that only a few inches separate the two of us.

"I trust you, Harrison." I reach up, touching my lips to his. "You won't hurt me," I whisper. He slides the palm of his hand along my cheek, caressing his thumb gently along my jawline.

"God, you're beautiful." His lips take control of mine, and my lips open for him. The moment we touch an explosion rises from deep inside. He slides a hand behind my neck, pulling me closer until the only thing separating us is clothes. I run my hand down his rock-hard chest, wishing I could rip the shirt off and expose him to the world. His other hand slides under the hem of my shirt, lying flat against my back. I sigh at his touch.

"Amelia," he whispers, pulling away slightly. "We need to stop."

"I trust you, Harrison."

"I don't." He steps back, putting space between us. His pupils are dilated as he stares into my eyes. "Please excuse me." He turns, entering the house and leaving me alone in a puddle of want and need.

I don't see him for the rest of the day. In fact, I don't see anyone for the rest of the day. Thomas and Colby have been out of pocket since the Mardi Gras party, and I'm not sure where Sara or Violet are hiding. I rummage through the refrigerator, looking for anything edible. My beignets wore off hours ago. I manage to find enough ingredients to make an egg sandwich, something I haven't had for years, and sit alone, staring at the countertops while I eat. My mind races through our kiss and the conversation that led up to it. Harrison said drinking my blood would be more intimate, sexual even. Does he think he will "dishonor" me if we share more than a kiss? That ship set sail years ago, I laugh, taking my last bite of egg.

I make my way to the library with my computer in tow. Even though I have an extension, I need to get this thing finished. It's funny. What seemed so important to me before, seems frivolous now. The smell of the books eases my frustration. It always does. After meeting Ophelia, I'm curious about witches so I pull a few books from the library about witches and their practices. Most of them are typical of what you find on a Google search, but one, in particular, catches my attention. It's a list of spells and the ingredients needed to cast them. I read through the list, laughing at a few of them until one catches my eye, *Casting Vampires Away*. I turn to the page but don't understand any of the ingredients or instructions. I write the spell down exactly how it is in the book. Maybe Opie will know.

Hours pass and my eyes begin to cross from reading in the dark. I work my way to my room, taking time to explore other rooms along the way. The rooms closest to mine are bedrooms, decorated similarly to the one I've claimed as my own. All are spotlessly clean, but it's apparent they've been empty for a while. I move to the floor above mine and find two more rooms. The room at the end of the hall is the only room with a closed door. Something about it draws me closer. Harrison's entire house is open. Why is this door closed?

I turn the knob, surprised to find it unlocked. The room is painted hunter green and dark mahogany woodwork lines the ceilings and floors. Against the far wall is a four-poster bed with heavy drapery surrounding the frame. Is this Harrison's room? Ancient tapestries line the walls, each depicting scenes I recognize from European history.

A large fireplace sits across from the bed and the mantle is the host to several old photographs and small paintings. My eyes are drawn to one in particular. A young woman with bright red hair and blue eyes sits in a golden chair. She's wearing a dress from the seventeenth century, and I recognize her face instantly. Penelope. Although similar to mine, there are slight differences. Her cheekbones are more rigid than mine, and where my eyes are large and round, hers are more almond-shaped.

I pull the small painting down, running my fingers over the thick brush strokes. "Are you me?" I whisper. I set the picture down, picking up a similar one next to it. This one is a picture of Harrison, and although it's apparent the image is old, he looks the same as he does today. His hair is long and tied with a ribbon at the back of his neck. He's wearing a high-collar waistcoat, and his green eyes are bright in the painting. Something about being in his room feels intrusive and wrong. I turn to leave and find him standing in the doorway.

"I'm sorry. I shouldn't be in here. It was rude of me to walk in like I belonged here."

"You do belong," his voice is barely a whisper. "I've been thinking about what you offered earlier."

"My blood?"

He closes his eyes at my words. "If we do this, we take every precaution we can." I nod, not sure what that entails. "If I go too far, I could kill you."

"You won't."

"How can you be so sure?"

I move closer to him. "I know in here." I touch my chest.

Harrison closes his eyes, leaning his head against the doorframe. "We will never be alone when I feed.

Either Thomas or Violet will be with us at all times." He sighs. "This goes against everything I believe in and have worked hard to overcome. Human blood, especially in this amount will change me."

"What will change?"

"I will be more aggressive, angrier, stronger, and angsty."

"So, basically a teenager."

Harrison smiles, relieving some of the tension. "Basically."

"When do we start?"

"Hello!" Violet says, peeking around Harrison's side. "I'm here to supervise." I suddenly feel awkward.

"Okay. How do we do this?" I ask, looking around the room.

"Why don't we go to your room? I feel like you'll be more comfortable there."

He turns, leading me down a flight of stairs and to the room that's become my own. I lie down on the bed while Violet makes a personal nest on a chair in the corner. "You look like a corpse," Violet laughs. I relax, realizing she's right. My arms and legs are straight as a board as I stare at the ceiling.

"Try to relax," Harrison says, moving closer to me. "I'm going to tell you everything I'm doing before I do it. If at any time you don't feel safe, call Violet. She will pull me off if I'm unable to."

"Can we have a safe word?"

"What's a safe word?" Harrison asks. Violet laughs from her chair.

"A safe word is the word you say if you feel uncomfortable with something. Usually, it's for sex, but I imagine it will work in this situation too." Violet fills in the blanks.

"Woodchuck."

"What?"

"Woodchuck. That's my safe word." Harrison stifles a laugh before lying beside me, and I resume the corpse position.

"Girl, you're going to have to relax." Violet closes the book she brought to read.

Harrison brings my wrist close to his mouth. "Wait." He stops instantly. "You're not going to use my neck?"

"I'd prefer to start with your wrist."

"Okay." I close my eyes in anticipation of the pain.

"Look at me, Amelia," Harrison's voice is soft, hypnotic, and sexy as hell. I turn, making eye contact with him. "My saliva will lessen the pain from the bite. I'm going to lick your wrist." In a normal situation, this would be super weird. He doesn't take his eyes off me as he licks. "I'm going to bite you now. If at any time you're in pain..."

"I know, use my safe word," I interrupt.

He laces his fingers through mine, before biting into my wrists. I gasp. Not from the pain I was expecting, but from the ecstasy of the connection. His fingers tighten around mine as he gently sucks my wrist, drawing part of me into him. Everything in the room disappears except for the two of us. My breath catches in my throat as he continues to feed. I don't know how much time has passed before Violet taps him on the shoulder.

"That's enough." He pulls away quickly, leaving me wanting more. The room around me spins, and my body feels like I've done some psychotropic drug and floating in complete bliss.

"Amelia?" He asks, sitting up. "Are you okay?"

"Mm-hmm," I mumble.

"Thank you," he whispers, standing from the bed. "I'll stay in the room until I know you're okay." The room disappears, and I sink into a hole of happiness.

EIGHTEEN

secrets are revealed

I WAKE up feeling more relaxed than I have in a while. The sun is bright in the sky, and I have no idea what time it is, nor do I care. The chair in my room is empty, which means Harrison left sometime during the night. I take my time getting ready for the day and notice my cheeks are more flushed than usual, but that's nothing out of the ordinary for a redhead. Most likely a sunburn from riding in the convertible yesterday. My wrist looks like it always does. There's no scar, no bruising, and no evidence of Harrison ever feeding from me.

Downstairs, Thomas is in the kitchen standing behind the stove. "Good morning, sunshine. I made you some breakfast."

"Thank goodness. I'm starved." He looks at me knowingly.

"Everything okay?" He sets a plate full of eggs and bacon in front of me.

I stop chewing. "Yeah, do I look weird or something?"

"You look beautiful, as always. Drink your orange juice. It'll help."

"Seriously. I feel fine, great actually." I empty my plate and glass before heading into the courtyard.

Violet is attempting yoga again. She's in a new position and frozen on her mat. "You're alive," she teases. "Want to join me?"

"Sure, what are we doing?"

"I don't know. Do what feels good." I move beside her, squatting into one of the positions I remember from my brief stint in yoga. "You did well yesterday."

"Thank you." I say, moving to a new position. "It wasn't bad."

"Because Harrison made it that way. Believe me, when someone who's trying to hurt you does it, it's not like that." I don't ask questions. "Well, look what the wolf dragged in." Colby stumbles into the courtyard.

"Is the sun always this bright?" He's using his hand as a makeshift sunshade.

"You know you missed an entire day, right?" Violet asks, watching him stumble toward us.

"What?"

"The party was two days ago."

"You're shitting me." Colby's hair is sticking

straight out on the ends, and a full beard covers his normally smooth shaved face. "Did I miss anything?"

"A shower." Violet is snarky this morning. "Oh, and Harrison is feeding off of Amelia now."

"What?" His voice is more alert than before. "Amelia?"

"It's nothing. I gave him permission. He needs his strength."

"What the hell did I miss yesterday? Why does Harrison need his strength?"

"Viktor. He knows she's alive." Violet nods her head toward me.

"Shit. Where's Harrison?"

"I haven't seen him," she answers.

"Me either," I add.

"Does Edon know about any of this?" He ruffles his hands through his messy hair.

"That's a question for Harrison." Violet picks up her yoga mat and heads inside. Her energy is off this morning, and I'm curious why.

"I'm going to take a shower and find Harrison. Are you okay?" He turns to me.

"Yes. Why does everyone keep asking me that? I feel better than I have in a long time."

Harrison comes from the garage into the courtyard after everyone else has left. "Hey." His smile brings the butterflies to life.

"Hey to you."

"How..."

I hold up my hand. "Nope. You're not allowed to ask me how I am this morning." I spin in a circle. "See, I'm fine. I feel great, and I'm in one piece. Thank you for making it easy."

He steps toward me, taking both my hands into his. "I'm the one who needs to thank you. I'm already stronger. I felt it immediately."

"Are you saying I have superhuman blood?"

He returns my smile. "Maybe." I stare awkwardly at the man I let suck my blood last night. That's not something you say every day. "Have you seen anyone else?"

"Thomas is in the kitchen. Violet just went inside, and Colby went to take a shower. I haven't seen Sara today."

"I've called a meeting with Edon this afternoon. I'd like for you to be there."

"About Viktor?"

He nods. "We're not going to sit around, waiting for him."

"Do you have a plan?" I ask.

"Always."

"Do you...will you need to *eat* more?" I don't know how to ask what I'm asking.

Harrison smiles. "Not today." For some psychotic reason, I'm disappointed. "Edon should be here within the hour."

"I thought you said the meeting was this afternoon?"

"I did." I look at my wrist where my watch normally

sits.

"What the hell time is it? Did I sleep past noon?" Harrison laughs, walking toward the house.

"If you'll let Colby know, I'll tell the rest of them."

I head toward the carriage house that's been turned into guest apartments. The shower is still running, and I decide to be nosey while I wait. Several photographs are displayed on the mantle, pictures of Thomas and Colby together before Thomas was turned. Pictures from Mardi Gras past, vacations spent together, and family time.

A high-pitched scream behind me grabs my attention. "Amelia?" I turn to see Colby standing in the door-frame, butt naked.

"Oh, I'm sorry." I turn quickly. "I found Harrison. He wanted me to tell you that your father is coming over for a meeting in an hour."

"Shit, okay." I hear scrambling behind me.

"I'm just going to..." I point to the door without turning around. "Sorry, I barged in."

"Nah, it's alright. You just gave me flashbacks from prom night." Although my curiosity is piqued, I don't ask for details and can't hide my smirk heading back into the house.

Less than an hour later, five lycanthropes, four vampires, and a partridge in a pear tree are sitting in the suddenly much smaller sitting room. They've mostly been sharing stories from the past and laughing at the memories. I never thought I'd witness werewolves and vampires "shooting the breeze," but here we are.

"As much as I enjoy catching up, it's time to discuss the issue at hand." Harrison spends the next few minutes filling everyone in on the details of Viktor, ending with our run-in at the French Market.

"With all due respect, Harrison, I don't see what this has to do with the Lycan. What you're describing is a vampire issue and a vampire issue alone. I don't like Viktor, hell, none of us do, but I'm not about to risk starting a war with him. I did my part by sending my son to take care of Amelia while she was held captive."

Harrison sits back in his chair, like the true Southern Gentleman he is. "Is it worth risking the lives of every human in this city?"

"From the story you just relayed to me, it seems Viktor isn't after the average human, running around our beautiful city." He turns toward me. "He's after one. Tell me why."

"Because he thinks I'm Harrison's wife Penelope, reincarnated," I interrupt.

"Well, shit. There's the reason. I knew there was more to the story." He slaps his thighs. "Seems you left a little bit of the story out, Harrison. That explains why he kept calling you Penelope."

"It doesn't change anything, Dad," Colby speaks for the first time. "If Viktor's allowed to do whatever he wants, it won't stop with Amelia."

Edon pats his son on the shoulder. "Colby, you have

connections here, and I understand your frustration, but this problem doesn't affect the pack. I won't risk the treaty over one human." He looks at me. "Forgive my bluntness, miss."

He's right. I'm not worth starting a war over. "No apology needed. Thank you for your honesty."

With my words, the lycanthrope stands. "I'm happy my son could help you, Amelia," Edon says. "I do hope everything works out for your good."

"You and me both," I tease, watching them exit the house.

Harrison sighs. "Colby, he's right. This isn't a pack problem. I understand if you don't want anything to do with this situation."

Colby looks at me. "My father sent me to protect Amelia the best I could while she was with Viktor. As part of the treaty, he had no choice. We became friends, and I don't want anything to happen to her."

"My life is not worth losing yours," I add quickly.

"I thought we discussed this. Viktor's going to have to catch me first." He turns back to the group. "Alone, we're strong but with the Lycan, we're stronger. Although I don't always agree with my father, I understand his hesitation."

"We're not completely helpless." Harrison moves to the front door. "Colby? I'd like to investigate a few of Viktor's known hangouts that aren't far from here. Maybe your nose will lead us to a clue that I've previously overlooked. Would you care to join me?"

Colby looks at me. "Will you be okay if I leave?"

"You've been hung over for twenty-four hours, and I've survived." I laugh.

"Do we need to discuss everything that happened in those hours?" Colby raises his eyebrows, looking between me and Harrison.

"I'll be fine. Violet and Thomas will come to my aid if needed. Besides, what's going to happen to me here?"

"Okay, I'm holding you to that." He turns toward Harrison. "I'd love to go. Maybe if we work together a little, Edon will see the importance of involving the Lycan."

"Agreed," Harrison answers, leading him out of the house.

"Where are they really going?" I ask Violet once they've left the house.

She sighs. "You heard him just as well as I did."

"Violet, what's your problem?" Thomas asks. "You've been a bitch all day."

"What's wrong with me? I think the better question is, what's wrong with Harrison? He's drinking her blood so he can fight Viktor, knowing it's not enough. He needs to hunt. This whole thing is screwed up."

"You're my maker, Violet, but I support Harrison. If he wants to go head-to-head with Viktor, then I'm there to support him."

"Thomas, you are nothing compared to Viktor. He would crush you before you knew what happened. None of us stand a chance against him, and Harrison's little Amelia meal last night isn't enough to help him. He's full of shit if he thinks we believe it does."

"What are you saying?" I ask.

"I'm saying, if Harrison wants to be strong enough to defeat Viktor it's going to take a lot more than a few sips. He's going to need every drop he can get."

"Are they going to fight him now?" I ask.

"Why? Do you think you can go save him?"

"Violet, stop. I never asked for any of this. I was happy, working on my pointless doctoral degree, and minding my own business. Viktor found me. He's the one who started this, not me. I refuse to let anyone die because of me. You're right. I'm not worth all of this."

"I didn't say that," she interrupts.

"You didn't have to. Where'd they go?"

She sighs. "I don't know. Harrison hasn't said anything to me."

"Yes, you do. You've known Harrison for a hundred years. You know how he thinks, how he works. Where'd he go?"

"Viktor's."

"I thought he couldn't go in there. Some sort of protection."

"He can't go in the house where you stayed. Viktor owns property all over town, many of which aren't protected." Her words make me angry.

"Take me there."

"Seriously? What are you going to do, read to them?"

"Damn, Violet. Chill," Thomas scolds.

"He's willing to risk everything for..."

"For a human," I fill in the blanks.

She looks up, wiping a tear. "God, I'm a horrible person."

"No, you're being honest," I retort.

"Amelia, I'm so sorry." She wipes a tear from her cheek. "It's not your fault. That's what makes it worse. You're right. You didn't ask for any of this."

"How can I fix it?"

"You can't." She lowers her head in defeat. "None of us can."

"Why would he go to Viktor's if he's not strong enough?"

"I don't know." She wrings her hands together. "Love makes people do stupid things. I've never seen him like this."

"If I may," Sara, who's been listening to every word without interrupting, stands from her spot on the couch. "Viktor has a weakness that might be helpful to know."

"We know." Violet nods toward me. "Amelia."

Sara moves closer to the three of us. "She's not his weakness. She's his obsession." She runs her hand through the end of her braid. "No, his weakness is locked safely in a house across the lake."

"What the hell are you talking about, Sara?" Violet is losing her patience.

"There is a child."

NINETEEN

an immortal child and a stupid human

"A CHILD? IS THAT EVEN POSSIBLE?"

I'm not sure what I'm asking.

Violet sits down, covering her head with her hands. "She doesn't mean an actual child of a vampire. She means an immortal child. A human child that was turned into a vampire at a young age."

"Oh, my God."

"God has nothing to do with it," Sara adds.

"How is that okay?" I ask.

"It's not. It's forbidden," Violet answers. "Imagine having a five year old, throwing a temper tantrum and killing everyone in sight."

"Did...did Viktor create one of these immortal children?"

Sara sighs. "I don't know who created her, but Viktor cares for her."

"How does Harrison not know about this?" Thomas moves closer.

"No one knows about her." She pauses. "Viktor loves Celeste even more than his obsession with Penelope."

"That poor child." Images of a beautiful child with blood dripping down her mouth flash through my mind.

"What are you suggesting we do, Sara?" Violet asks.

"I'm not suggesting anything. You asked for his weakness, and I provided you with one."

"We can't kill a child, can we?" I look between the two women. "Can we?"

"If it's discovered that she exists, she won't survive another day."

"Who would do such a thing?" I walk away from the vampires.

"There are rules, Amelia. Every society has rules. Vampires don't follow the rules of man, but we are held accountable to our own. The rules warn against the creation of such an abomination."

"She's a child, Violet. How can she be an abomination?"

"I once witnessed Celeste kill an entire family because one of the children took a toy away from her. Violet's right. She's an abomination."

"Why does he protect her? Why not just dispose of her?" Thomas asks the million-dollar question.

"Because he loves her," Violet answers. "She's his

family. The child that he and Penelope were never able to have." She sits heavily on the sofa. "She's the answer. She's the way we will control him." Violet stands, moving out of the room. "I'll be in my room. Let me know when Harrison arrives." Sara leaves close behind.

"Damn," Thomas says, moving closer. "I never thought about little vampire demons running around. That's some shit right there."

"Agreed."

"You hungry?" Thomas asks, heading toward the kitchen.

"No, thank you. I don't feel like eating at the moment." I spend the next few hours in the library, researching any information I can find on immortal children. Out of the thousands of books in Harrison's collection, there are only three that mention anything about them and even those are only a few pages. From the small amount of information I've found, it seems immortal children were all the rage during the medieval era. Some vampires actually had small collections of them. No wonder it was outlawed. According to what I read, the penalty for creating an immortal child is instant death for both the child and their creator.

The sun has already set by the time I wrap up my study session. I haven't heard anyone come in, but to be honest, this house is so large they could be back, and I wouldn't know. I work my way back into the main room and sit behind the grand piano taking up residence in the corner of the room. I play the only song I remember from YouTube University, *Hot Cross Buns.* The black and white keyboard seems to mock me for my lack of knowledge. I'm on the second verse when the door slams open, scaring the shit out of me. I stand in time to see Harrison burst through the door, carrying a lifeless body.

"Oh, my God! Colby?"

"Get Thomas!"

I run full speed to the kitchen, finding it empty. I don't slow down as I run into the courtyard and up to the carriage house apartments. "What the hell, Amelia?"

Thomas is sitting in front of the television and jumps up when I enter. "It's Colby."

He doesn't ask questions. He runs vampire speed into the house. When my human legs deliver me back to the main room, I find him hunched over a bloody and unconscious Colby. "Is he..."

Harrison comes to my side, wrapping his arm around my waist. He shakes his head, and I nearly collapse. Thomas has his arms wrapped around the lycanthrope, rocking him gently. "Colby. Come back to me, boo." He pulls away, shaking his shoulders. "Colby!" His voice sounds frantic. "What happened?" he screams at Harrison.

"Viktor."

"You let him die?" Thomas is angry. "How could you?" He pulls Colby to his chest, and opens his mouth, revealing his fangs.

"You can't," Violet says, coming into the room. "A lycanthrope cannot become a vampire. Their blood cannot mix with ours."

"How do you know? I need to try." My heart breaks at the panic in his voice. Thomas shows his fangs again, ready to bite into Colby's neck.

"I forbid it," Violet says. "As your maker, I forbid it."

"Fuck you, Violet. I don't care who you are, Colby is my life. I'm nothing without him." He bends down, trying to bite Colby's neck. Something prevents him from being able to get close enough to bite. "Dammit," he picks up Colby's wrist, trying the same. Again, an invisible barrier keeps him from making contact with his skin. "What did you do?"

"I forbade it. As your maker, you are not allowed to break my commands."

"Shit!" He screams. "I can't let him die."

"If you bite him, you'll turn him into something neither of you will want. Lycan blood does not turn into a vampire. He'll die an even more miserable death than he already did." Tears stream down my face, not just for the loss of Colby, but for Thomas's pain. "Once the heart stops beating, the blood exchange cannot happen anyway."

"I'm sorry, Thomas," Violet kneels next to the couple, offering her sympathy to her creation. Thomas pushes her away, pulling Colby closer.

"This isn't happening. This is a nightmare. Wake me up, please!" I don't know how much time passes as

Thomas rocks Colby's body, refusing to give up hope that he'll return. Leaving him alone feels wrong. Harrison keeps his arm around my waist, offering his silent support. "I want revenge," Thomas's voice is no louder than a whisper.

"Thomas, now's not the time."

He turns toward Violet. "I want revenge."

"I wasn't as strong as I thought I was," Harrison speaks for the first time.

"I could've told you that." Violet's words are harsh. "One light feeding isn't enough to make you strong enough to fight him." She stands, moving closer to us. "You need to hunt and feed like he does to stand a chance."

"Kill the child." Thomas's words are barely a whisper.

"What child?" Harrison looks between the three of us. "What child?"

"An immortal child," Violet answers. He unwraps his arm, moving closer to her.

"There's an immortal child? Where?"

"Viktor has been protecting her for years."

"How do you know?"

"Sara," Thomas answers. "She's met her."

"It's a girl?" Harrison sits on the piano bench. "What does this mean?"

"It means Viktor has a weakness," I answer. "According to Sara, his love for this child is stronger than his obsession for me and Penelope."

"This child, Celeste, is the answer," Violet says.

"I want her dead. Viktor took something I love away from me. I will take something he loves away from him." Thomas's tears have turned to anger.

"I thought she was dead." Harrison stands from the piano. His face is even paler than usual.

"You knew about the child?" Violet asks. He turns, facing the blank wall where Penelope's portrait once hung.

"She was Penelope's younger sister."

"What the hell?" Violet puts her hands on her hips. "I'm hoping I misunderstood you."

He sighs. "No, you heard correctly. Penelope was her maker." He turns, facing me. "When Celeste became ill, Penelope had already been turned. Two of her brothers had already passed from disease, and she couldn't bear losing her sister too."

"Her answer for that was to turn a child into a monster?" I ask.

"Yes." He pauses. "Penelope's maker was angry and killed the child. Or at least, we thought she did."

"Apparently, Viktor's brought her to New Orleans," Violet states the obvious.

"I don't know if I can kill her." Harrison sits, resting his head in his hands.

"Then I will," Thomas says, standing. "I have no problems killing a demon child."

"Does Sara know where the child is located?" Harrison asks.

"I do, sir." Sara walks into the room. "I'm sorry. I was eavesdropping from the next room."

"Is she guarded?"

"Always, but only by a few. She's stronger than her guards."

Violet stomps toward the corner of the room. "Of course, she is. She's ancient."

"Sara? What does the child look like?"

She wrings her hands together. "Well, she's a beautiful little thing with long red curls and bright blue eyes." Sara turns, looking at me. "She looks like a smaller version of Amelia, if you ask me."

Harrison looks at me knowingly. "Can you show me the house where she's kept?"

"Yes."

"I'm going, too," Thomas says.

"Amelia's going."

His words surprise me. "Me? I won't be any help in a fight with vampires."

"Celeste doesn't know Penelope's dead."

"Hold up a damn minute," Thomas interrupts. "You're going to dress Amelia up as Penelope and use her to do what, exactly? Kidnap a vampire kid?"

"Yes."

"Harrison? What are we going to do with her once we get her here? You know how these children are. One day she'll be the sweetest kid you know, the next she's killed everyone within a ten-block radius because her iPad battery died." Violet's anger pours from her.

"I'll worry about what to do with her once we get her here. You're right. She's Viktor's weakness, and losing her will be the catalyst we need to gain the upper hand."

"What kind of upper hand do you think we'll get? None of us are strong enough to fight him. All we're going to do is piss him off even more," Violet shouts. "Tell me how this is going to help."

Harrison looks at Colby's lifeless body. "With the help of the Lycan, we can defeat him. Edon will join our cause."

"Tell me you didn't do this on purpose. Tell me you didn't plan Colby's death so that the wolves would join our fight," Violet spews.

"No, I would never do something like that." Harrison makes eye contact with each of us in the room. "I swear to each of you, Colby's death was in no way planned. If I could take everything back, I would. His death happened because I was weak, both mentally and physically. I fooled myself into thinking I was stronger than I was. Thomas?" he turns toward his former cook. "I'm so sorry. I never intended for this to happen." Thomas doesn't respond. "I need to feed." He doesn't look at me when he speaks.

"Me, too," Violet answers.

"When we're strong enough, we get Celeste and with the help of the Lycan we'll put Viktor in his place."

"You can feed from me." My voice is shaky.

"No. The kind of feeding we need to do, you won't survive."

"Are you going to kill someone?" Violet and Harrison share a look.

"No," he answers, offering no other details.

"There are ways," Sara adds. "There are junkies that are willing to be drained almost to the point of death. It gives them a high."

I nod, not sure I want to know more. "How can I help?"

"You can stay alive."

I spend the next hour, helping Thomas clean Colby's body and placing it in a room in the carriage house. He hasn't said anything since we've been working, and I don't know what to say. Violet, Sara, and Harrison left to hunt, which brings horrible images to mind. Thomas dresses Colby in his signature khaki pants and a blue button-down shirt. If I didn't know better, I'd think he was asleep. "I need to tell his family," Thomas says, stepping away from the body. "I don't want Harrison to be the one to tell him." I nod, understanding. "Will you be okay, alone?"

"Of course."

He bends down, kissing Colby on the cheek. "Goodbye, my love." The sentiment brings tears to my eyes. He turns to me. "Don't do anything stupid while I'm gone."

I hold my hands up in surrender style. "Wouldn't dream of it."

An hour later, I'm in the library, searching for a book I remembered coming across several weeks earlier. It was a book on the voodoo practices of New Orleans. I remember reading something about a way to bring the dead back to life. An hour into searching, I find the text I've been searching for. *Only a shaman or high priestess can perform the necromancy ceremony.*

My mind flashes back to Opie and the potion that saved me from Viktor. I grab my backpack and head toward the garage. I'm relieved to find the keys inside my Nissan and pray it will start. Not only does she start, but she runs better than ever. I exit the garage, turning onto the main street. God, it feels good to be myself. I take a deep breath, clearing my mind of the insanity of the past month.

The drive from the Garden District to the Quarter is easy and doesn't take long. I manage to find a spot to park on the street only a few blocks from Opie's store. I look around, making sure nothing with fangs is waiting on me before making the quick jog to her door.

"I'll be with you in a minute," Opie says from behind the curtain when the bell above the door dings. I look through the big book of spells she keeps close to the door for tourists while I wait. "Amelia?" Her voice startles me.

"Hi, Opie." I smile at her familiar face. She looks behind me.

"Are you here alone?"

"I am. Harrison knows I'm here," I lie.

"Come to the back." She pulls me behind her curtain to the seance room. "You need to be careful coming out here alone."

"I'm not staying long. I have a question, and you're the only one I know that can help." Opie keeps looking around, nervously.

"Make it quick, girl."

"I don't know how to ask this, so I'm going to come right out with it." I sigh. "Can you perform a necromancy ceremony?"

Opie looks at me like I've lost my mind. "Girl, what have you been reading?" She puts her hands on my shoulders. "You need to leave, now. It's not safe here."

"Opie, please. Someone very close to me...they died, and I want to help him."

"Amelia. If this person was close to you then the last thing you want to do is turn them into a zombie. That's exactly what happens. Their body returns to life, but their soul isn't there. If you cared for this person, a necromancy ceremony is the last thing you should do for them." She looks around again. "You have to go, now." She physically turns my body around, pointing me toward the door. "Take this." She shoves a dark crystal into my hand.

"What is this?"

"Obsidian. Keep it in your hand until you're safely back inside Harrison's protections."

"Opie, I don't understand."

"Amelia, I'm trying to save your life. Go. Now." She

pushes me out the front door. Her nervous energy flows to me, and I literally run to my car. Once inside, I lock all the doors and hit the gas, nearly hitting two cars pulling into traffic. I top speeds of eighty miles an hour, swerving in and out of traffic and around pedestrians, while the crystal's sharp edges cut into my skin. I enter the Garden District and let out a sigh of relief.

Harrison's garage door is still wide open and less than two blocks away. Something slams into the roof of my car, denting the metal and causing me to swerve. "What the hell?" I scream, trying to keep my car on the road. Whatever's above me, runs its claws over the metal of the roof, piercing the metal. A large claw barely misses my head. Ahead I see the edge of the fence and push my engine harder. The creature slides to the side as I round the corner to the garage without slowing down. Its claws are still deep into my roof, helping it hold on to the top.

Remembering the obsidian, I slice the crystal into the creature's hand. A blood-curdling scream followed by dark blood, flows through the damaged roof. I see the shadow of something large and black as it rolls off the car and into the street behind me. I turn into the garage, slamming into the side of Violet's BMW before coming to a stop. I'm not sure if the garage is protected, but I don't take any chances. I'm out of the car and pushing the wall switch in a matter of seconds. The door slams shut, separating me from whatever the hell that was.

I run through the courtyard and into the house, not slowing down until I'm safely in my bedroom, with the door locked. It takes a few minutes before I'm breathing regularly and brave enough to look out of the window. The world outside looks like it always does. No one is any wiser of the creatures that surround them daily. I don't know how I'm going to explain the dent in Violet's car, or the roof being ripped off of mine, but right now, that's the least of my worries. Sliding my back against the wall, I let the tears flow.

sealing the deal

I WAKE to a pitch-black room and my body curled into a ball on the floor. The house is silent, and I strain to make details out of the shadows cast by the moonlight. I startle at what looks like the silhouette of a person, sitting on the floor across from me.

"It's me," the shadow whispers.

"What are you doing?" I sit up, not sure why he's in my room, watching me sleep.

"Making sure you're okay."

"I'm fine."

Harrison stands, turning the small knob on my bedside lamp. The light makes me blink quickly. "No, you're not."

I sit up, keeping my legs crossed in front of me. "I'm guessing you saw the cars."

He sighs. "That, and Ophelia called."

"Shit."

"What the hell were you thinking?" His tone is angry.

"What was I thinking? Are you serious right now?" I stand, matching his energy. "I was thinking I needed to do something to help Colby. I remembered reading something in the library about necromancy, and Opie was the only one I knew to ask." I step closer to him. "I was thinking I could help, that I could do something. Not be some precious plaything, kept safely locked in a tower for her protection. It's what I do. It's who I am. I help people." A tear threatens to fall, dammit.

"Do you know what you ran into while you were out there?"

"No, but I'm sure you're going to enlighten me."

"It was a strigoi."

"So, a vampire," I answer. Bitch tone activated.

"No. A strigoi isn't a vampire. A vampire is created when they rise from the grave after being drained by another vampire. Strigoi is a living human who's been infected with vampirism."

"That thing was human?" I open my hand, revealing the obsidian crystal that saved my life. "This saved me. I used it to cut the hand of the creature, and it fell off the top of my car."

"Amelia? Is that its blood on you?"

"Yes." I pull my hands up, realizing they're covered in dark goo, along with the sleeves of my shirt.

"Did any of it get in your mouth?"

"No, I don't think so. What happens if it did?"

"You need to get his blood off you, but you cannot ingest or let any of it into your eyes." He steps toward me.

"Harrison, what happens if the blood gets in my eyes or mouth?"

"It could turn you into one of them." Those are the words that break the camel's back. I can't stop the tears that flow uncontrollably.

"God, I'm an idiot."

"No, you're just overly passionate. Especially about the ones you care for." He turns me toward the bathroom. "Let me help you." I nod in defeat. Harrison strips me down to my bra and panties after setting the shower to the perfect temperature. He wraps a hand towel around my face and eyes, guiding me under the water. Harrison lathers my hair twice, gently massaging my scalp with each wash. In any other situation, this would be intimate, almost sexual. In this situation, it's embarrassing.

"Thank you."

He pulls the towel away from my face. "I think your hair is clean." I turn, facing him. He's fully dressed, and his clothes are soaked.

"You're wet."

He smiles. "That's what usually happens in the shower. I'm going to change, and we'll talk later."

I nod, not trusting my words. He steps out of the bathroom without speaking. I stare at the space where he stood moments earlier and the tears flow again.

How could I have been so stupid? I'm working on my damn doctoral degree, for God's sake. I finish washing and dress quickly. I'm disappointed when Harrison isn't in my room. I don't know if I should go find him or wait for him to come back... Being awkward sucks.

I decide to crawl into bed and wait until morning. As Scarlett O'Hara so famously said, *Tomorrow is another day*. I fall asleep quickly, and the world fades to nothing.

I awaken to scratching on my window. Did I imagine that? I focus on the sound, not sure if it was leftover from a dream or real. I hear it again, this time it's louder. "What the hell?" I move toward the window, pulling the plantation shutter open enough to discover that I have an overactive imagination, and nothing is outside. I climb back in bed, fluffing my pillow, and snuggle deep into the covers. I'm almost asleep when I hear the noise again. This time, it sounds like claws, scrapping against the windowpane. "Penelope," a voice whispers. I sit straight up in bed. Did I imagine that? "Penelope," the voice repeats. I slide out of bed, onto the floor and army crawl my way to the hallway door. "I see you, Penelope. Come outside, and play with me." I jump to my feet, running down the hall and up to the next floor. I don't bother to knock on Harrison's door. I turn the knob and enter at the same time, making enough noise to wake the dead. He sits up, startled.

"Amelia? What's wrong?"

"There's something outside my window." He

doesn't ask questions, he's past me and in my room in the flash of a second. I run after him, not wanting to be left alone. I enter my room, finding my window wide-open and Harrison nowhere in sight. "Harrison?" He's gone. "Oh, my God."

"What's going on?" Violet asks, stopping next to me.

"Something was scratching on my window. I ran to Harrison's room, and when I got back down here, my window was open, and he was gone."

Violet turns toward me. "Stay here."

"But what if it comes back?"

"It won't. Stay in this room. Do you understand me?" I nod. She flashes out of my room, leaving me alone with my imagination. I close the window and lock it, closing the shutters in front like they have the magical ability to keep whatever that was from coming through. My heart races, thinking of what could be happening below.

I'm not about to be a rebel and go looking for answers. I slip on a pair of leggings and a hooded sweatshirt and slide into my hiding place in the corner. This isn't fun anymore.

The sun is beginning to shine through my window when Harrison finally returns. He's covered in blood, and his clothes are torn, but he's here. I jump up, moving in front of him. "Are you okay?"

"Yes, are you?"

"I'm guessing by the amount of blood you're covered in, you found whatever it was."

He pulls his t-shirt away from him, assessing the blood. "I did. Just as I expected, it was a strigoi."

"How the hell did it get in? Isn't your house protected?"

"Strigoi don't follow the same rules as vampires."

"Was it the one from yesterday?"

"There's no way of knowing, but if it was, it won't be bothering you again."

"It called me Penelope." His breath catches.

"When?"

"When it scratched on my window. It called me Penelope. Does that mean Viktor sent it?"

"Probably. He has many strigoi working with him." He runs a hand through his disheveled hair. "Bastard." His eyes look me up and down. "I need a shower. Do you want to stay in my room while I'm in the shower?"

"Yes, please."

Harrison's smile calms the turmoil in my brain. I follow him to the third floor and into the large bedroom. "Make yourself at home. I won't be too long." He disappears through the bathroom door. Where do I sit? The bed feels way too intimate, but the only chair is the picture of a medieval torture device. The back is so rigidly straight, I'd almost rather stand. Several minutes of awkward standing later, I opt for the uncomfortable chair. On a small table next to it, sits an old book, frayed around the edges. Something about it feels very personal. Although the nosey part of me wants to open it, I resist the urge to invade his privacy.

True to his word, he steps out of the bathroom not long after. He's wearing nothing more than a towel, wrapped precariously around his hips. His bare chest is layered with muscles and long hair hangs past his shoulders. I swallow the lump that formed in my throat. "You okay?"

"Umm, sure. Are you?" God that sounded dumb.

"I'm good, thank you." He leaves the door open, stepping back into the small room and giving me time to reassess the situation. Obviously, I'm attracted to him. When we kissed, I felt a connection to him like nothing I have words for. But damn. Seeing him like this brings fire to places that haven't seen a match for years.

He steps back into the bedroom, still wearing only the towel. I can't stop watching as he walks across the room toward an antique wardrobe and carefully chooses something to wear. The damp towel is pulled tightly across his ass, showing every tight muscle and dimple, and I can't stop staring. He knows exactly what he's doing, and I'm enjoying every minute. "I'll be out after I change." His words bring me back to reality.

"Thank you." I instantly regret not being more of a party animal earlier in life. Maybe I would know how to not sound like I grew up alone, on a desert island, and this is the first time I've seen a nearly naked man.

Harrison smirks and heads into the bathroom. *Get yourself together, Amelia.* I manage to get in a few cleansing breaths before the door opens, revealing a halfway-dressed Harrison. He's wearing low-hung sweatpants, something I've never seen him wear, and no shirt. His hair is pulled into a messy bun, and I try to keep my composure.

"Do you want to talk about it?" I ask, not sure what to say.

"There's nothing to talk about. I hunted and killed the strigoi that dared come onto my property."

"It's going to keep happening, isn't it?" He looks down.

"Most likely." He sits on the edge of his bed.

"I've been doing some thinking." He looks up at my words. "We've established that Celeste is Viktor's weakness and that Celeste doesn't know Penelope died."

"We're going to get her without you," he interrupts. "I don't want to put you in danger."

"No, I want to." I swallow the lump in my throat and move closer to him. "If she's as wild as Violet says, she's not going to make it easy on the four of you, plus she's almost as old as you, which means she's strong." I pause, sitting next to him on the bed. "If I can convince her that I'm Penelope, it will make it easier." He wraps his long fingers through mine.

"Amelia, I don't want to put you in the predicament of having to pretend to be something you're not."

"That's the least of my worries. I can pretend with

the best of them if it will keep you alive." He doesn't take his eyes off mine.

"I don't want to lose you."

"You're not." In a moment of boldness, I stretch up, kissing him lightly on the lips.

"Amelia." He pulls away, looking at me. "Are you sure about this?"

"I've never been more sure of anything." In a scene straight from a book, his lips crash into mine, causing an explosion from deep inside. My soul comes alive at the contact. He moves us from the edge of the mattress to the center without me having any clue of how he did it. I pull away from the kiss just long enough to straddle his hips with mine. Harrison sighs at the contact.

I reach down, pulling my hoodie over my head and throwing it to the corner of the room. He slides his hands under the straps of my bra, gently guiding them down my arms until my breasts are uncovered. He doesn't waste a minute, covering one nipple with his mouth and the other with his hand. I gasp at the sensation and grind my hips into his, while evidence of his arousal hits me in all the right places. I bite my lip to keep from crying out.

"Amelia," he whispers, flipping me onto my back. He kisses his way down my body, ending at the waistband of my leggings. He looks up.

"Take the damn things off," I pant.

He slowly slides my leggings and underwear down my legs, driving me wild with need. I resist the urge to help him and instead enjoy the intimacy of his touch. Soft, wet kisses follow the fabric down until nothing is left. He slowly works his way back up my legs, kissing every inch of my skin until his mouth reaches my softest part. He slowly caresses me with his tongue, making sure not to leave any part untouched. Within seconds, a tight coil forms in my abdomen. One last perfect connection with his tongue brings me over the edge. I cry out in ecstasy as he slides his body even with mine. I spread my legs wide, giving him full access.

Wet kisses work their way up my neck and to my lips. The hardest part of him gently slides into the softest part of me, and I cry out from the connection. "Is this okay?" he whispers through kisses.

"It's more than okay." Grabbing a butt cheek with each hand I push him in further. He moves slowly, giving me what my body is begging for. It doesn't take long before we are moving in perfect unison, his tongue matching each thrust. I feel the coil forming again, this time stronger than before. Harrison's breathing matches my own as we explode together. He doesn't move in the few minutes it takes for us to return to breathing normally.

"That was..."

"I agree," I answer. We lay in each other's arms for a few minutes before I feel him begin to move inside me again, his erection still strong. This time he moves slower, taking his time. He flips me from underneath him to on top, putting me in charge. I sit up straight, taking every inch of him inside. Moving slowly, I make little circles with my body. I lean down, kissing his neck while slowly sliding on the hardest part of him. He grabs my ass, trying to speed me up. Taking each of his hands into mine, I pin him down to the bed. He laughs a low, sexy laugh.

"You're mine," I whisper into his ear and bite his ear lobe. He gasps, making this whole situation even hotter. I continue sliding up and down, bringing myself down on top of him as far as possible. Each movement brings another gasp and forms the coil once again.

"Say it again."

"You're mine." This time I bite his neck as he slams his body fully into mine, shaking with his release. I cry out from the connection as we release together. I collapse onto his body as he covers my face with soft kisses.

"I am yours," he whispers into my ear just as I drift off to sleep.

I wake to a stray sunbeam blinding me in my right eye. It doesn't take long to remember where I am and why I'm here. A smile forms on my lips, thinking about our time together. I turn and realize I'm in the middle of a king-size bed, alone.

"I'm here," a soft voice whispers from the uncomfortable chair.

"Come back to bed. Watching me sleep is a little creepy." He smiles, walking across the room and sitting on the edge of the bed.

"I've been thinking." He looks down at our joined hands. "I don't want you to risk going to get Celeste."

I sit up. "Why?"

"Because I can't lose you."

I move closer to him. "You're not going to lose me. We already had this conversation. I'm going to convince her that I'm Penelope, and she'll come willingly."

"Amelia, you act like this is something simple. Celeste is a vampire. A very old and powerful vampire and not just any vampire, she's an immortal child. That makes her volatile and capable of utter destruction. She would rip your heart out before you realized what was happening."

"I understand the risks." I lace my fingers through his. "I witnessed my friend die and was attacked by a strigoi all in one day. If there's something I can do to help keep you all safe, then I'm going to do it."

"You're human."

I stare at him. "Are you just now discovering this?" Sarcasm is my love language. He doesn't laugh at my weak attempt at humor. "Look, Harrison. I'm stronger than you think."

"I don't want to put you in danger."

"Then teach me how to be her. If anyone knows Penelope, it's you."

He looks at our joined hands. "That feels wrong on so many levels."

"On what level does a vampire, a strigoi, and an

immortal child feel right? That's the bingo card of a lifetime."

"Okay," he answers, reluctantly. He kisses the top of my hand. "I'll meet you in your room in an hour. I need another shower."

I crawl to the edge of the bed. "Yeah, me too." He wraps a hand behind my neck, pulling my face to his. "Don't start something we don't have time to finish," I say with a smirk.

"They'll be plenty of time later." He kisses me deeply, taking his time and exploring every detail of my mouth.

"Now, I don't want to leave."

"One hour." He disappears into the bathroom.

TWENTY-ONE

TRUE TO HIS WORD, one hour later, Harrison knocks on my door. I try to play it cool and walk to the door instead of running. "Hello." That sounded sexier in my head.

He gently takes a piece of my hair, bringing it to his nose. "You smell good."

"Thanks. I'll let the people at *Head and Shoulders* know you approve of their scents." He laughs, lacing his fingers through mine.

"Come with me." He leads me to a bedroom on the third floor, not far from his. "I had all of her...her things put in this room. I couldn't bear looking at them every day." The room is set up similarly to his with a king-size four-poster bed taking up the far wall. Instead of the rigid, straight-back chair he has in his, there's a soft plush chair, facing the fireplace. Next to the chair is a small round table, full of small paintings. I pick one up, tracing the paint strokes that surround a beautiful young child's face. Red curls surround her snow-white face and piercing blue eyes stare back.

"That's Celeste," Harrison says, moving behind me.

"She's beautiful."

"She was." His voice sounds sad. "Our families were too poor to have portraits painted. Years later, Penelope commissioned this painting." He takes the picture from me, copying my movements with his own. I move across the room to an old vanity. On top is an antique brush and comb set. "Those were hers." He steps in front of me, taking them from my hand and meticulously laying them back on the vanity. He pulls me to the front of an old wardrobe, opening it to reveal an overload of taffeta and fabric worthy enough to be in a museum. "These were her clothes."

"Harrison, don't take this the wrong way, but these clothes are from the nineteenth century. Penelope wouldn't be wearing them today."

"No, she wouldn't, but Celeste won't know her any other way."

"Celeste is an immortal child, but I doubt she's an idiot," I state the obvious. "She's not going to expect Penelope to be wearing these clothes."

Harrison closes his eyes. "Amelia. I want you to wear these. Please don't question me."

I stare at him, not sure how to respond. "I'm sorry. I didn't mean to upset you."

"You didn't. I apologize."

237

Being around his dead wife's clothes is clearly distressing him. I turn my attention back to the wardrobe, pulling the skirt of one of the dresses out. "How are these not damaged? They're in perfect condition."

He shrugs. "They've been enclosed in this cedar wardrobe since...since her death." He walks away from the memory. "Penelope always wore her hair tightly pulled behind her neck." He pulls the portrait that was hung above the fireplace out, leaning it against the bed. "This is how Celeste will remember her."

"Did she have an accent?" He nods.

"She had a mild French accent."

"I don't do accents, other than mimicking other people by accident." I think back to our first meeting at the university and my horrible imitation of his Southern drawl.

"You won't need to talk much. I'll teach you what you need to know."

Violet walks into the room. "Edon's here."

He nods. "I'll be right down."

"Want me to come?" I ask.

"Yes. Colby was your friend." He offers me his arm, and we head down to the awaiting lycanthrope. The five wolves from yesterday are back along with five I don't recognize. None of them are sitting, and the energy in the room is heavy. "Edon," Harrison says as we enter the room.

"What the hell happened to my son?" Edon doesn't mince words.

"Viktor," Harrison answers.

"What does that mean?" Edon steps toward Harrison. "My son is dead. I need more than a name."

"Colby went with me to search a few of Viktor's properties, looking for any clues that could lead us to where he was. Neither of us expected to find him." Harrison refuses to back down as the wolf moves closer.

"You led my son into a situation where you knew he would die?"

"That's not what he said, Edon," Violet stands from a chair in the corner. "They didn't expect to run into him. It wasn't Harrison's fault."

"Shut up, bitch," one of the younger wolves barks from across the room. "This has nothing to do with you."

Faster than my eyes can track, Harrison is behind the young pup, with a claw to his throat. "I've been lenient to you and your pack, Edon. Even allowing one of them to live in my home. However, don't mistake my leniency for weakness. You will not come into my home, threatening me or any of my people. Do I make myself clear?"

"Perfectly," the young wolf answers.

"Apologize to the lady," Harrison's words are no louder than a whisper. The wolf tries to pull away. Harrison draws blood from his neck. "Maybe you didn't hear me. Apologize to the lady."

"Jack," Edon warns.

"I'm sorry," the wolf mutters.

"I'm afraid that wasn't adequate. You get one more chance." Harrison's words bring chill bumps to my arms. Seeing him like this, like a predator, makes me question my sanity. Strangely, his behavior doesn't scare me. I find it kind of hot.

Jack turns toward Violet. "Forgive me, miss. I was speaking out of anger. Colby was my cousin."

Harrison releases the wolf. "I understand, and I'm sorry for your loss," Violet answers. She looks around the room, making eye contact with each of them. "Viktor did this. He's your enemy, not us."

Thomas stands. "I loved Colby. He was my life. Believe me, when I say I want revenge more than anyone in this room, but I agree with Violet. Viktor is to blame, not Harrison. The only way we're going to defeat him is by joining together."

Edon runs his hands through his hair. "I don't know."

"We have a plan," Harrison says. "Viktor has a weakness."

"Viktor has no weaknesses, if he did, he'd have been taken down centuries ago."

"There's an immortal child," Harrison speaks softly.

Edon looks up in surprise. "With Viktor?"

"He's been protecting the child for many centuries. The child is his weakness."

"What the hell is an immortal child?" Jack asks.

Edon turns, walking toward the grand piano. "An immortal child is a child who has been turned into a vampire."

"Is that real?" Jack asks, looking around the room.

"I'm afraid so," Harrison answers. "It's a practice that has been outlawed, but occasionally one is found. Viktor has been hiding this child for many centuries."

"What's your plan?" Edon asks, turning back toward us.

"We're going to get the child and bring it back here."

"Why not just kill it?" a young wolf who's been quiet the entire time asks.

"We're going to use the child to lure him where we want him. Killing it will only anger Viktor. He needs to hold out hope that he will get the child back."

"We'll help however we can, as long as I get to personally deal with Colby's killer." Edon moves toward the door, and the small pack follows. They leave without another word.

"Well, that went better than I expected," Harrison says, moving to my side.

"What's the plan?" Violet doesn't seem convinced.

"Amelia has agreed to help us retrieve Celeste. We'll bring her here and lock her in the holding cells below ground."

"How is that going to be a weakness for Viktor?" Thomas asks. "He can't get onto the property."

"He can if I let the protections down."

"The protections are out of your hands. Ophelia's the only one that can release them. Or someone from her family." Violet shares information I had no idea about.

"Why bring him here?" Thomas asks. "Why not one of the other homes?"

"Because Viktor is smarter than that," Harrison answers.

"Then he's smart enough to know this is a trap."

"We're going to bank on the fact that his love for Celeste will overtake any common sense he might have left in his head." Harrison sits on the piano bench and begins playing a song I recognize from freshman year music appreciation. "We'll get Celeste tomorrow evening," he says, ending the conversation. Thomas and Violet disappear, leaving me alone with Harrison and Beethoven.

"That's beautiful. Beethoven's always been one of my favorite composers."

"Yeah, mine too." He continues playing. "He was just as angry as his music sounds, though."

"You met him?"

"I did. Penelope and I sailed home a few times after arriving in New Orleans. It was on one of those trips that we met him. Attending the performance of his final symphony was one of the highlights of my life."

I stare at the man who hobnobbed with Beethoven. "Teach me what I need to know to be her."

He sighs, standing from the piano. "When Penelope

walked, she practically floated. She was graceful and had poise at all times."

"Well, we're screwed. I'm the opposite of grace and poise." Harrison laughs, stepping toward me.

"Keep your head held high when you walk and be confident as you move around. That's the difference. Other than that, you are more like her than you know."

"I'd like to come with you to get Celeste," Sara says, coming into the room. "She knows me, and it will make it easier."

"Agreed," Harrison answers. He turns back to me. "Get some rest, tomorrow will be here before we know it." He kisses me on the forehead, dismissing me for the evening.

"What does that mean?" What the hell?

"It means, get some rest. We'll get you ready tomorrow." He continues playing like nothing happened between us.

I don't know what to say. A few hours ago, we were wrapped in each other's arms, now he's sending me to bed like a child. I stare at him for a few seconds, not sure what to say before heading upstairs...alone. I stomp loud enough to be heard from the first floor as I enter my room. I don't know what I expected, but this isn't it. A tap on my door draws my attention.

"What?" I scowl.

"It's me."

"I'm getting some rest so you can get me ready for tomorrow."

"Yeah, I'm sorry about that."

I open the door, staring down the incredibly hot vampire that was inside me hours ago. "I'm not digging this Dr. Jekyll and Mr. Hyde thing. I'm not here to play games, Harrison. Either we're together or we're not. I'm not doing this hot and cold thing."

"I understand." He hands me a note, putting a finger to his lips. "I'll be in my room if you change your mind." He winks before walking away.

Closing the door behind him, I open the folded paper.

Amelia, please forgive my coldness. I don't trust Sara. Since she's been here, Viktor has been a step ahead of us. I have no doubt she had something to do with the strigoi and Colby's death. I didn't want her to realize our connection more than she already does. Get dressed now. The protections have been down since earlier tonight. Thomas and Violet are waiting for my signal. I'm going to send Sara on a scouting mission. While's she out, we will go.

I casually close my door and head upstairs to the room containing Penelope's things. I rummage through the ancient dresses, choosing a lavender-colored one that doesn't look overly complicated to put on. For the first time in my life, European history comes in handy. As part of my degree path, I took a class on the clothing of women from the seventeenth and eighteenth centuries. Without that, I wouldn't have a clue of what goes where. Using Penelope's brush and comb set, I brush through my curls, pulling them in a bun tightly behind my neck, the same as the portrait leaning against the bed. "Need any help?" Violet stops in her tracks. "Oh, my God. You look just like the painting."

"Can you help me into the dress?" I ask, bringing her back to reality.

"Yes, I'm sorry." She moves next to me, helping me slide the corset into place.

"How are these clothes in such good condition after all these years?"

"Because Harrison has them remade every ten years or so."

I stop wiggling into the corset and turn around. "What?"

"When the clothes get old or moth holes appear, he has her entire wardrobe remade, including the under-garments. He hires a seamstress in France to recreate them all." My heart jumps into my throat. He told me they were original, just kept in great shape. Why would he lie about that? "What's the matter, Amelia?"

"Nothing. Can you tie it tight?"

Violet tugs the corset string tightly, sucking my waist in and my breasts out. She helps me slide the skirt and jacket in place, making sure all of the pieces are straight and in the correct order. "This fits you like it was made for you." I turn, facing her with a grand spin. "Gorgeous," she says, looking me up and down. "Harrison's downstairs."

"After you." I slip on a pair of lavender shoes that are dyed the same color as the fabric. They fit perfectly. Not only do we look alike...we apparently have the same measurements. I follow Violet down two flights of stairs, holding the large skirt up enough to see the steps below.

"Wait here," she says at the top of the last flight. She continues to the bottom and to Harrison. "I feel like you need to be prepared." Her voice echoes up the stairwell.

"There's no need to be dramatic, Violet. Where is she?" I move down the stairs, joining Violet on the landing. Harrison's breath catches in his throat.

I spin, just for the hell of it. "What do you think?"

"Oh, my God. Penelope, it is you."

"*Amelia* looks beautiful, doesn't she?" Violet asks, staring at her maker.

"Yes, she does. I'm sorry, Amelia. You look so much like Penelope; it threw me for a loop." He clears his throat. "Shall we?"

I try not to be weirded out by his behavior. "Yes. Do we know where to go?"

"Edon's meeting us there," Thomas says, coming

into the room. "The rest of them are waiting for Viktor here. They're hidden throughout the property."

"Yes," Harrison answers my question. "We're heading across the lake."

"He has a house in Mandeville. That's where he keeps her," Violet answers.

"Sara?"

"She doesn't know, and it needs to remain that way." Harrison holds out his arm for me. I wrap my arm through his, and the four of us leave for victory or death.

TWENTY-TWO

what the what?

THE FOUR OF us climb into the back of a black SUV with Thomas behind the wheel. My dress takes up at least half of the back seat, which is good. After Harrison's slip up of calling me Penelope, I'm not sure I want him next to me right now. I get it. I'm dressed in his dead wife's clothing, but the fact that he lied about the age of Penelope's clothes and called me by her name makes me uncomfortable.

The drive across the lake is long and quiet. If there is a plan, no one has bothered to share it with me. Harrison's energy is off. In fact, all three of them seem...off. There's tension between them, and I don't have a clue why. We're nearly across the lake when the energy becomes so thick, I can't stand it any longer. "Is anyone going to tell me what's going on?"

"I'm not sure what you mean?" Harrison turns his head toward me.

"I mean, you three are acting like we're on the way to rob a bank. No one is speaking, and you're all staring out the windows blankly. I get the feeling you're not telling me something." Harrison reaches over, lacing his fingers through mine.

"We're just all anxious to get this over with." He smiles warmly. His smile doesn't reach his eyes and does nothing to ease the tension building inside.

Ten minutes later the car comes to a stop in front of a beautiful four-pillar home. "This is it." Harrison steps out of the truck. "Celeste will be inside," he announces after opening my door and helping me down.

"What do you mean? You're not coming?" He just finished telling me how volatile Celeste is and how she could rip my throat out in an instant but wants me to go inside, alone?

"She should see you first."

Violet moves to my side. "Harrison? What are you doing? Amelia can't go in there alone. Viktor will kill her on the spot."

"Don't question me, Violet." His tone is harsher than I've heard before, and she instantly backs away.

"What the hell, Harrison? Why are you acting weird? I don't want to go in there alone. I have no idea how to act like Penelope. Anyone with two brain cells will be able to tell I'm not her."

He closes his eyes, breathing deeply. "Fine. Violet, follow her to the door, but not any further." She nods, moving back to my side. "Thomas, keep the truck running."

"What am I supposed to do?" I ask, looking between the two of them.

"When she sees you, she should come willingly." Harrison doesn't offer any other advice. Yesterday he promised to coach me through this, and today he's sending me straight into the lion's den.

"Come on," Violet says, nudging me forward. I walk slowly up the front path and onto the porch while concentrating on walking with poise, the only pointer Harrison has given me about Penelope. Pulling the antique handle on the front door, a soft bell rings. An older woman wearing a black and white maid's uniform opens the door.

"Yes, may I help you, ma'am?" She looks me up and down, assessing my centuries-old clothing.

"Hello, my name is Penelope."

"Oh, my God. You look..." She stops her words.

"May I see her?"

"Excuse me," she says, regaining her composure and pushing the door closed.

"My apologies. Maybe I didn't make myself clear. My name is Penelope. I'm here for Celeste." I smile, flashing a warm smile. "May I see her?"

"I'm sorry, miss. I'm afraid that isn't possible. Mr. Luquire has specific rules about Celeste."

I push a foot through the door, blocking it from closing. "I'm fully aware of Mr. Luquire's rules. In fact,

250

he's the one who's instructed me to take her into the city with me." I've never been a good liar. I imagine the truth is written all over my face. "You know how he can be if he doesn't get his way."

"I suppose," she answers.

"Who's here, Fran?" a young voice calls from behind.

"It's no one, dear. Go back to your studies."

The door pulls open even further, revealing a beautiful, redheaded child. Her curls spring halfway down her back, and her blue eyes pierce into my soul. "Hello?" I smile.

"Penelope?" she whispers. "Is it really you?" A tear slides down her cheek.

"It's really me." I smile an authentic smile. Nothing about this child feels deadly or volatile. "I'm sorry I've been gone for so long. I've come to take you with me, back to our home in the city."

Celeste opens the door wide, running outside and wrapping her tiny arms around my waist. "I've missed you." She audibly sobs with her hug.

"I've missed you, too." Knowing this beautiful child's life was taken from her at such a young age brings familiar emotions to the surface. Our lives took different yet similar paths. Neither was in our control. I wipe the tears freely falling from my eyes. "Are you ready to go?"

She pulls away, holding on to my hand and pulling me into the house. "My home is with Daddy."

I kneel to her level, fighting the layers of fabric. "Viktor isn't your father, Celeste. You may feel that you're safe here, but he doesn't have your best interests at heart."

"You're so confused. I'm sorry for what he's done to you." My forehead wrinkles at her words. I don't understand what she's saying. She touches each of my cheeks with her tiny hands. "Daddy loves me."

"I'm...I'm sure he does. That's why he asked me to come and get you and take you home." Celeste moves further into the room and hides behind the maid's skirts.

"No."

"Come on, sweet girl. We need to get you to safety."

"You're not Penelope, and I'm safe here," Celeste announces. I stand, not sure what to do.

My mind races through the limited information I know about Celeste, searching for something to help convince her to leave. "Yes, I am. Do you remember the village in France?" She nods her tiny head. "Do you remember me turning you into a vampire to save your life?"

"That's not what happened." She takes off running, heading up the stairs.

"Celeste!" I call after her. Shit, what am I supposed to do now? I turn toward the door just as it slams shut. Standing in front of it is a vampire I remember from my nightmares, Viktor.

He looks me up and down. "Well, hello, Penelope." His smirk doesn't match his words.

"I'm not Penelope, asshole," I retort.

"Yes, I know, mon amour. I see he's dressed you up as his plaything, so I thought I'd continue the charade." What's he talking about? A loud pounding on the door interrupts his words. "Don't worry, he can't get in. This house is just as protected as the other against the likes of Harrison Chamberlin."

"Penelope!" Harrison calls through the door. "Dammit, Viktor! Don't hurt her!"

"Why would I hurt her, Harrison? That would be your agenda, not mine. Her name is Amelia, by the way." Harrison continues pounding on the door, and I fight the panic rising from my core. Memories of my first experiences with Viktor flash to mind.

"What's the matter, Amelia? Starting to have second thoughts?" Viktor uses my real name.

"Daddy!" Celeste runs down the stairs.

"There's my girl, mon petit amour." She runs into his arms. He picks her up, spinning her around.

"Daddy, she tried to take me. Just like you said she would. Are you sure she's not Penelope?"

"No, my dear, she isn't. This is Amelia, and you did amazing, just like I knew you would." He sets her back on the floor. "Why don't you go upstairs with Aunt Fran, and I'll come practice your languages with you later?"

"Okay." She wraps her tiny hand inside Fran's, who walks her upstairs. "Good night, Amelia."

"Um...good night?" Watching her climb the stairs leaves me feeling confused. Harrison continues to bang on the front door. I'm not sure how the door is still standing, considering the strength he's using. Viktor watches until the child is out of sight and walks toward a bar cart, pouring a glass of dark liquor.

"You're going to need this." He toasts the air before handing the glass to me. "Why don't we move to a quieter part of the house?"

"Viktor, I'm not doing this again. You can't keep me against my will." I set the glass on a table.

"See, that's your problem. I'm not the one keeping you against your will. You're looking at this entire situation through skewed lenses."

"Really? How the hell am I supposed to look at it then?" Edon walks out of the back room just as I finish my words. "Edon? What are you doing? You're supposed to be helping." I look between the two of them. "You told him we were coming?"

"I *am* helping," he answers.

"How could you betray Harrison?"

The two men share a look. "She really doesn't know, does she?" Edon asks.

"Stop talking about me like I'm not in the room, asshole! I'll tell you what I *do* know. Viktor tried to kill me in my apartment. In fact, he set up the entire scenario so I would rent from one of his buildings. Not long after being there, he tried to kill me. Harrison was the one that saved me. He took me back to his house and offered me a place to stay when I had none. What did you do, Viktor?" I spew.

"I'm sure you're going to tell me." He sits on an overstuffed couch, crossing his legs at the knees.

"Damn right, I'm going to tell you." I clear my throat. His odd behavior is distracting me. "You killed Thomas. Right in front of me."

"What makes you think that was me?"

"Harrison told me it was you."

He smiles. "I'm sure he did. What else did he *tell* you?"

"You kidnapped me from the street."

"You've got me there. That was me." He takes a sip of dark liquid.

"You took me to that house and forced me to watch you feed."

"Did you actually see me feed?" I think back to the dinner party with the young blonde girl. He's right. He didn't feed from her.

"No, but...but that was her head on the table the next day."

"Or could it have been a fake head made to look real?"

"Stop, you're trying to confuse me. A fake head is dumb. Why would you do something like that?"

I turn to the wolf sitting next to Viktor. "Edon, you

were there. He killed Jeremiah, right in front of you. How could you believe anything he says?"

"Jeremiah was playing on the wrong side. I'm on the side of honesty and truth. His death was necessary." He pauses. "Harrison isn't who or what you think he is."

I cover my ears with my hands. "Stop!"

"Listen, Amelia," Viktor instructs. What's he talking about?

"To what?"

"Your beloved is gone. He left you here because he knows the truth is going to come out, and you'll finally know who he really is."

I turn, looking out the window. Just as he said, the SUV is gone. "Harrison?"

"He's not who you think he is," Edon repeats.

"You blame him for Colby. That's why you're here. Some sort of crazy revenge thing."

"You're right. I do blame Harrison for my son's death because he's the one who killed him. I sent Colby to keep you safe. I knew Harrison would trust him because of his connection to Thomas. But it was Harrison who killed my son."

"No, it was Viktor."

"No, my dear, it wasn't. I have no issues with the Lycan, nor would I have a reason to kill one of them. Especially the son of the alpha. Harrison killed Colby in hopes of involving the Lycan in his delusional plan." Viktor looks bored with our conversation.

"What are you telling me?"

"I believe that's my cue." He stands, clearing his throat. "You might want to sit down."

"No." I cross my arms in front of my chest.

"Suit yourself." He pours another glass. "Penelope and I were in love." He ignores my laughter. "She was the most beautiful person I've ever known. Inside and out, she was perfect." He takes a drink. "We grew up together, the three of us. Harrison was the runt of our group and the first one to get sick at the start of the plague." I look up quickly.

"That's a lie. Harrison said *Penelope* was the first to get sick."

"Of course, he did. His view of the past is…skewed."

"You're crazy."

He takes another drink. "No, my dear. I can assure you, I'm perfectly sane. Shall I continue?" I nod, not sure why. "He was one of the first ones in the village to get sick. It took some convincing, but he managed to get someone in the village to take him to the healer in the mountains. We were just kids, and no one wanted a sick kid around, so they agreed to take him."

"To the vampire?"

"To the vampire," he confirms. "Of course, we didn't know at the time that's what she was. There was no such thing as modern medicine, and she was the closest thing we had to a doctor." He empties his glass, reliving a memory. "Afterward, he was out of control. The plague took its share of villagers while Harrison took even more. Most of them were killed when he drained them, but some were reborn."

"Penelope?"

"It haunts me to this day." His voice is softer. "We'd been married for several years."

"Married? You were married to Penelope?" Suddenly feeling an overwhelming need to sit down, I find an overstuffed chair opposite the couch.

"Very happily, I might add. She was and will remain the love of my life. We had a child, a daughter."

My mind flashes to the young girl upstairs. "Celeste?"

He nods. "Harrison turned them both."

Oh, my God. Is this the truth? I don't know who to believe anymore. "Celeste is yours and Penelope's child? Why would Harrison lie to me? He told me Celeste was Penelope's younger sister."

"Because no matter how he spins the truth, he was in love with Penelope, and his jealousy drove him to do the unthinkable. He turned my wife and child into vampires, and brought them here, to New Orleans." He pauses, trapped in a memory. "I forced the vampire that turned him to turn me, and I spent the next century looking for them." He takes another drink. "Damn, I wish this was alcohol." He pauses. "I was never able to free Penelope from the bastard."

I take a deep breath. "Okay, let's say any of this is true. What does Harrison stand to gain from taking Celeste away from you?"

"He gains control," Edon answers. "It's all about control with him."

"He would hold her captive like he did her mother, refusing her food until she eventually starved to death. What he couldn't have in life, he wants in death."

"He's started hunting again to be strong enough to fight you." I don't know if I just gave away a secret or not, but at this point, does it matter?

Both Edon and Viktor laugh. "Don't be fooled, young one. He never stopped hunting. Harrison feeds on the poor and the weak."

"That's not true." My voice is no louder than a whisper. "He drinks goat blood."

"Why? Because that's what he told you? I suppose he told you the strigoi that attacked your car was sent by me?" He laughs. "Those vile creatures are not worthy of my time. No, my dear. Harrison is the one responsible for all of this." He takes another drink. "He's a master manipulator, Amelia. He always has been. You're just a means to his end."

Oh, my God. Is this true? "Why did you hold me captive and do all those horrible things while I was there? You treated me like a creature that you could torture and play games with." I fight the tears threatening to fall.

He sighs. "You had to believe. This is the finale of a plan that has been in play for nearly twenty years. We couldn't risk you discovering the truth of who I am or who he was until now. You weren't ready for the truth."

"Not ready for the truth? What the hell does that mean?"

"Would you have believed me? If I had told you the opposite of what Harrison's been spoon-feeding you, would you have believed me? You had to believe the lie in order to protect you and to bring this plan to culmination."

I stare at the creatures in front of me. "You used me? You scared the living shit out of me, all in the name of what exactly? Tricking Harrison? Is this some kind of a sick game the three of you are playing?"

"I can assure you. My son's death was no game." Edon's voice is angry. "That bastard killed Colby in cold blood."

"Forcing me to believe your narrative didn't do any of us good. All you did was make this whole thing even harder to understand. God, I don't know what to believe." I stand, flipping the miles of fabric behind me. "I want out of this freaking thing."

"I'm sorry for scaring you. Harrison had to believe. The only way he would, was by using you. I'll admit, maybe I played my part too well."

"Fuck you, Viktor." I sling the fabric around again. "Where can I change?"

"I'll take you to your room," Sara says, stepping into the room and toward me.

"I should've known you were here, traitor. Harrison was right about you." My tone is rude. "Let me guess. The door to my room will be locked for my safety?

Should I go ahead and put on a blindfold?" I fling my anger toward Viktor.

"You'll find that you are free to leave anytime you wish. However, I can't guarantee your safety anywhere away from this home."

"Dammit. This conversation isn't finished." I follow Sara upstairs and into a bedroom off the main stairway. Unlike the room at his other house, this room is decorated comfortably and straight out of a *Better Homes and Gardens* magazine.

"You'll find clothes in the closet and before you ask, no, there are no cameras or microphones anywhere. Get some rest." She moves toward the door. "Things will be clearer tomorrow."

"Sara, wait. Can you unbutton this damn thing?"

TWENTY-THREE
who do i believe?

I OPEN and close the door to my room at least ten times, checking to see if I'm actually free to leave or locked inside. True to his word, the door is unlocked each time. With Sara's help, I've changed from seventeenth-century Penelope to grad student Amelia. The sun is setting low in the sky, and my mind races through the information dump Viktor shared earlier. What if he's telling the truth, and Harrison has been behind everything? I always thought I was a good judge of character, but now, I have no idea who to believe.

A soft knock on the door draws me back to the present. "Yes?"

The door creaks open, slowly. "Amelia?" a soft voice calls.

"I'm here." The door opens wide, revealing the adorable redhead. Her clothes are not as old as the ones Harrison dressed me in, but not from this century.

"Are you hungry?" she asks.

I think back, trying to remember the last time I ate. "Actually, yes, I am."

Celeste smiles. "Good. Sara sent me to get you. She said she's a better cook than she pretended to be and has a small feast waiting on you."

I smile at her words. "Is Viktor still here?"

"Yes. Daddy's downstairs somewhere." She turns toward the door. "He asked me to remind you that I am nearly one thousand years old and capable of destroying a small village if needed." She smiles warmly.

"Duly noted." I follow her to the kitchen and discover Sara setting a grilled cheese sandwich and tomato soup on the table.

"There you are," she says, sitting in an empty chair. "Thank you, Celeste. You may go."

"Do I have to?"

Sara turns, giving the girl an incredulous look. "Yes." She watches red curls bounce out of the kitchen before turning back to me. "I thought you might want to talk."

I dip the edge of my sandwich into my soup. "I don't know what I want." I take a huge bite and roll my eyes at the flavors that attack my mouth. "Actually, that's not true. I want to return to my life before all this vampire and werewolf shit happened."

"Don't forget the witches," Sara adds. "Would it help to share what I know with you?"

"It couldn't hurt." I take another bite.

She sits on the chair across from me. "Harrison is my maker."

I stop chewing. "What? At the house, you said Viktor was your maker."

"I did." She smiles. "I lied."

"Why was it necessary for everyone to lie to me? Why this elaborate production?"

Sara looks down. "Edon and Viktor decided that was the best way to protect you and the only way to make Harrison believe. If you knew the truth, he would've been able to sense it from you. They couldn't take the chance."

I stare at the vampire in front of me. "Seriously? It seems like there could've been another way besides scaring the shit out of me."

"I don't know all the details, but I do know Harrison has had his claws in you and your life since you were a child. The only way to keep you safe and prevent him from knowing what was going on was to trick both you and him into believing Viktor wanted you dead."

"Well, the plan sucked."

Sara laughs. "Can I tell you my story? It might help ease some of the confusion you're having."

"I'd like that."

She takes a deep breath. "It was the early nineteen hundreds when Harrison found me. I wasn't anything special, just a meal, his next possible donneuse." I set my sandwich down, already enthralled by her story.

"He was crueler than any human I'd ever known, and believe me, I'd known cruelty in my life. When he fed from me, he would bleed me nearly dry, to the point of death, only to release me and repeat the process months later. One day he went too far. Whether out of guilt or cruelty, he gave me some of his blood, making me reborn as a vampire."

"How did you get away?"

She looks down. "I was an old woman, and eventually, he stopped caring. I wasn't any use to him as a vampire, which meant he didn't care what I did or where I went."

"How'd you end up with Viktor?"

"I asked." She shrugs. "He needed someone to take care of Celeste, and after years of proving my loyalty to him, he allowed me to be her primary caregiver."

"But I saw him break your neck."

She rolls her head around. "All in a day's work, my dear. A broken neck is merely a hindrance to a vampire, not death. I was back to normal within minutes."

"Why would Harrison do all of this? Was it for me?" I push my nearly full bowl away, suddenly not feeling very hungry.

"This will sound cruel, but Harrison does nothing for anyone except himself. Only he knows the reasoning behind his obsession with you." She pauses. "Viktor didn't own the apartment building you rented a room from, Harrison did. Ms. Esther was his donneuse, not Viktor's." I suddenly feel sick to my stomach.

"What about Violet and Thomas?"

"They each have their own story, but from what I gathered while there, neither is fully aware of who Harrison truly is. Although, I think Violet might have some suspicions."

"He told me the story of how he saved Violet from taking her own life," I remember the conversation we had about his companion.

"If you speak with her, I think you'll discover she has a different version of that story." Sara stands, taking my bowl back toward the sink. "Amelia, you're safe here. I know you don't know who or what to believe right now, and that's perfectly understandable. But listen when I say, Harrison's had this entire scenario in play since he first found you as a child. He's crossed every T and dotted every I to ensure you become the Penelope he could never have. In his mind, he truly believes he's the good guy and Viktor is evil. Everything that's happened in your life has been at the hand of Harrison Chamberlin, and every aspect that Viktor's been involved in has been carefully planned for your protection and Harrison's fall."

I pull my cell phone out, realizing I have over a hundred missed calls and one missed text from Violet. If what Sara says is true, Violet is as much a victim of Harrison as everyone else. I decide to test the water and send her a text. Utilizing an app on my phone that disguises numbers, I type four simple words.

> We need to talk.

Moments later, I receive a response.

> Amelia? OMG, are you okay?

> I'm fine. Can you meet, alone?

Several minutes pass before I receive a response.

> No.

She doesn't send anything else. Shit. "Finished eating, Amelia?" Celeste bounces back into the room. "I thought maybe we could play a game or something."

I don't know why her words surprise me. "Sure, I guess. What do you have in mind?"

"I have a kite in the backyard. The breeze from the lake makes it fly really high."

A kite? "Sure. Sounds like fun." She takes my hand into hers, leading me into the backyard. Green grass, the color of Astroturf, greets us as we exit. The grass turns into light brown sand and eventually leads into the murky water of the lake. "This is beautiful."

"Eh," she shrugs. "Here, take the string. I'll get the kite flying." In an instant, the kite lifts off the ground as Celeste jumps, holding it in her hand. She's hanging on to the bottom of the kite, as it lifts high in the sky. Within seconds she's nearly out of sight.

Oh, my God. "Celeste?"

"She's fine. She's just a little show-off." Viktor comes around the corner of the house with a smile on his face.

"Won't she get hurt?"

He laughs. "It would take a lot more than a fall from that height to do her any harm. She's tougher than she looks." Even so, I grip the string with all my might, not wanting to be the one responsible for her flying over the lake and into oblivion. He reaches up, taking the string from me and tugs slightly.

"Is she safe up there?"

"You try telling a thousand-year-old immortal child they can't fly anymore." He laughs at his words. "To answer your question, yes, she's safe." Just like he said, Celeste floats back into the yard, wearing a huge grin.

"Daddy, did you see me? I was super high."

"I did, pumpkin. I think maybe you tricked Amelia into helping you get up there."

"Maybe." She smiles. "Thanks, Amelia!" She wraps the string around the kite and runs inside.

"Why do I feel like I fell into a trap?" I ask, trying not to smile.

"Because you did. She has a magical way about her." His eyes soften as he speaks. "Have you had a chance to think over everything?"

"I spoke with Sara earlier. She told me some things about Harrison." I look up at the vampire who I've despised since day one. "Did Harrison own that apartment building?"

"Yes."

"Were you there to turn me that night?"

He looks over the water. "No. I was there to get you away from him. I knew he would come, and I wanted to get you out of there before he showed up."

"Why did you say those things? Why didn't you just tell me why you were there?"

He smiles, lifting an eyebrow. "If I had walked into that apartment and told you the truth, would you have come with me?"

"Probably not."

Viktor laughs. "Probably? You would've told me where to go and how to get there. I knew the only way to make you believe was to show you who I was." I think back to that night. He never threatened me. In fact, he told me he was there to save me.

"So, the coffin in the closet?"

"Harrison's. More of a prop really. No one uses those things. They're creepy."

"How did you know I was there?"

"Edon. His wolves have been tracking you since you were a child. They knew who you were and what Harrison wanted from you."

"The Lycan are tracking me? Why?"

"That's a very good question and one that I can't answer."

I turn, facing him. "Everyone except me was in on the ruse the entire time?"

"Well, you and Chamberlin. It was the only way we could trap him."

"What *does* he want from me?" I rub my arms, fighting the cold wind blowing off the lake.

"He wants you, and now that he knows Celeste is still alive, he wants you both. The woman he could never have and her child he could never produce. He wants the family he thinks he deserves."

"Sara telling him about Celeste being alive was part of the plan?"

He sighs before answering. "Yes. Knowing she was alive was the catalyst to bring his insanity to the surface."

"What if he hurts her?"

"He won't. I won't allow that to happen."

I stare into the open water. "Am I Penelope?"

Viktor turns to me. "No one will ever be Penelope. You are you and she was..." He doesn't finish his thought. "There's no denying your similarities, but no, you are not Penelope. Harrison worked with a witch who cast a spell on you at some point. Any feelings or soul contracts you might have felt with him were nothing more than her spell." Viktor turns, walks inside the house, and leaves me alone.

The pain in my stomach returns. Harrison tricked me into believing I could possibly be Penelope, reincarnated. How could you be so naive, Amelia? You're smarter than that, yet you fell ass over tits for the first man who pulls a one-liner on you. My phone buzzes, drawing me out of my personal reprimand session.

Can you get out?

I stare at Violet's text, not sure how to respond. Do I want to get out? Strangely, I feel safe here. I slide my phone back without responding.

I turn, following Viktor's footsteps into the house, and find him in the living room, sitting on the floor and playing a board game with Celeste.

"Amelia! Do you want to play?" she asks, trying to hand me a metal game piece.

"Last time we played a game, you tricked me into letting you fly." Celeste laughs. Her giggle reminds me of a childhood lost.

"You can't fly in Monopoly, silly."

"Good point," I sit on the opposite side of the board. "Actually, I wanted to talk to your dad for a minute." Viktor looks up as Celeste sets the pieces and cards in their correct spots. He raises his eyebrows in question. "I don't want to spend the rest of my life running from him."

"Are you saying you believe me?" I look between the beautiful vampire girl and her father several times before answering.

"Yes. How do we stop this? How do we stop him?"

"Harrison must die."

......

After a wild game of Monopoly, and me being the only one who needs sleep, I excuse myself to my room. My phone buzzes just as I drift off to sleep, pulling me back into reality. It's another text from Violet.

Harrison is planning on attacking.

In an instant, I'm wide awake.

When? I answer.

Soon.

Soon? What kind of an answer is that? I jump out of bed, dragging my phone with me. The bottom floor of the house is silent and empty. "Viktor?" I call into the darkness. I run upstairs, looking for someone to share the text with. "Viktor?" I whisper.

"Amelia?" A door at the end of the hallway cracks open. "I thought you went to bed."

"I did until I got this." I hold the phone up for him to see.

"How do you work this thing?" He squints at the screen. "It's a cell phone. Just swipe up." He bats at the screen for a few minutes, not achieving anything. "Oh, for God's sake." I read the text to him. Viktor doesn't respond. "Did you hear me? Violet says he's planning on attacking."

"Of course, he is. I would expect nothing less."

"Aren't you worried?"

"Not at all. Bring it on. Isn't that what the young people say?" He closes the door to his room. "Good night, Amelia," he calls through the closed door.

TWENTY-FOUR

the end and the beginning

IT TAKES a few minutes to realize where I am when my eyes open. The sound of feet running in the hall and giggling as Celeste passes my door, warms me from the inside out. "Amelia?" a loud whisper echoes under my door. "Are you awake? Aaa...mee...leeeaaa?"

"I'm up!" I yell toward the door.

"Yeah! Come and play. Daddy told me to let you sleep, so I did."

One look at my phone tells me it's six o'clock in the morning. How kind of her to let me sleep in. I roll my eyes and smile. "I'll be there in a minute. I need to take a shower."

"Ooohhh...kayyyy...." she whispers.

I take a quick shower and, thankfully, find a pair of leggings and an oversized hoodie to slip on. Pulling my hair into a high bun, I head downstairs, toward the giggles. "Amelia!" Celeste exclaims as I enter the kitchen. "You're awake!"

"I didn't realize it was an option."

Sara has a plate of eggs and bacon waiting for me, and my stomach growls at the sight. I eat every bite before being pulled into the living room. "I thought we could build a farm." She motions toward a box full of wooden blocks and carved farm animals. "Aunt Fran and Aunt Sara aren't fans of getting on the floor to play." I sit next to the large box of blocks where we spend the next hour building the farm of her dreams.

"Did you let Amelia sleep in?" Viktor asks, coming into the room.

"I did!" Celeste answers.

"Can I borrow Amelia for a while?" He sits on the couch behind his daughter.

"As long as you keep it short. She'd rather play farm than talk business."

"She's not wrong," I add, moving to the couch next to Viktor.

"Don't encourage her." He laughs. "Edon stopped by earlier. Harrison has demanded we meet him tonight."

"I hope you told him to kiss your a..." I stop, looking down at the immortal child in front of me.

"It's okay. I've heard bad words before," Celeste says. "You can say ass."

"As much as I'd like to, we need to end this thing.

He's never going to leave you alone until he has you. Do you want to live your life that way?"

"No," I whisper.

"Where are we meeting?"

"*We* are not meeting anywhere. You are staying here where you're safe. Me, Sara, Fran, and the Lycan will meet with Harrison."

"That's crap."

"What exactly do you think you'd be able to do? Hit him with your laptop? Or perhaps you could throw a shoe at him?"

"Ouch." I cross my arms in front of me. "Don't hold back for the sake of my feelings or anything." As much as it hurts to hear, he's right. I would be more of a hindrance than anything else. "I understand. What time's the meeting?"

"Midnight at Jackson Square. He likes an audience."

"What's going to happen?" I ask, not sure what to expect.

"Knowing you and Celeste are in the same spot and he has a chance to get you both has… altered his way of thinking, just as we hoped it would. We're going to take care of him. He won't bother you or anyone else again."

"How can you be so sure?"

"Unlike Harrison, I don't halfway do things. This will be over tonight." I look down to see Celeste lying prostrate on the floor, surrounded by her farm pieces.

"Are you okay down there?"

"Yep, just waiting for you to finish your boring

conversation." She sits up, handing me a carved goat. "Here. The goat is you, and I'm the horse."

We continue playing until Celeste gets bored and begins to put the farm away. "Are we done?"

"Yeah, I'm getting tired of playing farm."

"Why don't you let Amelia get some work done? It's time for you to study your languages. What language are you working on right now?"

"Portuguese," she answers, heading upstairs. "Thank you for playing with me, Amelia. If you need any help with your work, let me know." I watch her turn the corner, heading toward the third floor.

"She's..."

"I know. Not only does she look just like her mother, but she acts like her too. Penelope was brilliant. Smarter than I could ever wish to be. Celeste is the reason I'm here." Viktor looks lovingly at the stairs where his daughter was standing moments earlier.

"You must miss her."

"More than you can imagine." He slaps his thigh, clearing the ghosts from his mind. "I've asked one of Edon's pack to stay here with you and Celeste tonight."

I don't argue. I feel safer having a mythological creature in the house with us. "What if something..."

"No, we don't do what-ifs. The Lycan have a plan, and I've had a many years to learn his weaknesses."

"Why now? He killed your wife and turned your child into a vampire. Why wait until now? Why not take him down after Penelope's death?"

His eyes take on a faraway look. "I've wanted him dead for longer than I've been a vampire. After he turned them, I tried to kill him. For years I hunted him and came close to killing him many times. But when I found her..." His voice catches. "When I found Celeste, my priorities changed."

"I feel like an idiot for believing the lies he spewed at me."

"Don't. You had no way of knowing the truth. He's a master at his craft and had many years to perfect it."

"To be honest, you didn't help the situation any by being the psychopathic asshole you were." I cross my arms over my chest.

"You had to believe the scenario. Terrifying you into believing I am the murderer Harrison says I am was the only way. I apologize." He walks to a desk in the corner of the room. "Sara brought your laptop." He hands me my MacBook, holding my thesis work.

"Why does this feel like a lifetime ago?" I open the computer, reading the opening statement out loud. "*Mythological Creatures of Europe and the Theories Behind Them.*"

Viktor laughs loudly. "By the end of this, you'll have enough information to write an entire book."

......

The day passes relatively quickly, despite the anticipation of tonight. Viktor seems unfazed by future events, and despite our first few weeks together, I've lost the urge to murder him every few seconds. He's growing on me. Not in a, he's hot, and I want him kind of way. Been there, done that, and got the t-shirt. But in a, I was wrong, kind of way. Observing the love he has for his daughter has helped me realize the truth about him, and to come to the realization that I suck at judging people.

Before I realize it, it's eleven o'clock, and the three vampires are preparing to leave. "Jack is outside. He will keep watch from there," Viktor announces, heading toward the door. "The house is secured, but even so, don't open the door for anyone. If someone is supposed to be inside, they'll know how to get in."

"I understand." I don't know why I'm nervous. My job is to stay here, they're the ones heading to a fight. "I'll keep Celeste safe."

Viktor smiles at my words. "You do that."

"Be careful, Daddy," Celeste says from the bottom of the stairs.

"Always, mon amour." He wraps his arms around her. "Keep Amelia safe," he whispers loud enough for me to hear.

"Okay," she whispers back.

I watch the three of them leave. Viktor is wearing a pair of black jeans and a sweater. He looks more human than I've ever seen.

I turn toward the young vampire. "What should we do while we wait?"

"Aren't you tired? Daddy said you'd probably go to sleep."

"Normally, yes. Tonight, there's no way I could sleep. How about we watch a movie?"

Her eyes grow twice the size as normal. "Ooo, I don't get to watch many movies. That sounds fun." I look around the room.

"Is there a television here?" I ask.

"Daddy doesn't believe in having them in the house."

My laptop is still on the table in the sitting room. "Never mind, we'll use this." I pull up Netflix, praying my account is still active. "What kind of movie do you want to watch?" I flip through the kid's movies, not sure what a thousand-year-old vampire would want to watch.

"That looks good." She points at the Halloween classic, *Hotel Transylvania*.

I laugh out loud. "I don't think you could've chosen anything more appropriate. Celeste spends the first thirty minutes telling me how everything in the movie is wrong and whoever did their research on vampires and werewolves was completely confused. After explaining the concept of fiction to her numerous times, she finally starts to enjoy the movie and gives up trying to fix it. I nervously find myself looking at the clock on the top of the screen more than I should. It's midnight, which means whatever's going to happen should be starting.

Celeste turns toward me. "Are you okay?"

"I'm good, why?"

"You smell different than you did earlier."

"Okay, that's weird, and it's just my nerves. Not knowing what's going on makes me anxious."

She sighs. "Daddy's okay. I can tell." I nod and we continue watching the computer. Celeste sits up in fright. "Amelia?" she whispers. She covers her lips with her finger. Oh, my God. What? She points to the window off the side of the house. In an instant, she's in front of it and lifting the curtain. This is the first time I've seen her move like the predator she is. She moves up the stairs in the blink of an eye, and I freeze in my spot. What the hell does she sense? In a flash, she's back at my side, holding a notebook and pen.

Vampire outside.

Shit! I grab the pen from her.

What do we do?

We stay quiet. They can't get in

I stare at the angelic immortal child in front of me, not sure what to do. I can't protect her from a vampire. Where's Jack? Isn't he supposed to be on the grounds?

Wolf?

I scribble quickly. She shrugs.

Almost on cue, something taps against the front door. My eyes are as large as saucers as I turn to Celeste, not sure what to do. "Amelia?" Violet's voice sounds through the door.

Violet! She's my friend.

I scribble before moving to stand from the couch. Celeste pushes me back, forcing me down. She shakes her head.

Not Violet, not friend!

"Amelia, I know you're in there. Let me in, please. I left Harrison and Thomas in the city. I'm here to help you, and I'm hurt." Celeste literally holds me down with strength I didn't know a five-year-old child could have. "Amelia?" Something slams against the front door, making me jump. "Dammit, Amelia. I need your help. Don't you want to help me? I thought we were friends."

I try to move. Celeste shakes her head, warning me not to move. *"No,"* she mouths.

"Amelia?" Violet's voice sounds different this time.

More guttural and deeper than before. "Amelia, let me in."

Celeste looks at me with an "I told you so" face.

"I can hear you." Whatever it is sniffs through the door. "I can smelllll you."

Hide!

I scribble.

Don't move

"Your wolf is still alive but won't be for much longer." What sounds like a body, slams against the porch. "He needs your help. I know how you like to help everyone, Amelia. Like you helped me the other night." The voice turns into one I recognize instantly, Harrison. "Remember how it felt to have me inside you?" Oh, my God. I cover Celeste's ears with my hands, and she rolls her eyes. "Come to me, and we can be together every night." He sniffs the door again. "I can still smell you on me. Come outside so we can be the family we were meant to be. You, me, and Celeste." He's batshit crazy. How could I have been such an idiot?

Celeste sits up, covering her lips.

Daddy's here

She scribbles in a hurry. Two weeks ago, I never

283

thought I'd be happy to hear Viktor was anywhere nearby. "Harrison!" I hear him yell toward the door.

"Daddy says for us to hide in the basement."

"What? You spoke with him?"

"Dammit, Amelia. Move!" I resist the urge to reprimand her for her choice of language. Instead, I let her drag me through the house and toward a locked door in the kitchen. She kicks it, nearly knocking it off its hinges before dragging me down a set of stairs straight out of a haunted house. We round a corner, heading toward another area and dodging antiques along the way. "Come on," she urges. Ahead of us is a door from the future. She puts her tiny hand on a glass screen and the door pops open, revealing padded white walls and rows of shelving, each containing hundreds of bottles of red liquid. Celeste slams the door behind us, locking us inside. "We're safe in here." She curls up beside me, pulling her tiny legs under her dress. "They're fighting." Her voice sounds sad.

"How do you know?"

"Daddy's talking to me in his head. We're connected." I don't ask questions.

"Is he...okay?"

She nods. "Everyone is here. He says when they got to Jackson Square there wasn't anyone there. Jack managed to call Edon before...before."

"It's going to be okay." I wrap my arms around the tiny killing machine. "Viktor will make sure we're okay."

"I know." Her words don't match her tone. She's not convinced, and neither am I.

Several minutes pass, and we sit in silence, not sure what's going on with the battle outside. Celeste suddenly looks up. "What?"

"Your friend is hurt."

"Violet?"

"She's alive but injured." I nod, pulling her close. Something bangs against the door of the room we're hiding in. We both jump.

I move to the small window at the top of the door, trying to figure out what or who's out there. Sara's face appears. Her eyes are open, but her face looks strange, almost frozen in time. "What is it?" Celeste asks.

"It's Sara."

"She's not alone," Celeste answers. "Amelia, get behind me." I move behind the small child as she stands, facing the door.

"No one can get in, can they?"

"Sara can," she whispers. The door to the safe room slides open, revealing Harrison. He's holding Sara's head and hands. Oh, my God, he's holding her head and hands that aren't attached to her body. I stare in disbelief. It takes a minute to register exactly what I'm seeing. I cover my mouth, stifling a scream.

"That came in handy," he says with a sickening laugh. "Viktor's weakness is thinking I'm not smart enough to know he trusted this bitch enough to let her open the door." He throws what's left of Sara into the room with us before stepping inside. "Both of my girls in one place. How perfect!"

"Harrison. What did you do to Sara?" I fight to keep my voice calm.

"I would think it's obvious." He points to what remains of her on the floor. "She was a liability from the beginning. I should've known she was playing both sides. Stupid bitch. I should've let her die to begin with." He kicks her head, slamming it against the brick wall.

"Why are you doing this?"

Blood is dripping from his mouth and his eyes look nothing like the Harrison I know. He resembles a wild animal on the prowl. "Because you're mine." He turns toward Celeste. "Both of you. Viktor stole you from me. We were supposed to be together. It was always supposed to be us." He reaches both hands toward us. "Come, my girls. It's time to go home."

"Stop!" Celeste yells. She moves so fast that I barely track her movement. She's on his back with her teeth sunk into his neck before I realize she's moved. He reaches around, grabs her by the hair, and throws her to the ground.

"Is that any way to treat your father?"

"You're not my father!" she yells. She repeats the move from earlier, this time hitting him so hard, he falls backward a few steps.

"Looks like someone needs a time-out," he says, regaining his footing.

"Go!" Celeste yells as she drags Harrison to the corner of the room. The two of them are moving so quickly that I don't know if either is winning. "Go, Amelia!" she yells for a second time.

Leaving a child to fight an adult goes against everything I know to be true. But Celeste isn't an ordinary child. I run out of the room and up the stairs, barely making it past the threshold when Harrison appears in front of me. "Leaving so soon?" I refuse to back down.

"What did you do to Celeste?"

"Nothing. I wouldn't hurt that little darling. She'll be a little sore in the morning, but nothing a good rest won't cure."

"Celeste!" I call behind me. She doesn't answer.

"All of this could've been avoided if you would've just followed directions. I told you to get the girl and bring her to the truck. But no, you were too dumb to do any of that, weren't you? Penelope was smarter than you could ever be. Hopefully, when you change, you'll pick up some of her intelligence."

"I don't give you permission to change me!" I scream.

"I don't need your permission, Penelope. We're meant to be together, forever." His mind is flipping from knowing who I am to thinking I'm Penelope. In an instant, Harrison is on top of me. I'm not strong enough to fight the inevitable as his teeth sink deep into my neck. The shock of pain hits fast and is nothing like before. When he fed from my arm, it wasn't painful. In fact, it was enjoyable. This is different. He's making it hurt on purpose. I can feel my life draining slowly through my vein as he continues to feed.

"Harrison," I choke on my words. "Stop, please." My voice doesn't sound human.

He doesn't stop. A black circle forms around my line of sight and slowly begins to close in on itself. Scenes from my life flash before my eyes, taking the pain of the attack away. My body becomes weightless, and the feeling of being pulled away offers relief. This is what it feels like to die.

An inhuman scream pierces my ears as Harrison's weight falls heavily on top of me, and his teeth slowly withdraw from my neck. A faint image of Violet holding a long piece of wood, dripping with blood, is the last thing I see before the room fades to nothing.

TWENTY-FIVE
awakening

"AMELIA?" a soft voice calls through the darkness. Something about the voice feels familiar. I don't know why.

Electricity shoots down my arms and legs, a constant memory of when I was seven and stuck my metal barrette into a light socket during carpet time. The fire that shot through my young body was nothing compared to the fire I feel now. Every pore is alive as my veins carry the flames of death to each inch of my body. A million tiny pins are embedded into my skin, slowly peeling each layer back, one by one. Is this what it feels like to die? Am I already dead? Is this what an eternity of damnation feels like?

Visions from my childhood play through my mind. Glimpses of a man that watches me. Memories that I've forgotten over the years. A man I remember seeing in the courtyard of my building after my mother left. The same man sitting in a car, watching me leave school and following close behind as I walked the streets of the Quarter to my home. I focus on his details, blurry but visible. Long brown hair, tall and thin, and a smile I can't forget, Harrison.

"Hello, Penelope," he says. "You won't remember me and that's the way it will remain, but we'll meet again." He smiles, showing fangs. The same fangs that sank into my neck, bringing this pain with them. He takes my hand into his. "Remember, you're mine. You've always been mine and always will be." His voice has the same Southern Gentleman accent I remember from the university, the day we first met. The scene pulls away like I'm watching a movie on a screen, and reality hits me like a ton of bricks. He groomed me from childhood to be his Penelope, and I fell for it like a little lovesick puppy.

"Amelia?" The familiar voice is back. "I miss you. Wake up so we can go fly a kite again. This time I promise not to go so high."

Celeste? That's who the voice belongs to, Celeste. The pain is less than before, but still there. I struggle, trying to open my eyes. Nothing works. I'm frozen in place, unable to make even the smallest move. What happened to me?

Something happens. The fire and pain burning through my veins stops instantly. "Amelia?" a deeper voice calls. I struggle to answer, my mouth still not cooperating. A hand takes mine into it, squeezing gently. "If you can hear me, squeeze my hand." I put every ounce of energy into returning the squeeze without success.

"She'll be out for a few more days," a female voice says. "Hopefully she's through the hellfire stage and now in the recovery stage. There's no way to know for sure, but she should be able to hear you."

I can hear you! My mind screams. *Am I dead?*

"I'll be back to check on her tomorrow. Thank you, Viktor, for allowing her to stay here. And thank you, little one, for being at the right place at the right time." The soft click of a door closing echoes through my ears. The voice sounds familiar. Violet?

Viktor? Am I alive? As the pain recedes, I'm able to rest for the first time and drift away from the burning that's plagued me. I wake with a startle at something crashing to the ground. It takes a minute to realize my eyes are open, and what I'm seeing isn't a dream. The walls are dark green, but my eyes are too blurry to determine any details of the room. Light streaming through the windows is painfully bright, causing me to blink faster than normal. "Hello?" my voice doesn't work. Not even a whisper escapes my lips. My arms weigh a million pounds each as I try to lift them into the air. I don't know how high they reach before falling back to the soft mattress beneath me.

"You're awake?" a young voice calls as the door opens. "Daddy, she's awake!" the voice runs out of the room, leaving me alone again.

"Amelia?" I focus my eyes on a tall figure standing in the doorway. Opening my mouth to respond, nothing happens.

"See! I told you she was awake." Small fingers wrap around mine, as little lips shower my hand with kisses. "I told you she'd be okay."

"Celeste don't squeeze too tightly. She's still transitioning. Be gentle." I turn toward the deeper voice. Even though I can't make out any details, I'm sure it's Viktor.

"I'm not going to hurt her. Do you think she can hear us?"

I blink my eyes quickly, hoping they'll understand that I can. "I don't know, honey."

Celeste sighs. "Amelia, I'm sorry I didn't protect you." I force every ounce of energy I have into squeezing her tiny hand. "Daddy, she squeezed my hand! She can hear me."

"Let's give her time to heal," Viktor says.

"I'll come to check on you later," she whispers, following him out of the room. My eyes close in exhaustion.

Sometime later, I awaken to the sound of water dripping so loud, it bangs off the metal surface it's hitting. What the hell is that? I try blocking out the sound, only to be drawn to another. The second hand on a clock pounds so loudly, it echoes off every bone in my ear. I manage to pull my hands up to my ears, covering them to block out the sounds. I sit up, swinging my legs around to the side of the bed, and try to stand. Surprisingly, I'm more stable than I expected and wobble my way to the door. I open it to see Viktor on the other side.

"Amelia?" He grabs me just before I collapse, pulling me into his arms. "What are you doing up?"

"Noise," I'm able to whisper. "Loud noises."

He carries me back to the bed. "That's normal. All of your senses will be heightened for a while. It's part of the process."

"What process?"

He pulls the covers over me, tucking me tightly into bed. "The transition is the hardest part. Especially when the person was almost dead."

"Dammit, Viktor. Answer my question. Transition to what?"

He sighs. "The transition into a vampire. Get some rest. You'll need it."

"Don't leave me alone, please?"

He pulls a chair closer to the bed. "I'll stay right here. Guess I should've brought a book with me." He smiles, making me feel better.

Vampire? Am I a vampire now? Do I want to be a vampire? Viktor said the transition is harder when the person is almost dead. Does that mean Harrison killed me? Is Harrison my maker? Questions flow through my mind in rapid succession as I drift off to sleep with Viktor sitting next to my bed, staring out of the window.

I awaken to find Viktor sitting in the same spot, his

feet propped on the end of my bed and my laptop on his lap. Oh, my God, he's reading my thesis. "Don't read that," I croak.

"You look better." He closes the laptop and sits up straight. "How do you feel?"

"Shitty."

"Then you're doing better." He smiles. "There are some interesting facts in here." He shakes the laptop at me. "Some of them are way off base, however. I can help you if you need it."

"I'll keep that in mind, thanks." I clear my throat, trying to get rid of the giant frog taking up residence inside. "What happened?"

Viktor takes a deep breath. "What do you remember?"

I think back, trying to separate dreams from reality. "Harrison and Celeste were fighting. She told me to run, and I did. He got in front of me and…" The memory of him biting my neck makes me flinch. "He killed me."

"He nearly did," Viktor answers. "Violet killed him." The memory of her holding a bloody stake comes to mind.

"She stabbed him in the heart?"

"Yes. She ended his life. He was so distracted with you that he let his guard down. Idiot."

"Violet? Is she okay?"

Victor smiles. "She's fine. She's been here nearly every day since it happened. In fact, she should be here before too much longer to check on you."

"Is she the one?"

"I'm not sure what you're asking." He stands, stretching his legs.

"Is Violet my maker?"

He laughs. "No, your maker is much smaller." On cue, Celeste bursts through the door.

"Amelia! I heard you talking and came to see if you were alright." She jumps on the end of the bed.

"I'm okay." I smile.

"I missed you so much!" She gently rubs my legs as she speaks.

"Celeste? Are you my maker?"

She smiles ear to ear. "Yep! You're my first. Daddy forbids me from turning anyone, but I broke the rules. When you wouldn't wake up, I was worried I did it wrong."

"You did it perfectly." I return her smile.

"Amelia? Are you angry at me for turning you?" She looks at my feet. "You were dying. I could hear your heartbeat slowing. It was barely beating, and you were in so much pain. I couldn't let you die like that. You didn't deserve it."

Truth is, I'm not sure how to feel about being a vampire. It hasn't sunk in yet. "I'm not angry. Thank you for saving me."

"You mean it?"

"I do." My stomach growls loudly.

"I'll get you something to drink," she says, bouncing off the bed. "Be right back!" She runs out of the room and down the hall. Her footsteps pounding through my brain.

"It gets easier," Viktor says, moving back to my bedside. "The sounds. They get easier to block out. Everything is amplified as a vampire. Our senses are kicked into overdrive. It's the hardest part. Well, that and the blood lust."

"Blood lust. Is that what this hunger is called? I don't remember feeling this hungry before."

"Yes. The blood will help."

"I have it!" Celeste exclaims, carrying a glass full of red liquid. She hands it to me and then watches me like I'm opening a present at Christmas. I stare at the liquid, not overly excited about drinking blood.

"Is it human?"

"Nope, goat. Drink it," Celeste encourages.

I lift the glass to my nose, taking a long sniff first. My mouth waters as soon as the smell enters my nostrils. I intend on taking a small sip, but as soon as the blood reaches my lips, I don't slow down. I drink the entire glass in one gulp. Immediately, the hunger subsides. "Oh, my God. That was good. I didn't think it would be, but it was. Can I have more?"

Viktor laughs. "One glass for your first time is plenty. You don't want to get sick."

"I want a shower."

Viktor rubs his nose. "I think that's a wonderful idea. Would you like me to get Fran?"

I stand from the side of the bed, sturdier than before. "No, I think I'll be fine."

"I put some of your clothes in the bathroom for you already," Celeste says. "This is Daddy's room. His clothes won't fit you."

I look around the large room. "I'm in your room?"

Viktor shrugs. "I don't sleep in it. Someone might as well." He stands, holding his arm out for Celeste. "Come on, mon amour. Amelia doesn't need an audience."

I step into the hot shower and audibly sigh so loudly that I'm sure the entire house heard. The hot water is an answer to prayer. I scrub every part of my body at least twice before finally turning the water off. The mirror is fogged up from the steam. I wipe it dry with the towel, surprised to see my image. Guess that one's not true. I can see myself in the mirror. The girl staring back at me looks different than I remember. Her skin is plumper than before, and the dark circles that have been present since she was a child are gone, replaced with smooth, bright skin. Even though her hair is wet, it's curlier than before with no visible frizz. This is the new me.

True to her word, there's a pair of leggings and a sweatshirt folded on the back of the toilet. I slip into them, relishing the feel of the soft fabric against my overly sensitive skin. I don't do anything to my hair other than run a brush through the curls before heading downstairs. Since drinking the blood, I feel like myself, only with more energy.

I move down the stairs quicker than intended, nearly falling on the way down. "Amelia, you look great!" Celeste is at my side in an instant. She holds my hand, pulling me toward the couch. "Come, sit down." As soon as we sit, she leans her tiny head against my arm. "I thought you were gone." Her voice sounds sad.

"I'm here. I'm not going anywhere."

"Good. Daddy said you can stay here if you want." I look at Viktor. He shrugs.

"I know you're homeless at the moment. You are welcome to stay here for as long as you need."

"I...I couldn't take advantage of you like that."

"You're not taking advantage," Celeste says. "As your maker, I'm asking you to stay as long as you need."

I look between the two of them. "Thank you. As soon as I can get some money flowing, I'll find a place of my own."

"You don't need money." Celeste looks at me like I'm insane.

"That's the way the world works. Without money, I can't afford to do anything."

"No, you don't need money. As your maker, you have my money. It's how *our* world works." I look at Viktor, not sure what she's talking about.

"She's right. When a vampire makes a new vampire, they are required to share their wealth with them." He looks at his daughter. "Little Celeste is quite a wealthy lady."

I don't know what to say. "Thank you."

"Violet's here," Celeste announces. Less than a second later, a soft knock sounds on the door. "I'll get it." She bounces to the door, opening it wide and welcoming Violet inside.

"You're awake!" Violet moves at vampire speed in front of me and wraps her arms around my back. "I was so worried."

I pull away from her grip. "Violet, thank you."

She wipes a tear. "You're welcome."

"I'm so sorry you had to kill your..." I don't know what word to use for Harrison.

"My maker." She completes my sentence. "Don't be. I'm not."

"Celeste, why don't you come with me, and we'll let the ladies talk?" Viktor ushers my tiny maker from the room. She turns back, making eye contact with Violet. I have a feeling her eye contact is meant as a silent warning.

Violet sits, pulling me beside her. "The Harrison I knew was not the Harrison that I killed. He's always been a bit eccentric, but those eccentricities changed over the last few decades. He wasn't the same person I once knew." She takes my hand into hers. "I'm sorry I let it go this far. I should've stopped him before he brought you into the house, but I didn't. And, for that, I'm eternally sorry."

"Violet, I…"

"No, let me finish," she interrupts. "I need to say this." She takes a deep breath. "I saw bits and pieces of his obsession throughout the years, but never to this extent. I found these in his office." She pulls a bunch of letters from her designer handbag.

I recognize the letters from Viktor's library. "These are the letters Penelope wrote and hid in the desk in Viktor's library. How—how did Harrison get them?"

"Harrison wrote them."

"Why would he do that?"

"He was obsessed with Penelope and Celeste. What he couldn't have in life, he would take in death. He somehow got those letters inside of Viktor's house and knew you'd find them."

I stand, moving toward the window. "I don't understand."

"Amelia, he's planned this since you were a child."

"I want to believe you, but how would he know I would grow up to look like Penelope? That doesn't make sense."

Violet moves to my side. "They grew up together. He had known her his entire life. Maybe it was a coincidence, or maybe it was fate. We'll never know."

"I believed him." Tears threaten to slide down my cheeks.

"Me, too," she admits.

"Thomas?" Violet knows what I'm asking.

"He's good. He's having a hard time with the truth."

I scoff. "Understandable."

"I need to go." She wraps her arms around me, pulling me close. "Keep in touch. I'm here if you need anything."

"Thank you, Violet. For everything."

......

"Are you sure you're ready to go out on your own?" Celeste gives me the look of a parent of a new driver, about to venture out on their own.

"Yes, Mom. I'll be fine." I smile at my words.

My tiny maker props her hands on her hips, clearly not convinced. "Have you had your blood today?"

"Yes, I'm good. We've been working on my control for the last six months. I'm not going to accidentally eat the entire city of New Orleans. Maybe just one or two."

"Amelia, that's not funny."

I hold my hands up in surrender style. "I'm not going to eat even one. I don't have any desire to feed from a human. I promise I'll be fine. I need to turn this thing in, and I'll officially be Dr. Lockhart." I hold up the two-hundred-page thesis, shaking it at her for effect. "I'm going straight to the university and straight back here."

"Are you sure I don't need to come along?"

"Celeste, you have to let her grow up a little," Fran says from the dining room. "There comes a time when you have to let her out of the nest and watch how well she flies."

"Why do I feel like I'm being parented by a five-year-old?" I laugh.

"Because you are." Fran laughs with me.

"Okay, but I don't like it." Celeste gives up her fight. "Call me when you get to the university and when you leave."

I bend down, kissing her on the forehead. "I'll be fine." I step outside and into the garage, finding the SUV Celeste picked out for me. I open the sunroof and windows, filling the car with fresh air as I drive across the lake. I'm in the city before I realize it and find my way to the university. A parking spot directly in front of the history building makes life even easier.

"Good afternoon, Miss Lockhart."

"Good afternoon, Dr. Cavish." I set the copies of my thesis on his desk. "Five copies, as required."

He takes the top book off, flipping through the pages quickly. "This looks great. I'll let you know when the team meets so you can defend your thesis and receive your degree."

"That sounds perfect. Thank you for the extension."

He smiles. "Sometimes life gets in the way. I understand." He walks me to the door. "Are you doing okay? You look different than the last time I saw you."

I smile. "Yes, I'm doing great actually. I'm working as a nanny on the north side of the lake and feeling much happier than before."

"Glad to hear it." He returns the smile. "I'll let you know as soon as we have a date." He waits for me to get inside my car before shrinking back inside the building. I zoom out of the parking place, heading back to my maker and her rules. Since the weather is beautiful, and I haven't been out for six months, I decide to take the long way through the Quarter before getting on the highway to head across the lake.

Just like always, the mass of people walking through the streets, unaware of the mythological creatures walking past them, or driving SUVs next to them, is strange to witness. A familiar store catches my attention. Opie's Voodoo Shop has the door wide open, welcoming visitors inside. I pull the SUV to a stop in front of her store and stare at the door. Why am I here? I slide out of the vehicle and through the front door of the store before I have time to think about it. A loud buzzer sounds as I enter. "I'll be right there!" Opie calls from the back. I don't answer.

This is dumb, and I promised I'd be smart. I head back to the door when a familiar voice passes through the curtain. "I'll work on that spell and get it to you next week."

"Next week will be too late. You know what I expect, sorcière. You also know the consequences if my demands are not met." The woman speaking has a hint of a French accent. I pretend to flip through the large potion book while they talk.

"Yes, I do. I'll get on it right away," Opie answers the

stranger. I turn in the direction of the woman and run straight into a ghost. Standing in front of me is my doppelgänger. Long red curls hang down her back, and piercing blue eyes take in every inch of my face.

"My, oh my. We do look alike." The woman smiles. "Hello, Penelope."

"Garden of Mystery and Intrigue"-VONO Book 2 is available for pre-order NOW!

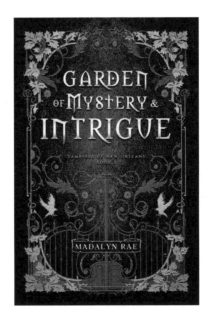

about the author

Madalyn Rae is the pen name for an author who loves telling a story. As a teacher of tiny humans during the day and author by night, she hopes she's able to draw you into her world of fantasy, make-believe, and love, even for a brief moment.

She lives on the Gulf Coast's beautiful white, sandy beaches, with her husband and two loyal, yet mildly obnoxious dogs, Whiskey and Tippi. She's the mother of two amazing adult children and a brand new son-in-law.

When not teaching or pretending to write, Madalyn is immersed in the world of music. Whether playing an instrument or singing a song, she is privileged to know that music is the true magic of the universe.

also by madalyn rae

The Elementals Series

Birth of the Phoenix-Adria's Novella-Prequel

Phoenix of the Sea- Elementals Book 1

Guardian of the Sea- Murphy's Novella

Ashes of the Wind-Elementals Book 2

Embers of the Flame-Keegan's Novella

Fire of the Sky-Elementals Book 3

Salt of the Earth-Elementals Spin-off

Spring 2024

Vampires of New Orleans Series

Garden of the Past-Prequel Novella

Garden of Secret and Shadow-Book 1

Garden of Mystery and Intrigue -Book 2

Winter 2023

Garden of Discovery and Love- (Working Title)

Winter 2024

Ravenwood- VONO Spin-off

Spring 2024

Printed in Great Britain
by Amazon